The Legend of Dragon's Doom
A Young Warrior's Vow

R.S. Revels

ISBN 978-0-578-03594-9

Cover graphics by Gayle Noble

Dedication

This book is dedicated to my parents, Raeford and Nardie Stepp, who have always believed in me and supported me every step of the way. They are my inspiration.

A special thank you to those who have walked with me as we discovered the legend within, Gayle, Jul, Jeff, DR, Barbara, Craig, Rhonda and Lynn. Your help in this adventure is much appreciated. May grace always go with you.

Prologue

In a land by the mystic wood
where the winds of magic blow
stands a castle alone on a hill
where waves of sadness flow.
With walls of crystal and gold
no happiness sounds within
no song nor joyous laughter
has been heard since this curse did begin.
'Tis a place known of legend
a home of strange tales,
it is where silent secrets loom.

Here in a place
called Dragon's Doom.
As the tale goes quietly spoken,
words shared in hushed, whispered tone.
While the years drag slowly by,
one hope stands alone.
Past knowledge kept silent and hidden,
locked away in corridors carefully sealed.
Hidden away, what has gone before
ne'er to be revealed.
In a cold and lonely room
kept mum, forever silent,
here in a place,
called Dragon's Doom
Where gentle hearts have been broken,
lives will ne'er be the same.
As each wander the corridors
cursing the name
As they seek for the rescue
deeply sunk in their own gloom,
from the miseries they must suffer
here in this place called Dragon's Doom.
Legend has it one will be called,
whose destiny it shall be.
When the day and the time is at hand
to set each captive free.
And those suffering look to the future,
a better future than they hold.
Appearing dark and bleak and empty,

they cry out for the one brave and bold.
This legend can come none too soon,
to be savior of the ones that are lost.
In this place
called Dragon's Doom.

ONE

From the turrets tall, towering high above everything, I look out across a vast and magnificent land. Glayemour, land of my home, filled with beauty, overcome with sadness. From one window I see, rolling hills repeating until they blend in with the distant horizon. Fields ripe for harvest, golden in the afternoon sun, as the workers toil diligently, their movements sure, but hurried. They know that to be out in the open is not safe. I hear the watchman as he moves about above me, his armor clattering with each step. In my mind I can visualize the scene above. How many times I myself, even in my youth, have stood in that very place. Taking my turn at standing watch for those working below. In my mind I see it all. The watchman stands bravely, almost arrogantly, in the center of the tower. Giving him the ability to see uninhibited the surrounding sky. Able to see, the fields and hills around us as he watches constantly, vigilantly, never faltering in his keep. Knowing the workers below, depend fully on him. The farmers and field hands trust in his presence as they work, harvesting the grains that will feed them over the long cold winter ahead. Still yet, even in the trust they have, anxious eyes wander toward the skies. The least unexpected noise, has all in hearing searching for the source. Fear is a constant, unwanted companion.

Rumors have run rampant through the castle. The stories grow with each telling as does the source of their caution, and their fear. From ten feet, to twenty, to fifty feet long it grows. Towering as high as the castle's turrets, with wings that can block the sun's light leaving the land dark and afraid. The smell of sulfur and smoke giving away its presence. With angry eyes, yellow and cold, yet full of internal flames, as tendrils of smoke escape flared nostrils. Footsteps that shake the ground, and all who feel them, tremble in fear. As still it grows, sixty, seventy feet long. Eyes dart repeatedly to the skies, and eyes search the fields as hands hurriedly toil, feeling their security stands tall on yon turret. A specially trained and chosen knight watches. A guard in armor, shined to the point it reflects the sun, weapons at the ready, sword of steel sharpened perfectly with a shield emblazoned with his crest, easily within reach. It is a silent and tedious task as the guard moves but slightly, turning to scan the skies, watching constantly, ever vigilant of his surroundings. It allows time for the tales to run through his mind of the mystical, magical, and mysterious properties of this monster of a dragon. Though carefully watching, the mind still wondering how much is real, how much fantasy and how much was created by the long nights by the fireside, fueled by ale. I have been there, I know the loneliness of the time spent there and the potential for disaster.

From my position here, I can hear him as he walks, his armor giving him away. It is the shout, cut off suddenly that brings me back to this place. I listen, though I hear no more I am afraid. From the window where I gaze upon the outside world, I see a shadow begin to grow. Blocking the light, covering the ground below, covering the workers, those, that up until that point had been unaware. A sound that could come from nowhere but the depths of hell was heard across the fields. Birds deserted the trees, squirrel and rabbit, fox and snake fled before the evil one. The screams of terror and pain began, joined by many more, echoing across the fields. Sounds of those fleeing , rushing back toward the castle, running, desperate to get to safety. Welding their worker's tools as weapons they try only to survive. The shadow, ominous and evil covers the ground as death swoops down upon the weak and upon the small. Try as they might to reach safety, in truth, they are all doomed to a horrible death.

The dragon's evil intent, seen in its yellow eyes, felt in its hot, blistering breath, breathing down the backs of the helpless as they rush toward the castle. Pain screaming through their body at the exertion, with their lungs about to burst as they struggle to keep running. Safety is near, safety, is unreachable. The gate to the castle grows closer, their eyes fill with hope, but it is nothing more than a game of cat and mouse. As dragon's claws swing outward and all that were still outside are lost.

Standing here, in this window, slamming fists of rage onto the wall, I know that tonight once again, the tears will flow. Great wailing will be heard throughout the castle, as it is draped in the colors of mourning. Candles will be lit, in memory of all of those that on this day were lost from this life.

Preparing myself, I left this chamber for the lower part of the castle. I stood off to the side dressed in mourning black, quietly, respectfully, listening to the cries of loss around me. I watched from the shadows as families held each other close. Supporting each other, while trying not to fall apart as tears fell and their cries went up to the heavens, asking why. It did not matter the person, there is no shame in grief, as knight as well as mothers, squire as well as maiden wept openly. So many this time, there were just so many that were lost. A draft from the window caused a candle to flicker and I watched as a shadow, for a brief moment, blocked the light of the moon over Dragon's Doom.

It was then that I knew, in my heart what must be done. But not until after this time of mourning. Out of respect for those who have lost, I would wait. The required fortnight would give me time to prepare. Without haste, I could gather all I needed. Without haste, I could make ready and no one would be the wiser.

I remained in the shadows of the great hall, keeping watch. The candles must not go out. The souls must have the light to find their way to their final destination. If one candle grew dim, if one candle so much as flickered,I was there, trimming a wick, draining wax, blocking a draft. As dawn's first fingers of light reached out, pushing away the curtain of night I wearily watched the sky, a brilliant red marked the start of this day. I could mentally hear the words, take warning. Looking to the mourners behind me, pain etched deeply into each face, the marks of their tears appearing permanently drawn as they travel down weary cheeks, I shook this dread away.

I turn again from checking the candles to the morning sky, listening to the best and strongest of the knights wandered the great hall, taking care of the weary, covering the weak from the morning chill. In every eye, was the same emotion, even this pain could not cover it as they looked to the window and beyond. As their hands rested on the sword at their side, fingers clinching tightly their hilt, anger born in the pain. Their thoughts are of a dragon's demise. But all must wait, out of respect for the dead. Out of respect for the ones left behind. I planned it carefully, thinking a fortnight after all, was not that long, and there was much to be done.

The list ran through my mind, as the strength built in my heart and the anger grew in my breast. This had gone on for too long, too many had died, too many mourned. I knew not the reason why this had been so allowed. I only knew that it must end, the dragon must die. I looked again toward the morning sun, blood red in rising, and I made a vow as did all who were gathered together in the great hall. Quietly, in the hearts of the wounded, the vow was made, sealed in the wax of the mourning candles that burned at Dragon's Doom.

Waiting for the fortnight to end was agony. To see so many, suffer so greatly and not be able to act, was enough to drive one to madness. I tried to fill the time with preparations when not trapped in the daily rituals. The candles burned, day and night and must be watched carefully. I was reminded often that the candles must not go out. There were memorials placed on the altars of faith and remembrance, these must be tended, great care must be given to the gifts for the dead. Times of prayer for the souls making the journey to eternity. Moments of remembering and sharing thoughts of those loved and lost. Rituals of importance and respect for the lost, and

11

the ones left behind.

The castle was quieter now, the wailing from the mourners now no more than quiet sobs, and silent tears as they slowly gave in to the realization of what had happened. Acceptance seemed impossible, but something necessary if we were to go on.

My usual custom was to stay out of the way of all. That was paying off greatly now as I could come and go and not be missed. I gathered daily what I would need, checking and rechecking conditions and quality, knowing that one cannot go into battle with weapons of inferior make. I carefully hid it all away for safe keeping. I continued following my plans step by step, item by item, I made ready for what I knew I had to do. Having been taken into training early, I had many weapons of my own. This fact made it easier when I approached the sword smith in the lower most rooms of the castle with my request. Entering his smithy shop I waited.

Turning to me he smiled and asked, "Yes, Young master? What is it I can do for you this day?"

Holding out my sword for his inspection I asked, "Is this sword the finest possible made? Is it crafted of the strongest steel? Does it have an edge sharp and true?"

With a look that gave way his thinking my sword merely a method of futile protection should I find myself outside and the dragon return, he still inspected the sword. "No Young Master, this is not the finest of swords. This is a sword meant only for training, not battle."

He turned away and removed something from the wall. Turning back, he handed me a sword of the finest kind. I looked in awe as light reflected off the steel blade, dancing across the ceiling. In the precision of its make, sharp and flawless I could see myself reflected. My still somewhat rounded face of youth, pale from lack of sun, with that cursed blond hair falling into my eyes. Eyes as blue as I remember my mother's were. Stopping that train of thought I returned to the here and now. I had to keep my thoughts on my vow. My hand closed around the hilt of the sword tightly as I accepted this masterpiece in weaponry. I held my breath as I held the sword, feeling its weight and grip, gaining balance as I practiced a swing and a thrust. This sword felt right in my grasp. As I slowly slid the sword into my sheath I heard a noise. When I looked up, the sword smith was again reaching to the wall. This time, he turned back with a helmet of strange design.

"Take this, Young Master. It is a gift for you, a new creation of mine." the sword smith held out the helmet, offering it freely. "It is made to fit snugly over the head so as not to move about. Open in front, this face plate is attached so that when in place, the face is protected as well. Yet the wearer can still see their enemy and can still fight." the sword smith carefully explained.

"I do thank you sir for all of this." I told him as I turned to take my leave. Carrying my new acquisitions back into my own area of the castle I placed them carefully away. Hidden along with the chain mail that would protect me, and hide my form, while not being too heavy as armor would. I needed speed, with the chain mail, I would still have it. My shield was a gift given upon completion of a segment of my training. This I worried about as it was full size and heavy. Some how I would manage, I would not allow anything to deter me now. Placed carefully beside the shield was my crossbow and arrows. The arrows that I had struggled over, and made of my own design. The arrowhead was made of two parts, one part of stone, one part steel. The stone, jagged of edge meant to rip and tear where it entered. The steel so sharp as to cut the strongest of metals, should it come across its edge. These two were bound together tightly, to hold their grasp in flight. Yet were constructed so as to come apart on impact, deadly and destructive.

My crossbow, I checked time and again. Specially made for me, its construction well done, it would hold up to the most fierce of battles. Placing each item carefully back I stood deep in thought. The fortnight would soon be over, I needed to be ready. Hearing footsteps in the corridor, I closed away my secret place and moved across the floor.

"Son?"

"Yes Father?"

"Are you well?"

"I am Father, I was just seeking a moment's rest. I was preparing to return to my duties now." I answered carefully.

"As you should." was all he said before walking away. When the footsteps continued on I left my room and went back to my duties as I had said. I could not destroy my chances now, the fortnight would soon be over. Vows had been made. Vows would be kept.

Two

As the dawn's first light began, I was already gone. Having quietly made my way through the castle and out its massive gates, drawing the attention of no one. A single torch at the end of each corridor was all that had lit my way. The silence of the castle would have been unnerving but for my quest. I had made sure that no one in the castle knew of my departure, leaving when all still slept. I knew where each guard would be and timed my passing to when their attention was directed elsewhere. The drawbridge was down, but so was the iron gate that prevented entrance. Slipping between the bars, it was the only time I appreciated my youthful size. Before the sun broke over the edge of the horizon I had collected my weapons from their hiding place and was making my way toward where I had heard lay the dragon's lair.

No one would know of my departure for a while. If I moved quickly enough, I had time to make my way across the open fields before even the dragons stirred. Crouching low, I hurried through the tall grains, eyes constantly looking to the lightening sky. The chain mail I wore under my cloak, an unaccustomed weight that was reassuring in its presence as was the helmet I carried. Each a reminder of my quest. With every step the weapons I carried shifted, the sounds they made comforting me, as with haste, I made my way ever forward. The fields seem to go on forever, appearing to stretch out toward the horizon so far away. A horizon that did not seem to grow any closer. I feared I would not make the forest before the sun rose bright. I knew that early morn and eve was the favorite time of the dragon's

15

to hunt and I did not wish to be caught out here, with none of nature's own protections to hide me. It was also in my mind that I did not wish for the sharp eyes of the guards to see me, alerting the others of my leaving. I looked back only once. In the slowly brightening sky I could see the light reflecting off the golden walls of the castle. Its image, I knew from memory danced on the surface of the moat surrounding it. As of yet, no one moved about. There was but two guards that watched through the night, it would take them a while to make their rounds on their assigned posts. All others were still tending to the mourners. That would change soon enough. Flags that were lowered for the fortnight would today be raised to the top of the masts. Today, life would return to some semblance of normal. Today, I was on my way, to fulfill my vow. Turning away from the castle behind me I resumed my journey.

When finally I reached the edge of the fields I hesitated, listening carefully I identified every sound before moving forward into the forest. Immediately I felt the change, the coolness of the wood eased the heat of my skin, as the canopy of the trees concealed my presence.

Carefully I examined the area, looking for a safe place to rest. Finding a collection of boulders grouped in a manner creating an enclosure, I entered and with my back to the rock I rested, knowing would be but for a moment. Yet ever watchful, ever on guard, my hand resting on the grip of my sword. Within moments I was easing away from my resting place, my mind focused once again on my quest. My vow replaying through my head. While I traveled as quickly as one on foot could, weighed down as I was, I still did so warily, I could not risk allowing a careless move to destroy my chance at success. Somewhere in this wood, was the dragon's lair, I promised myself and those that had been lost, that I would find it. I walked, whispering promises into the air, sending them to the departed souls, sending them to the ones left at the castle. I walked, repeatedly whispering promises of my vow of this dragon's demise. To my mind came reminders of the tales from long ago of the great knights traveling from so far away, their only reason being to slay a dragon. Appearing on dancing stallions, decked out in ribbons and bells they came. Knight and steed alike, dressed in armor. Knight and steed charging off into the distance, never to return. And here was I, not yet a knight, daring to enter this place alone. Determination was my driving force. The salvation of my kin, my cause. As I made my way deeper into the forest wood my resolve did not waver.

It was the smell that first warned me, sulfur and smoke assailed my nose and throat. Crouching to the ground, hidden among the boulders and brush, I listened closely. There was no mistaking the sound, the ground trembled and trees shook as the dragon walked. Its weight causing each step to sound as thunder. Hidden, I watched it pass, waiting patiently as it spread its massive wings and lifted itself skyward.

Once it was gone from sight I moved out into the open, looking toward the dragon's lair. Halfway up the side of the mountain of fire. I began my climb, intending to go inside to wait for the dragon's return I was stopped by the smell. Horrendous and nauseating, the stench drove me back away from the entrance. Peering into the cave I could make out bones gnawed white, scattered about inside. I tried but could not tell whether they were of animal or human beginnings. Suddenly I heard the unmistakable roar of the dragon, directly behind me. My

17

moment of distraction may have cost me everything. Turning I stood watching as the dragon swooped downward toward where I stood. Each breath sending searing flames ahead of it. Smoke circled its head and was lost in the wind from its flight.

Tossing aside my cloak, I made ready. With my shield I hoped to deflect the dragon's flames in the attempt to get close enough to strike with my sword. I stood determined to succeed, or to die in the trying.

I watched as the dragon drew closer, then passed just out of reach of my sword. The wind from those great wings nearly knocking me off my feet. Still I stood, carefully watching my foe, as it circled around, watching me, watching it.

The dragon's flight was at times strange. Oddly it appeared almost as if it were swimming in the air, floating on the waves of air currents. Its great wings barely moved as it sliced the sky. The scales on its body shifting and flowing as each muscle moved. These scales were better than the finest armor made. It was these very scales that were going to make my success difficult. I watched, as each circle brought it in closer, just as it passed it swung out its massive tail, attempting to spear me with the spiked end. I was ready, reflexes sharpened from training, quickened by testing I dodged the assault and watched as the dragon moved away into the sky. I was at the moment holding my own in a battle not yet fully begun. I watched closely, placing my full attention on the dragon. I could not allow another distraction. I knew the consequences should I allow that to happen. Slowly, very slowly I eased my crossbow to the ready, just as slowly I set an arrow in place, eyes still on the dragon as it circled around yet again. Patiently I watched, as the dragon began its descent toward me. I took aim and fired the arrow from my crossbow. My aim was not true as the arrow struck the dragon's side at a wrong angle, merely bouncing off and angering the great beast at my audacity. The roar that came from deep in the dragon's throat, sounded as if it came from the depths of hell itself, so was the anger. Flames erupted from the dragon's mouth coming toward me, flowing around me. Surrounding me in its extreme heat. The pain was intense, and I feared this time 'twas not the dragon's doom, but mine.

Using my shield I tried to deflect the worst of the flame even as the steel kept growing hotter in my hand. My thoughts, for one fleeting moment, were that I had failed. The vow I made was in vain, I had, in my arrogance came up against an adversary stronger than I and I had surely failed. In that failing, I had let everyone down. No one would ever know what had became of me. In my haste to leave, I had left no note, no message, nothing in my chamber would tell them where I had gone. Now I would die here, alone with no one to mourn my passing. Only for the briefest of moments did I allow this thought reign, then I remembered my training, each lesson, every move played through my mind, I remembered the words told me time and again "as long as you breathe, you have not failed. As long as you live, fight." Fight I would, as long as I had the strength to lift my sword.

Reaching behind me, seeking anything to stop the dragon's flame, I searched blindly, desperately, ready to use what ever I might find. When my fingers closed around the ankle of a man I all but dropped my shield. Taking tighter hold of the shield I backed again, in an attempt to protect this unknown person. The laughter that greeted me was unexpected.

"I don't know whether it is your determination that impresses me, or your foolishness in this battle so against you that gives me cause to laugh."

"While I do not wish to interrupt your entertainment at my expense," I managed to say, "I do wish to understand how you can find this, my possible death amusing. And how is it you stand here in the flame untouched and bothered not?"

"Oh you are a foolish one indeed, and an uneducated one at that. Dragon- be gone!"
When the flames suddenly stopped, and the dragon's roar I heard no more, I lowered my shield just enough to see. The land before me where once the dragon stomped and roared, where his footprints marked the ground, where the trees bore the scorched marks of the flames, stood empty. The dragon, was there no more.

I turned with haste to see the one behind me that had caused such a thing. Before me stood a man not much taller than I, yet the look of his skin and the white of his long hair bore proof he was much older. The marks of time around his eyes did not disguise the brightness within, nor did they cover the proof of his wisdom and mirth. The smile that played along his mouth embarrassed and annoyed me, yet I held my tongue. His clothing was like nothing I had seen before. The tunic material dark, but still it shimmered with a light that seemingly traveled through the threads. His fingers long and lean, fussed with the material as if trying to quieten it as one would a willful child. In his other hand was a staff, carved with the likeness of many beasts covering it from top to bottom. What stood out, was the dragon and snake that were carved circling the staff, wrapped around all the other beasts and rising to the top to meet face to face. Resting on his breast was a medallion made of the finest gold. The design engraved upon it I had seen before, on the tapestry than hung in the great hall. Not only was this medallion weaved into the fabric, but also the portrait of this man. A man whose name was never spoken aloud. Even the whispers stopped around the young ones. Now, I would finally find out why.

"Tell me, who you are. How is it that you did this, and where is it, that you sent the dragon? Tell me, it has not returned to the castle."

Leaning upon his staff he silently watched me, he appeared to be waiting for something, but I knew not what. Finally he spoke, but only to ask a question of his own. "Did your master instructor only attempt to teach you how to battle? Or is it, that as obvious as it is that you did not learn to fight, you also did not learn manners?"

I was angered at his words, until I realized what it was he waited for. "I do sir, most humbly offer you my gratitude for stepping in and preventing my death. I did learn my manners well, as I did learn to hold my own in battle."

At this the strange man did laugh aloud, then without answering my questions he turned to walk away. Reaching the edge of the forest he turned back, "Don't just stand there gawking, come along, come along. There is much to do if you intend to slay this dragon. Unless of course you have changed your mind, If that be the case, remain where you are. The dragon will return soon enough and finish what it had begun."

Embarrassed at his laughter, I none the less picked up my crossbow and shield and followed him into the wood. He walked quickly, never once turning back, never once slowing down. I held my tongue, even as my sides ached and my lungs felt as if I had quit breathing long ago. I remained silent as each part of my body screamed

in the agony of exhaustion and exertion. Still speaking
not one word, he walked ever deeper into the wood and I
wondered, just what is was that I had fallen into now, all
because of a vow for a dragon's doom.

Just when I felt that my last strength was fading,
when I forced concentration on each step so as not to
stumble, for I did not wish in any way to appear weak in
this man's eyes, we came to a small clearing. On the far
side was the solid rock face of the mountain.
"What do you see?" asked this strange man I
followed.
"What I see with my eyes is a rock wall. But what I
feel, is that all is not as it seems."
With a nod he walked on, straight into the rock,
disappearing before my eyes leaving me no choice but to
attempt to follow. The wall before me trembled and then
parted as water around a stone, closing silently behind
me, as if it had never been disturbed. Inside I stood
amazed at the sight, and in my heart, I must admit to the
feeling of fear. Large torches burned from the walls,
casting shadows across the room. Containers of every
known shape and size lined one wall and covered the
table in front of it. Great volumes of books and
scrolls lined shelves and were stacked haphazardly along
the adjoining wall. To one side was a place carved out of
the wall for the fire that burned high. Near to it, the one
cot in the room.
Strange beasts stood and approached this man as
he entered the room. Beasts that bore the head of a
dragon yet with the body of a lion, across the shoulders
and back were the strong green and brown scales of the
dragon. Their legs and underbelly the golden fur of the
lion. On their feet where claws like daggers, their tail also

22

bore the spikes of a dragon. Their eyes a pale yellow, but
not weak. Tendrils of smoke escaped from their nostrils
giving evidence that this creature could also breath
flames. Its walk one of sleek beauty, arrogance in its
presence, anger underlining, but all was controlled.

I watched more confused and amazed by the
moment as these fierce looking creatures under his
touch acted as tame as the cats that roamed the castle
halls. I watched carefully, remaining ever on my
guard from just inside the wall, unsure of this turn of
events. Clutching my crossbow tightly I watched as each
creature in turn, moved to look at me. While none left the
presence of their master, they watched me intently
appearing to determine whether I was invited guest, or
interloper in their domain. Deciding whether I was friend,
or enemy and I knew, without hesitation, an enemy stood
no chance here.

At a signal that I did not see, one by one the
creatures stood and approached me. Tightening my
grasp on my crossbow and shield I watched their
approach. Instinct took hold and I took the stance of
battle. Then panicked when my weapons disappeared
from my hands. Moving a step back I did not remove my
eyes from the approaching creatures but turned my
head at the sound of the strange man's voice.

"Stand your place," he commanded "they cannot
befriend you, if they do not know you. Fear the caTragons
not, you are safe here."

Fighting to hide my trembling, I watched warily as
they drew closer, each step deliberate, each step silent.
Stopping before me, never taking their eyes from me they
sat gazing intently at me, looking as if they waited for
something from me. Swallowing my fear I reached out to
the nearest of the beasts. As it took the scent from my

hand, it's eyes never left my face. Satisfied it stood and returned to its master's side. Each beast in turn did the same while I stood quietly, unmoving but for the holding out of my arm. When the last and the largest of the beast approached it did not take the scent from my hand, it sat before me, watching me as if waiting for something that I knew not. I held my breath, waiting for what was to come from this creature. Finally it too stood and returned to it's master. Respect for these beasts, respect for their master and his home had me acting carefully. When all had returned to him, standing close around him, he spoke again.

"Rest for the night, on the morrow. your training begins." Walking to the cot he stretched out, the great beasts resting at his feet and sides, leaving me to find for myself a place to rest. Spreading my cloak on the floor near the wall where I stood I made ready for the night. Tomorrow, I would show this man, this person who still had not revealed his name, that I needed no training to fulfill the vow I had taken. Still, sleep was a long time in coming.

Three

When the morning came it was a rude awakening that awaited me. A sandaled foot shoved against my side, brought me to my feet instantly. Confusion at where I was and what was happening clouded my thoughts as I quickly had my sword drawn and ready. My training had me taking a fighter's stance even before I was fully erect.

The roar of several angry beast brought me back to the here and now. Slowly, I returned my sword to its sheath as they crouched ready and waiting to pounce. A mere glance in their direction from their master had them returning to their place by the fire that roared in its pit. A large pot hung over it with something bubbling inside. The aroma nothing I had ever smelled before. Before I had chance to move a bowl was shoved into my hands with the command to eat,

"You'll need your strength for what you are about to do." was all he said as he walked away.

Looking into the bowl, the scent assailed my nostrils, pungent but not fully unpleasant. Lifting the bowl to my lips I closed my eyes and took a small sip. The thick broth poured onto my tongue. I did not know this food, but as the taste was not disagreeable I soon finished the portion given me. The one without a name was standing before me as I brought the bowl down.

"Will you tell me now, your name? Will you tell me why you are only spoken of in hushed tones in the castle? I need to know, just who it is I will soon prove my

25

abilities." I was not expecting the laughter this brought. The sound humorless and seemingly full of self reproach, yet holding a sound of frustration as well.

"So they still hold their anger do they? Do they, themselves even remember? Or is now more a legend and vague memory than anything else?"

"What is it that you have done that would bring anger that would last this long?" I was beginning again to wonder just what I had fallen into.

"The thing that was done, or not done, is of no concern here. At some time, I may tell you, but not now. I am sure that after the years of telling their version has grown to proportions of great exaggeration. Be that as it may, the name that I am known by, the name spoken as you say in hushed tones, is Guillaume, now come, we have much to do."

Looking for a place to clean the bowl I still held in my hands I heard Guillaume speaking behind me, "Just place it near the table, the caTragons will clean it as they always do."

Glancing at the beasts that were watching the bowl in my hands I did as I was instructed, while my belly churned in disgust. Reaching for my cloak I picked it up from the floor along with my shield and sword. Turning I followed Guillaume from the room. We walked, following a large cavernous tunnel back into the mountainside. Torches protruded from the cavern walls along the way, seeming to light themselves as we approached. Torches that burned brightly, but should not have been enough to light the tunnel this well, yet the way we traveled was lit as if we walked outdoors in the light of the sun. We walked on a stone floor, yet Guillaume's footsteps made no sound. I wondered at these things, but I did not question. Not yet. The tunnel opened into a room that was larger than the Great Hall of the castle. The walls shone with light reflecting off of many precious stones embedded within. Colors of the rainbow danced across the room, reflected from the crystal prisms mounted on a stone table in the center of this place.

Leading me to an open area, Guillaume turned to me. Staring at me intently as if trying to take my measure he finally spoke, instructing me, "Show me what you were taught. Show me, how you fight."

Now I knew I could prove my ability. I could prove that I knew how to fight, not only that I knew how, but that I could fight well, and this, would seal the dragon's fate.

Sliding the sword swiftly from its sheath I began to move. A great elaborate showing of thrusts and blocks. First with the shield, and then without. I went to great lengths to show all that I had learned. When I finally returned my sword to its sheath I turned to Guillaume with an arrogant flourish. My great pride was destroyed when I saw him laughing. Laughing at me. Anger flushed across my face quickly, my voice became tight and strained as I asked what was so funny.

"You were taught the mechanics of battle, you know how to swing that sword. What you were not taught is the mystic part. What you do not know, is how to hold and to actually be, that same sword. In your hands it is merely a weapon. When in your hands, it should be a part of those hands. That, is what you will need to learn. That is what you will have to learn, before you can even consider approaching that dragon, or any dragon with thoughts of its doom."

His laughter angered me, who was he to dare laugh at me? Who was he, one that the elders had

apparently sent away for some wrong doing on his part, to laugh at me? My grip tightened on my sword as my eyes drew closed to mere slits. Feeling my whole body tighten in angry response to his laughter I considered my options. I was after all a bright person, a worthy opponent in a battle, I had been trained well. My mentor, my master teacher is the best in all the land.. but if this he was saying would make me a true fighter in every word, I then was willing to hear what he had to say. If this, that he spoke of would make my chances of success greater in fulfilling my vow, then what he offered, I wished to learn.
"My name, is Adwr, I am your student. Teach me this that you speak of."

"I know what you are called, I have been waiting for you for many days. Your arrival was foretold in the stars and in the cauldron. I have made ready for you, and the task at hand. I tell you now, if you listen to me and learn well what I am going to teach you, by the time this quest has ended, you will be known by a different name."

I watched as Guillaume turned and walked across the cavern to a far wall. At the base of this wall was a table of enormous proportions. Made of stone and polished wood it shone in the light of the torches, an unnatural glow emanating from the center.

"Lay your weapons where you stand and come here."

I did as I was told and then slowly crossed the room to stand at his side. On the table were weapons of such strength and beauty as I had never seen before. Each glowed with a mysterious light, seeming to come from somewhere within them. I reached out slowly only to have Guillaume stop my hand preventing my attempt at grasping the weapons before me.

"You will not touch these until you know them and

28

they know you. You will not hold these, until you understand how to make them become a part of you, an extension of who you are. They will become you."

Once I acknowledged his words with a nod he released my hand. Bringing it back I rubbed my wrist absently as I looked longingly at the sword glowing softly on the table. I wanted this weapon now. I wanted to hold this thing of beauty and death in my hands, but I did not voice my thoughts nor did I reach for it again. I would wait- for now.

"Go back and pick up the weapons that you brought with you and bring them here."

Moving away from the table reluctantly. I walked to where my weapons waited. Turning back I was startled to find Guillaume directly behind me, dagger raised as if to strike. My shield too far away to reach and my hands bare of weapons I could do no more but raise my arms to ward off the blow. Instead of feeling the blade of the dagger pierce my flesh I felt the sting of Guillaume's words.

"You claim to have been taught well, and yet you did not hear nor feel my approach behind you. Just as you were caught unaware by the dragon. You must learn to use all the senses given you, if you are to survive." With those words Guillaume disappeared. I glanced frantically around the room. It was empty but for myself and the torches. I moved quickly around the cavern, in an ever widening circle I searched. In my mind a jumble of thoughts. I knew he had to be here, somewhere. My determination to find him, to prove to him that I was as good as I claimed had me acting without forethought. I searched the room, turning in circles where I stood only to move across the floor and search again.

That was when I heard that cursed laughter. He

was laughing at me once more. I was growing weary of this being nothing more than his entertainment. Stopping where I stood, chest heaving as I sucked in air from my exertions. I wiped the sweat from my brow as I fought to regain control of my thoughts and actions. Somewhere in this fantasy tale where I found myself, was reality. He was here, somewhere. Then a flicker in the air, a disturbance of the dust floating in the light caught my attention and I watched it carefully. Taking one step toward it I concentrated on that ripple. I began to feel, a presence there. Then just as quickly it was gone. The place I watched, was empty. Then I had a feeling, similar to a chill run along my back, turning I glanced about the room, attempting to focus on the unseen. Closing my mind to the real, I sought the surreal. There, just for a moment, was another wave created in the dust. This time I did not step forward. This time I waited. By centering all of my concentration on the feelings I had, to recognize the unseen movements while ignoring what my sight was trying to tell me, I could feel him moving closer. Still I stood, waiting, turning my head slowly around, making that I was scanning the room for his where abouts while I felt his slow approach. I could feel the changes taking place in my senses, the hair on my arms and along my neck raised, my breathing grew shallow as I prepared for his appearance. So attuned to him now I could feel his approach, almost hear his silent footfall on the rock floor. Another ripple in the dust mere inches away from me had me flexing my fingers in anticipation. He was here, I knew he was here. Then he was gone, just like that.

"So," came Guillaume's voice back over at the polished table, "you can do that. It had been foretold, and now it is proven. You do have the ability to sense the presence of what you cannot see. It has just gone unknown and untrained. We will sharpen and strengthen that in your lessons."

"And just how will you do that?" I had to ask.

"With practice." was Guillaume's response, just as he again disappeared leaving me standing once more alone in the room. Taking a cleansing breath, I began to close out the sounds of the real, and allow my growing sense of the surreal to gain in strength and focus. Concentrating on what lay just behind the curtain of sight. This time, it was just a slight shadow across the torch light, the sight of Guillaume's hand the only acknowledgment he had been found. He was again gone, disappearing into the hidden world. Hour after hour passed as we played this game of cat and mouse. Hour after hour even as my body grew tired, I grew stronger in vision. I listened to instructions that seemed to sound more inside my head than be heard by my ear. I learned to shut down the sight of the real, and feel with an inner vision, watching with that inner eye, the unseen in the room. In the midst of that training I saw a form that moved silently through the mists of reality and magic and before all my eyes, Guillaume was there. I watched as he moved, not realizing yet that I could actually see him. When he stopped, my eyes stopped, when he moved again, I followed his steps. My stance did not change, my body did not move. It was only with my eyes that I followed him. I controlled my breathing to hide the excitement that ran through my body. The feeling a giddy one almost like the feeling brought on by the fine wine served back at the castle. Yet something, gave me away.

"So you can now see me, even here." came Guillaume's voice. "good."

I watched as he stepped through the curtain from that world to this and stood before me. "Enough for today, we will begin again tomorrow." with that he turned and walked to the entrance of the corridor that would take us back to his chambers. Leaving me once again no choice but to follow.

Following Guillaume back down the corridor I was not surprised to see that the torches were going out behind us as we passed. Seemingly all on their own. I wasn't surprised that even though I listened intently, Guillaume's footsteps made no sound while I sounded like a clumsy mule tripping my way along. The weaponry that I carried rattling with each step, the sound echoing off the chamber walls.

The moment I entered Guillaume's chamber he spoke up. "Go outside the wall, off to the left you will find wood for the fire. Gather enough wood and bring it back inside so that we can prepare our meal."

I really should have thought first but I didn't. "Why do you not just use your magic and make the wood appear?"

"Young Warrior, it is only because of your ignorance in this that I do not get angry. Understand this, when one has a talent, any talent...when one has a gift, a training, that ability is to be used only as intended and only for good. When talents are used for selfish reasons, then no good can come from that. When one takes advantage of a gift for the wrong reasons, they become lazy in body and lazy in spirit. They begin to feel self important. They feel that their gift makes them better than others in some way, they are above others and that all of those below them should pay homage to them. In fact, it is the opposite of that. If you have a gift, that gift should only be used in the service of others, carefully and respectfully. Do You understand that?"

When I only nodded in response he glared at me, waiting. "Yes, I understand." Even though, I wasn't fully convinced he was right I went for the wood. Walking across the room toward the wall that I hoped would allow me outside I noticed a movement. Turning to see I watched confused as a caTragon stood and stretched. The creature now had the head and mane of a lion on the body of a dragon. The dark scales covered its body from just behind the mane all the way back. While it stood only four feet tall it had to be nine feet long from the end of its snout to the end of its tail. Its front feet still bore the razor sharp daggers for claws.

Guillaume watched me closely while I stood looking at the caTragon my thoughts racing. There was a lesson here, I knew there was, but what? Turning to Guillaume I spoke slowly, "Never expect anything but the unexpected. What I think is true, may in fact be false. What I think is set, could change at any given time."

With that Guillaume almost smiled, instead he looked down at the caTragon at his side waiting for attention and spoke whether to it or himself, he spoke loud enough for me to hear. "There may be a chance for this one yet."

Watching as he scratched the caTragon behind the ears absently I turned and stepped through the wall. Again it parted as water around a stone, opening and then quickly coming together behind me. Finding the wood just where Guillaume said it would be I gathered as much as I could carry in my arms. Having never carried wood in this manner before it took a couple of attempts before I could balance the sticks in my arms to where I wasn't dropping them every time I tried to move. A student in every form, I muttered to myself as I walked back toward the rock face.

Fighting with every step to balance the wood I carried, I walked slowly around the side of the rock. My mind repeatedly going over the events of the day, move by move. Distracted, I almost made an error that I felt was intended by Guillaume. Stopping before I attempted walking through the wall I looked at it carefully. To the average eye, the entire face of the rock looked solid. Just to prove a point I kicked a stone toward the rock and it bounced off the surface and back almost to the toe of my boot. I slowly and carefully searched the rock wall for a sign, any sign of where the opening was. As my eyes roamed down the rock I concentrated, seeking the normal so that the abnormal would show, finally coming to rest on an area just to the right of center. Smiling I walked to this place and through the wall into Guillaume's chamber. Carrying the wood over to the fire pit I placed it against the wall, returning one piece to the stack that fell, with not a little noise to the floor.

Guillaume spoke not a word to me, he in fact did not look in my direction, but I knew, yes, I knew that he had watched my movements. Looking past him to the pit I noticed that a fire was already burning. Leaning in to see what he had used for wood I saw that it was the wooden bowls from the morning meal. Before my mind had time to gather the words for a question Guillaume spoke. "You didn't really think that I would eat out of a bowl after a caTragon did you?"

"I would not have presumed to state my opinion either way, being that our acquaintance is such a short

34

one." I answered as I moved to sit on the floor in the
place where I had slept the night before. Pulling my bag
close to me I ran my hand across the soft leather.
This bag had been created just for me. Tanned until it
could not have been softer, yet stitched in such a manner
that it had lost none of its strength. I only allowed a
fleeting thought of the castle and those I had left there.
How they were faring, whether the dragon had returned
to cause more destruction, whether they had discovered
my disappearance, whether..... knowing that this was a
dangerous road to allow my thoughts to travel I forced
myself to leave that line of thinking and opened the bag.
Reaching inside I removed the items I had brought to
make more arrows for my crossbow. Placing them by my
side I began to work as Guillaume added things to the
bubbling cauldron. Things I was not about to inquire as to
their identity.

Guillaume's feet suddenly appeared before me, I
looked up as he was reaching down. I watched as he
picked up one of the cut stones from the floor beside me.
Turning the crystal in his hand he examined it. The purple
colors inside the otherwise clear stone seemed to glow in
his hand. "I see you are using Grandite, what made you
choose to use this stone?"

I thought for a moment whether to answer that
question, then after recalling the events of the day went
ahead. "I was searching for the stone to use to make the
other half of the arrowhead. I entered the wood on the
north side of the castle and followed a trail that looked to
have not been traveled in a great while. This trail was
covered in various stones, but I did not choose any of
them. When I came to a fork in the trail I thought long
over my choice. The path to the right was still covered in
stone. The path to the left, was all but bare. Still,

something seemed to draw me to the left. I chose not to ignore the feeling but to follow it and I went left. The path began to go up into the mountains. The longer I walked, the steeper the climb became. At the edge of the forest, there were great boulders in a line. I hesitated but the feeling still pulled at me, so I stepped between the stones and onto the nearly bare hillside. There before me were these stones. As soon as I set foot inside and saw the stones, the hillside began to glow with a purple light. The air became warmer, but not uncomfortably so. Looking closely I saw that many were of the perfect size, they would only need be shaped and sharpened for the arrowhead. I had never seen such stones as these before, but I somehow felt inside that these stones were special.   Stepping further out onto the hillside I collected only enough for two dozen arrows. Leaving the rest undisturbed and untouched."

Stopping to take a deep breath and collect my thoughts I looked up to see Guillaume listening and watching me closely. "Continue..how did you shape these stones into this form?"

Turning a stone over slowly in my hand I felt it as it began to warm. I watched as in my hands, the same purple light that I had witnessed in the stone in Guillaume's hand, began to shine. Hesitating, fearing sounding like a madman, I answered in a low voice. "I thought in my mind how I wanted the stones to look, seeing in my mind a picture of it. I was holding a stone at the time, in my left hand. When I reached across to get a chisel I rubbed my right hand across the stone. The edges of the stone simply fell away, leaving it shaped exactly as I had pictured it."

Guillaume returned the stone in his hand to me, then turned to walk back to the cauldron. I could hear as the spoon scraped against the side as he dished up our meal. Crossing the room to the table he set the bowls in place and took his seat. He waited until I had joined him before he finally spoke again.

"Grandite is a stone that is as old or older than this sphere that we dwell on. It is a stone that is more than a mere rock. Grandite is a stone that has life within it. It has a power, a magic that exceeds any other magic known in this lifetime. One could search all of history, or look to the stars for what is to come in the times after this. They would find nothing with the powers that this stone has."

"Is there not a great danger in it then should it fall into the hands of one bent on evil?"

"There would be yes, but Grandite has the ability to protect itself. It is only found when it wants to be. It is a stone with a powerful magic, but it is also a stone that is designed for service. When it saw what you needed it to be, it became that."

Spooning a portion from the bowl before me I took a bite of the meal Guillaume had prepared. I didn't even taste it as the words he had just spoken tumbled about in my head. "And what about a stone that is made into an arrowhead and is shot at the target but somehow gets lost. Whether the target carries it away or it misses and goes off into an area where it can not be found. What of it then?"

"I can only speak here on what I know of the legend as I have never lost a stone. Legend tells that if a Grandite stone is lost while in service, rather than risk falling into the wrong and possibly dangerous hands, then the Grandite loses its magic. It becomes a mere piece of quartz. Never again to shine."

The rest of the meal was finished in

companionable silence. The only sounds were of our spoons scraping the bowls and of the caTragons smacking their lips as they waited for the remains.

Once the meal was finished Guillaume stood and taking both bowls motioned in the direction of the wall. Turning I was only mildly surprised as the sight of the cot awaiting me. "Rest,"Guillaume told me, "tomorrow is another day."

Exhaustion brought sleep on quickly, but my mind refused to slow as thoughts raced about as madly as the few jousting matches I had been privileged to witness. Running crazily, directly at each other then trampling one over the other as horses hooves pounding across the jousting field, kicking up dust and chunks of earth. Rest, was not had on this night.

Four

The dreams were back. It had been many a fortnight without them, I had hoped that they were gone for good but no, they had returned. Bringing with them once again the feeling that something was missing, something was so very wrong. Try as I might, I could not understand the dreams. The pictures were not clear, the images moved past too quickly to catch. I knew though, that I was running. I could feel myself moving quickly, I could feel the air leaving my lungs. At the same time, I could taste the fear that was making me run. I didn't know if I were running to something or away. I just knew I had to hurry, yet no matter how hard I tried, I was getting nowhere. Corridors stretched out endlessly before me, turning and twisting left and right as I ran. My destination somewhere unknown, as I still ran on.

I woke abruptly, chest heaving, I moved carefully, sitting up in the cot I pushed my hair back from my face. Soaked in sweat it clung to my face and neck. A shiver ran down my back as I looked out into the darkness. The only sound was that of Guillaume and the caTragon's breathing on the other side of the room. Finally my breathing slowed and my heart's pounding eased. Relaxing back onto the cot I pulled my cloak back up across my shoulders as I once again sought sleep. Never before had the dreams came more than once in a night. On this night, they did return. Only this time, there was a difference. I knew exactly where I was in the dream. I was in one of the sealed corridors of the castle, standing off to the side I watched myself, an observer yet still a participant to a never ending terror.

Running I could hear my sandals as they

slapped against the stone floors. The sound echoed along the many corridors, following me with each turn. I could see the tapestries along the walls, the colors running and blending together into a blur of indecipherable hue. Tapestries that would blow in the breeze created as I ran past them on my way-- to where? Where was I going? Where? And why was it so important that I get there so quickly?   Trapped in the nightmare I tossed and turned on the cot until I managed to roll from it onto the floor. Landing with a crash as the cot turned over onto my back. I heard the hiss as a torch came to life, sending light across a small area of the chamber. Shoving the cot away I sat up and turned to look at Guillaume.

" How long have you had those dreams?" was all he asked.

Seeing no condemnation, nor any ridicule I decided to respond honestly. "I have suffered from them for as long as I can recall. I had gone many nights without them, until tonight. They torment me in that I can never see them in a way that is understandable, only in pieces that are disconnected. There is something that has happened that causes me to run. In every one of the dreams I am running as fast as I possibly can. I know not why, or to where. It is mostly the feelings that I carry with me. Feelings of something.......gone so terribly wrong."

"And you do not know what that is?"

"No, Guillaume, I do not know what it is that has gone so wrong. I just know that it has and that I have to run for help. Yes, that's it, I'm running for help. I just never get there." I turned again in Guillaume's direction to see him and the caTragons watching me. There was nothing in his eyes but a look of thoughtfulness.

"Go back to sleep," he finally said, "tomorrow is

another day of lessons."

When the room was once again in darkness, I settled back onto the up righted cot and stared into the night. The thought returning again and again.. I was running for help..for who? Who was it that needed help so desperately? Finally sleep once again claimed me, this time, the dreams did not return.

The morning brought a manner of awakening unexpected. Feeling a hot burst of air and then something wet across my face I opened my eyes. Standing beside my cot looking down at me was the largest of the caTragons. Watching the beast carefully I was relieved when it turned and walked away, back across the room. Slowly moving to a sitting position I attempted to shake the night from my head and move into this new day. The remnants of the night's dreams still clouded my brain as I fought to understand.

"Here, drink this." Guillaume commanded as he handed me a mug of something hot and steaming. With the first tentative sip I knew this was something I had never tasted before. Bitter but not intolerable, it stirred my being enough that I felt sleep falling away. Standing I followed the caTragon's path across the room to the table. Taking my place, I leaned forward resting my arms on the table as the caTragon and I both watched as Guillaume approached bowls in hand. Placing a bowl in front of me Guillaume sat down and began to eat. Bowing my head I offered a silent grace to the Higher Power and upon opening my eyes reached for a spoon. I could feel

Guillaume watching me but I did not look up. When I lifted the last spoonful of food to my mouth Guillaume spoke, "What do you remember of your dreams?"

I did not wish to discuss it, but saw no way out of it. "Mostly what I remember is feelings. The feeling that something has gone terribly wrong some how. Some one that I never see is in trouble and needs help."

"Do you know who it is? What else do you remember?"

"No, I never see anyone, its just a feeling that there is someone else. The only thing that I can remember seeing, are the halls of the castle as I run. That is all I see. That is all I ever see."

When Guillaume did not respond I looked up at him. He was sitting with his head bowed staring at nothing. A single tear fell from his eye and landed on the table creating a very small stain on the wood. Confused at what I was seeing, I said nothing.

Finally Guillaume stood, carrying his bowl back across the room he spooned out another portion of food and set in on the floor for the caTragon. Taking my bowl and repeating the process he then walked toward the same corridor we had traveled just the day before.

"Come, you have a lot to learn."

Unsure of what today's lessons would entail I retrieved all of my weapons then followed Guillaume down the corridor. I watched as up ahead of me the torches flared to life moments before Guillaume reached them. Entering the cavern I was surprised to find the room filled with smoke.

"Guillaume? Guillaume? Are you here?" I shouted as I eased my way into the room, struggling to see. Pulling my cloak up across my mouth and nose I walked into the room. My eyes and throat began to burn but I still moved forward. The smoke began to boil and roll before me, growing thicker by the moment. Bumping into the table in the center of the room I stopped and grasped the edge trying to figure out what to do. Suddenly I had a clear memory of how the room looked and it dawned on me, there was nothing in this room that would burn in a way creating this much smoke. Just as the thought came to me a large dragon rose up directly before me. The roar emanating from somewhere deep in its throat causing the table behind me to shake, rattling the crystals resting there. Its yellow eyes creating an eerie glow in the smoke. Swinging its massive head it approached where I stood. With each roar from the dragon flames danced across the air before it.

I drew no weapon, but I did not back away. I watched closely as the beast approached. All of my instincts told me to stand my ground. Even as memories from my nightmares tormented me, I stood my ground. From somewhere in my memory I heard a voice shouting, still I couldn't understand the words. When the dragon was within a foot of where I stood it stopped. Lowering its head it looked me directly in the eye. Determinedly standing my ground a battle raged with in me, one voice screaming run, the other instructing me to stand still. As my hands trembled and my stomach churned I stood where I was, waiting. When I did not move the smoke suddenly swallowed the dragon and I was left alone. The room, was silent. I did not move from where I stood.

Some thing quietly moved into the room. Remaining as still as I possibly could I waited, straining to hear. The smoke danced before me, but all was silent. There was a presence in the room, it moved to one side, then the other. No, there was more than one presence in the room. They were circling around me, behind me. I

43

could feel what ever it was closing in, the circle around me growing smaller. When the smoke shifted I found myself surrounded by several large caTragons. Snarling and growling they circled around me. One or the other would jump in close, snapping at me only to back away, rejoining the group slowly circling. I watched them carefully, but did not move from where I stood. When the smoke closed in I held my breath, listening to my feelings I knew they were gone. Only then did I breathe again.

When a snake larger than any I had ever seen before suddenly dropped across my shoulders I instinctively grabbed it and tossed it away into the smoke. It was then I heard that cursed laughter from Guillaume. As the room cleared of all the smoke I saw Guillaume sitting on the floor across the room. He continued to laugh as I stood staring at him. Tears rolled from his eyes as he held his sides while he laughed uncontrollably. Leaning back against the table I crossed my arms over my chest and waited for him to regain control.

When he stood the caTragons trotted silently across the room to stand beside him. Absently he reached down and stroked the nearest beast which reveled in the touch.

"Your name, what you are called by, is wrong. Before your quest is over, it will be changed. It will be corrected" Turning away from me Guillaume left the room with the caTragons trailing along obediently behind.

Gathering my weapons from where I had dropped them in the smoke I wondered at his words. All the while a lost memory teased the edges of my mind. Dancing away before I could grasp what it was.

I walked into the chamber to see Guillaume

44

tossing the last piece of firewood onto the flames burning under his ever bubbling cauldron. I turned toward the wall even before I heard his words, "We need more wood."

Stepping through the wall, feeling it flow closed behind me I blinked in the bright light, blinded momentarily. Once adjusted to the glare of the afternoon sunlight I turned toward where I knew the wood pile was located. As I walked, my mind repeatedly going over the past couple of days. Recollections of my dreams, foggy and unclear floated in and out of my thoughts, teasing me with understanding that was just out of reach. Lost in thought I reached for sticks balancing them in my arms. Without warning every fiber in my being went onto alert. Someone was here. Dropping the wood I swung about in one smooth move turning to face who ever or what ever was there as I drew my sword. The area before me was empty. Without moving I could see the trees around me, the low growing brush that fell away in to the small clearing before Guillaume's rock. Sight told me, there was nothing there. Instinct told me otherwise. "I know you are here." I spoke aloud then waited.

Feeling a presence to my right I turned quickly, holding my sword at the ready. Standing before me was a giant of a man, no not a man. This was a being I had only heard mentioned in whispers. "So, you are not a legend after all. The mindful whisperings and ranting of one too far lost in drink. Are you friend or are you adversary?"

At my bravado the Cyclops before me merely smiled. Odd that the smile seemed tinged with sadness. "So, it is true, you do not remember. I am Opsis, I am your friend. Guillaume told me that you were soon to be here. I see that he was right in his predictions. You have grown tall since last I saw you."

Standing straighter, eyes narrowing in suspicion I

45

grasped my sword tighter "When did you ever see me?"

"It was a time long ago, before the banishment. It was before you became known as Adwr."

"Before.." the question I intended to ask broken off by Guillaume's voice interrupting.

"Opsis, I see you have arrived. Come my friend, join us at our table in a meal." Looking to me, his expression one of amusement and yet, somewhere in the depths of his eyes, I could have sworn I saw a prideful satisfaction. "Bring the wood." was all that he said as he turned to walk away with Opsis.

Now, I had yet another addition to the puzzle that this quest had become. Another question added to the confusion that tormented my thoughts.

I carried the wood into the chamber and stacked it carefully in its place. Removing my sword I moved to rinse the dirt from my hands before joining Guillaume and Opsis at the table. The steam drifting upward bringing the mouthwatering scent of the food to me as I bowed my head to offer grace. Upon opening my eyes I saw I was being silently watched.

"Why do you do that?" Opsis asked.

Seeing that it was an honest inquiry and not an insult I shrugged. "I offer thanks for the meal, I ask for blessings for days to come. That the food give strength of body for what ever is to come in those days. I ask blessings on behalf of those that cannot ask for themselves."

Opsis nodded in response and turned again to Guillaume. Not before I had noted that far away look in his eye. There again was that hint of sadness, the reason

46

for it going unspoken, even though I knew that both
Guillaume and Opsis knew the cause. I finished my meal
in silence, allowing the talk to flow around me even
though I paid it little mind.

When the caTragons that had been sitting off to
the side of the table stood and began to growl oddly we
three as one looked up to see what was the cause.
Guillaume turned from the caTragons and looked to the
wall. In a moment, with the simple lifting of a hand, it
changed from the appearance of solid rock to an opaque
shimmer. Together we watched as outside there was a
movement among the trees. Shaking violently, causing
leaves to tear away and fall to the earth. Smoke
appeared in bursts and disappeared. The dragon was
here. Excitement rose in my chest as I watched it walk
from the forest. Slowly it approached the rock wall of
Guillaume's hideaway. Standing just on the other side it
glared unmoving at the wall.

"It knows we are here." I spoke in a whisper.

Swiftly raising his hand Guillaume silenced me.

The dragon stood still for what seemed an
extraordinary length of time. Simply standing and staring
at the wall. With a roar that sounded from the depths of
somewhere evil flame erupted from its throat bathing the
wall before it. Involuntarily I jumped back. Remembering
the feel of those flames. Yet, they did not enter the room.
It knew we were here, but it could not see us, could not
get to us. It could only stand on the outside and vent its
frustrations on the rock wall it faced. Finally turning away
it lashed out one last time. With a vicious swipe of its
muscular tail it struck the rock wall violently. Pebbles
rained down from above, rolling off the hillside and
directly to the dragon's feet.

I turned slowly and reached for my sword behind

me. Held fast it would not move from the wall where it stood in its sheath. Turning angrily to Guillaume I spoke, the words barely audible from a tight throat. "Release this. Give me my sword and allow me do what I have vowed to do."

"It is not yet time." was all he said.

"What do you mean? How can it not be time? The dragon stands before us, within reach of my sword or in the very least my crossbow. Release them from what ever hold you have placed them under and allow me to fulfill my vow.

"It is not yet time." Guillaume folded his arms, his hands shoved into the voluminous sleeves of his cloak, resting them on the table before him. He watched the dragon closely, never taking his eyes from the beast as it disappeared back into the forest.

Slamming my fists onto the table in frustration the bowls and mugs jumped and threatened to over turn. The growl that began in my own throat sounding more animal than human. Slowly it turned into a wail of anger and frustration. Jumping to my feet, the bench I had sat on overturned, slamming to the floor. Crossing the room I stood by the wall, looking out into the deserted clearing. Staring still even as the wall closed away leaving me glaring at the gray, granite surface. Turning swiftly I nearly shouted, "Why?"

"It is not yet time," Guillaume answered, continuing before I could interrupt, "you will understand, in time. When it is right, all things will be revealed. Now, the time is not right. There is still much to do."

When his raised hand stopped further comments I moved stiff and angry over to my cot. Stretching out I turned my back on them. Refusing to acknowledge their existence. Before sleep overcame my anger and took me

48

into a place of rest I heard Opsis speak softly.   "He is still young, even as he becomes a man." Then, I heard no more.

The next time I awoke it was to a completely different situation. Both Guillaume and Opsis sat at the table, bowls and mugs before them as they talked. Several caTragons lay close by hoping for hand outs. Rising from the cot I walked over to the cauldron and spooned out a helping of its contents. Pouring a mug of Guillaume's steaming brew I crossed the room and took my place at the table. Ignoring the looks I bowed my head offering grace before I began eating.

"You do not speak when you enter the presence of your elders?" Opsis asked me. "Have you lost all of the manners I know you have been taught? Many of them by me."

Placing the spoon carefully in the bowl I looked up at Opsis and Guillaume."I did not wish to be rude and interrupt your conversation."

"He does have a point there Opsis old friend." Guillaume spoke, coughing to cover the laughter in his voice.

"No, no he does not actually have a point," Opsis argued, "he was taught how to approach any given situation, with his elders or with anyone else. Be they parent, teacher, knight or blade-smith. Now, whether he was expected and made to use them after what happened, that is something that I do not know. What I do know is that he now has to remember those lessons- and use what he learned. You, yourself should know that I am right, in the face of destiny, all lessons have their place."

I watched as Guillaume thought about what Opsis

had said and then slowly nodded. "You are correct in this and I am in error." Looking to me he continued to speak,"Get up from the table, take your bowl and approach it as you were once taught."

Clenching my fists tightly I glared at Guillaume. I could feel my mouth drawing tightly closed as I bit the inside of my cheek. I sat in my place very still, my back straight and shoulders back as I stared across the table. I had agreed to be student to Guillaume's teaching, who did this Opsis dare to think that he was to now demand of me? Only once did I allow the thought that I am not a child- I am a warrior- to pass through my mind. I knew, that to voice that thought, would to give me the very appearance of what I denied being. Slowly I rose from the bench and picked up my bowl and mug. Silently and with movements made stiff by the indignation I felt, I walked back across the room to the cauldron. Waiting a moment I then turned and crossed the room back to the table. Guillaume and Opsis were again deep in conversation. This time I stood behind my place at the table, bowl in hand, waiting. I feared that they would add to my indignation by ignoring me and forcing me to stand in place for an extended time for their entertainment. Even the caTragons were watching the unfolding events as if they understood.

Suddenly I noticed that the room was quiet, Opsis and Guillaume had stopped speaking and were watching me. Feeling a betraying blush creep up my cheeks I tried to ignore it as I spoke. "Good morning Guillaume, Opsis. I trust you are well and would not mind that I join you at the table for a meal."

"All is well indeed young student, you are more than welcome to join us at the table." Guillaume spoke as he waved his hand across the table in form of invitation. Once again taking my place I returned to eating.

Between mouthfuls I looked to Guillaume, "I have told you my name, yet you refuse to address me with it, calling me anything other than what I have said or even nothing at all."

Guillaume looked directly at me, staring solemnly for several moments before answering. "I will call you by your name, when it is by your name that you are called."

Dropping my spoon into the now empty bowl I looked from Guillaume to Opsis and back again. "What is it that you know, that I do not. Or that my mind hides away from me. What secrets do you carry? Why were you banished from the castle? What, if anything does that book you now carry with you always, have to do with all of this?"

"Questions, that will all be answered in their time, when the time is right." Guillaume responded to my outburst.

"And just when, will the time be right? How will I know, when the time is right?"

Opsis spoke up, "You will know that the time is right, when you have the answers. Let us go now, your lessons await you."

Giving in for the moment I carried my bowl over to the cauldron for the third time. This time I filled it then placed it on the floor for the caTragons. Gathering my weapons I turned to follow Opsis and Guillaume from the chamber.

FIVE

I walked down the corridor head bowed muttering to myself. "Everything will be understood when the time is right.. when the time is right, you will know it all..I will call you your name, when your name is what you are called..circles, he talks in circles. They could tell me. It wouldn't hurt for them to share something, anything to give me a better idea what's going on here."

Still muttering my discontent I wasn't paying attention when I walked into the Great Chamber. At the sound of a dragon's roar I stopped suddenly and looked up. I wasn't in the Great Chamber, I was outside the walls in the forest and standing before me was a dragon. A very large, very angry looking dragon. It wasn't the dragon that I sought, still, it looked as if I were about to go into battle. Reaching for my sword my hand found an empty sheath. Taking my eyes off the dragon just long enough to look I saw that my sword was indeed missing. Pulling my bag quickly from my shoulders I blindly searched for my crossbow, it too was gone.

I slowly began to back away as my mind considered and rejected various ideas. As I retreated the dragon moved forward. Swinging his massive head from side to side he continued to approach. With a roar that frightened the birds out of the trees and mice from the grass beneath them, the dragon drew closer. Backing up against a tree I fought panic. I couldn't understand how I had gotten outside, or where and how my weapons disappeared. As the dragon drew closer I knew I had to forget worrying about what I didn't have for the moment and start thinking of a way out of this mess.

Swinging around to the back side of the tree I

searched the area behind me. Deciding that the best course of action would be to put myself in action I moved away from the tree to run. As I stepped away from the tree my tunic caught on a broken branch. Grabbing it I tore it away from the tree and began to run. Blast if the dragon didn't decide to chase after me into the woods. Dodging in and among the trees I tried to either lose the dragon or find a safe hiding place. Something though was bothering me, I just couldn't quite figure it out as I ran. Then trying to keep up with where the dragon was, I listened as it followed. To be as big as it was, it didn't make much noise as it ran. I didn't hear trees crashing to the ground as it forced its way through. Why had it not taken to the air as a way to catch up with me or find me quicker than running through the woods?

As I ran, something in the tree ahead of me caught my eye. Running up to the tree I swung in place behind it and pulled the colored cloth free from the tree. It fit perfectly into the hole in my tunic. I was running in circles. No, that wasn't possible, I hadn't made any turns. I was running straight, but I ended up back where I had started, unless I hadn't really ran anywhere at all.

Guillaume's voice came back to me, "Understand that not all things are as they seem. Stop and look to see if things are actually as you think you are seeing them."

"What is it about the dragon that is wrong? Think think think.." I instructed myself, I could hear it approaching. It wasn't running though, it seemed to know I was close by and that it had plenty of time to find me. Almost as if it were playing a game of some sort. Still I thought, running possibilities through my head as to what was wrong with this particular dragon. "To be a dragon the thing is quiet as a cat...or a caTragon."

Stepping away from the tree I yelled out to

53

Guillaume, "I've figured out your game this time Guillaume..I know I am still in the great chamber and I know its really a caTragon that stalks me."

With that said, the forest disappeared and I found myself standing just to the right of the table in the center of the great chamber. Opsis stood behind the table holding my sword and crossbow.

"Well done." he said as he handed my weapons back to me. Then placing a hand on my shoulder he turned to Guillaume. "The boy did well, he still learns quickly."

"Yes, you are correct in what you say." Guillaume answered as he stood near the entrance, the caTragon at his side. "Still, he is not yet ready. He will need to learn when to and when not to use those weapons that he so quickly reaches for. "Come, let us go. This is enough for one day."

Guillaume's words angered me and I spoke without thinking, "What do you mean this is enough? I am not tired, I am ready to learn more. I want to learn what you have to teach me- now- so that I can finish my quest. I want to do more- now." In the center of the room, I stood with feet slightly apart braced for what was to come. I watched as Guillaume and the caTragon turned almost as one to face me. I could see Opsis out of the corner of my eye as he too watched Guillaume.

Guillaume stood silently watching me, the look on his face was unreadable. I didn't know how badly I had angered him with my outburst, or even if I had angered him at all. He spoke not a word, merely stood in the entrance of the great chamber watching me. Not about to back down I stood just as I was, waiting, returning Guillaume's look stare for stare. The longer I stood in place, the warmer the great chamber became. I could feel the sweat running down my back, ignoring it I stood still. At one point the sweat dripped from my hair into my eye, the pain intense, yet I was determined not to show any weakness in my stance. I stood, unmoving as I waited. While the room grew ever warmer.

Opsis crossed the room to stand near Guillaume. He spoke low, but I still heard his words, "Don't you think this is long enough, old friend? Can we not return to your chamber now?"

"No, I think not," Guillaume finally spoke. "He wants another lesson, he shall have another lesson." Looking down he spoke to the caTragon at his feet with words I did not understand. The caTragon obediently rose and crossed the room to stand in front of me.

Guillaume finally spoke then to me. "On the day I saved you from a dragon's fiery death, you yourself indentured yourself as my student. You, asked to be taught. As student, it is your position to listen to the master, not turn and give instructions as if the positions have been reversed. A dragon lives forever unless felled by warrior's sword, this one is no different. It will still be here when you are ready. You are not yet ready. But, rather than take time and give yourself a chance to reflect on what you have learned and absorb it into your very heart and spirit, you want to rush through as if this dragon will somehow disappear, or maybe you fear that someone else will kill this dragon before you get to it. You need not fear that. This dragon waits for you, only you can end its reign of terror. But since you seem to be in such a rush and you demand of me another lesson, another lesson you shall have."

When Guillaume fell silent again I waited. I could feel my spirits rise, the excitement growing within me. Even after all he had said, my thoughts were still, the sooner I get these 'lessons' out of the way, the sooner I can take care of that dragon. My warrior's sword was aching to sink into the monster's heart. I stood waiting for the lesson, feeling the room still growing ever hotter. Even the air seemed to smolder as if about to burst into flames. Each breath I took burned my throat and lungs. Soon it would be unbearable in here. I longed to mop the sweat from my brow, but again I refused to show weakness. My mouth dry I ached for water, yet I was quiet.

"I am going to give you a lesson in patience. You will stand right where you are, since you seem comfortable there, until I say you may walk away. You are not to speak. You are not to move. You are to wait. To keep you company and to keep you honest in this, the caTragon will stay with you. I would recommend doing as I had just instructed as peaceful as they seem, caTragons can get ornery when they wish. This particular caTragon has the worst disposition of the lot of them."

When I looked down at the caTragon it snarled angrily at my movement. Raising my head back up I faced Guillaume for the rest of his instructions. Opsis stood behind him silently watching me. It was difficult to tell with him but I could swear that he wanted to say something to Guillaume, or to me, but did not. There was in his expression, lurking just in the depths of his eye that hint of sadness and possibly pride.

"You will have noticed by now that this great chamber has grown rather warm. If you will take the time to remember your lessons on the land, you will recall that Fire Mountain is only a good day's run from here. While

Fire Mountain has slept peacefully for many ages now, its fire is not gone out. The lava that feeds it flows from many parts of this land directly to the mountain. Just as the seas flow in and out on the phases of the moon, so does the lava flow. Now is the time that the lava flows to the mountain, under this very chamber. It will flow for the rest of this day. The floor to this room, the very air in this chamber will grow increasingly hotter as the day passes. I had hoped to spare you of the discomfort but since you are not tired, and you want another lesson -now- you shall have it. You, and your warrior sword will remain where you are until I give the caTragon the command to allow you to leave."

With that Guillaume and Opsis turned and left the Great Chamber. Leaving me standing in the center of the room, alone with a caTragon that was watching me too closely for comfort. It seemed as if this beast was just waiting for me to make a mistake so that he could inflict punishment. While the room, grew increasingly hotter.

After Guillaume and Opsis disappeared from view down the corridor I listened as the sound of their voices slowly faded away. I kept watching the entrance hoping against hope that Guillaume would relent and return to call off the caTragon so that I could leave this place. Long moments passed and Guillaume did not return. While the room continued to get hotter. I watched as areas of the floor seemed to glow from the heat while the air shimmered and steamed above it. Water ran down the walls only to evaporate into steam before reaching the floor. All of this gave the room the appearance of melting, just what I felt that I was doing. My tunic was soaked in sweat, clinging to my back, just as my hair clung to my face. Looking at the caTragon, the beast showed no sign of discomfort. In fact he seemed at ease in the heat and almost to be enjoying it.

"You could at least pant of something." I spoke to the beast, which earned me a growl and an angry glare.

Falling back into the commanded silence I waited. I closed my eyes in the hope of preventing any of the sweat that poured down my face from making it into them. I was burning enough, I didn't need to add that to it. As I stood there, I felt my mind begin to wander. As the heat in the room stole the air from my lungs it broke my concentration and took my mind back to a time long forgotten. A time hidden and locked away far back in the back of faded memories.

I was hearing what sounded like laughter, like the giggles of a young child or rather children at play. I felt that one was me, then there was one, maybe two others judging by the sounds. Nothing I was seeing was very clear, it was as if I were looking through a heavy fog that shifted and moved, almost revealing things only to hide them once again. Watching this I began to see where I was, it was the Great Hall in the castle, but not as it was when I left it. This room was different somehow. The fireplace was the same, and as it normally is, there was a fire burning low, I could see a spark dance out ever so often. The great banquet tables looked the same in the brief moments I had to see them. There was a tapestry hanging over the fireplace that I did not recognize. For some reason it had large golden cords that hung down on either side. I couldn't make out the design on the inside of the hanging. I heard a voice calling to me.. " Come and help us, please.." the rest became muffled and I watched as through the fog someone was reaching for the golden cords. The figure turned back to me, I saw what appeared to be a girl, but I only guessed because of the manner of dress, as the figure was but a blur. I watched as they motioned for me to come help move a chair. I began shaking my head no, "No, we're not to bother with that, come away"

When the figure continued to motion for help and I continued to refuse I could see the figure turn stiffly in my direction. Pointing at me I plainly heard an angry voice taunting me, "Adwr, Adwr Adwr.. you have a new name and its Adwr!"

"No, that is not my name."

"Yes it is, yes it is..Adwr, Adwr Adwr. new name new name new name new name.." the voice began to fade into the recesses of my mind from where it had come.

"That's NOT my name, its NOT my name!!" I shouted over and over again..

I turned angrily toward the sounds but just as they had come, the visions were gone. Feeling I wasn't alone I opened my eyes to see Guillaume and Opsis watching me. "That is not my name..but, if that's not my name...then what is it?" Neither answered as I looked from one to the other and back.

"Guillaume, who was it in the castle besides me? Who was I trying to tell to leave the tapestry alone?"

"We will discuss these things later," Guillaume spoke, "for now, lets leave this room before the heat grows any worse."

I followed Guillaume and Opsis from the Great Chamber and down the corridor. The farther we walked the more the heat began to dissipate allowing my head to become clear. Thousands of questions raced through my mind but I only gave voice to one. "Guillaume, what have I forgotten?"

He did not turn around as he answered, " That is for you to remember."

Not giving up quite so easily I turned to Opsis," Opsis, what have I forgotten? What memory hides from me?"

Opsis slowed until we were walking side by side. Placing his large hand on my shoulder, his gesture of friendship somewhat comforting in my confusion. "Memories are strange things. They can be a beast or they can be a blessing. They are also an individual thing. You may remember something one way, while I viewing the same thing, remember it differently. Over time, what we think we remember, is not actually a memory at all. It was just a thought passing through that became lodged. Understand, brave one, we can not answer your question because they would be our memories and not yours. Our memories, would mean nothing to you."

We walked in silence as I thought of what he had told me. I tried to hide the frustrations at the lack of answers as I tried to find truth is what he said. "If it is a true memory why would it hide? Why would the mind forget?"

"That is the beast or blessing of the thing. A memory of good times, is a blessing. It gives you a comfortable feeling, makes you smile. Like a warm cup next to a fire on a cold night, it is like a friend. A treasure the heart holds onto tightly. Memory of a bad time or event, that is the beast. It can haunt you forever, making living a good life impossible as the hurt one suffers refuses to allow healing. Or, the mind in seeking healing, may hide the memory away. In an attempt to live as happily as possible."

"Opsis, are you saying something bad happened, and that is what I can not remember?"

"That is for you to discover."

"How can I discover anything, when I do not know what I am seeking?" I asked a little too loudly as I swung away in frustration. Opsis merely looked down at me, refusing to be drawn into my emotional quagmire.

Not about to give up I asked him, "Why then are pieces of memory seeming to haunt me?"

"The mind is something we know little of. What gives us thought, what holds the memories. How we know to walk or to breath or wake up after we sleep. So to this question, I can only offer a guess. I believe, that the mind tests us, attempting to see if we are ready to remember. Testing to see if our spirit has healed enough to handle what it hides."

I looked up at Opsis, speaking in barely audible tones. "To me, it seems to be playing a cruel game. Teasing and tormenting, sitting back waiting until I feel safe and then attacking again." Opsis did not answer, understanding I did not expect one to this comment. Resuming walking I was silent, lost in my thoughts. Trying to come to an understanding of what I have learned, wondering the reasons, while fighting with errant questions that danced about. Even though Opsis had answered my question in the only way he could, I still could not release the frustration at not knowing. I still had to have answers from somewhere, to something.

My next question seemed to spring out unexpectedly even though it had been running through my mind as well, "Opsis, what is my name? My real name?"

"That young, brave and noble warrior, will come with the rest of your memories." When I started to interrupt he continued. "I could say your name all day long and it would mean nothing to you. Until you remember it

61

yourself, it would be just another word among many."

Stopping suddenly I turned to Opsis, grabbing his arm to gain his attention. "Can you not just try? Can you not, WILL you not at least just try and tell me my name?" the frustrations obviously winning as they burst forth unrestrained.

I was not prepared for the look of unhidden sadness that crossed Opsis' face. He stood looking down at me for what seemed to be a long while before he answered. "I have spoken your name. It meant nothing to you at that moment, it would mean nothing now."

"Opsis..I wasn't" I wasn't allowed to finish as Opsis interrupted. An act that was something that I some how just knew that, Opsis, as a personal rule didn't do, but this time did.

"I will not say it again until you remember it yourself." Turning from me he continued his walk down the corridor leaving me standing where I was.

SIX

When I entered Guillaume's chamber he turned to look at me. Shaking his head and for the world we know, looked as if he were fighting laughing at me once again. "Go outside..."

"And get wood." I interrupted.

Guillaume continued, ignoring my outburst. "go past where the wood pile stands, you will go around the rock wall. There you will find a rather large pool of water, fed by a waterfall from the top of this hillside. You can cleanse yourself and your garments there."

I stared at Guillaume for a moment, seeking the correct response. I wanted to apologize for my rudeness, but yet I did not like being treated as a child.

Opsis spoke up preventing any mistake on my part, "Any man, would appreciate the chance to get clean over walking about smelling worse that a wet caTragon."

"You are correct Opsis, thank you Guillaume, I shall return shortly."

As I turned to leave Guillaume spoke up, "Bring wood back with you when you come."

Stifling an exasperated sigh I walked through the shimmering wall into the sunlight. Standing still for a brief moment I waited for my eyes to adjust to the change in brightness. Once I could see without straining I turned to follow Guillaume's instructions. Passing the pile of wood I noticed that it was in shambles. Logs lay scattered all about the ground. A couple of the pieces appeared to have been shredded leaving nothing much more than kindling pieces. Odd I thought as I went past. There was no evidence showing what may have done this. There were no tracks anywhere.

"Its almost as if something dropped from the sky, wracked havoc on the wood and then disappeared as it had come, but that's not possible." I spoke aloud to myself as I walked. Guessing and second guessing what had happened. "What ever did it, I don't doubt that Guillaume will have me stacking that wood back as it once was."

Walking around the hillside I spotted the pool. The waterfall cascading down from a great height creating a mist that covered a large area of the water. Walking over to the edge of the pool I could feel the coolness coming off the surface. Placing the weapons that I had carried with me down on the bank I made ready. Thinking to take care of two needs with one action I remained dressed as I entered the water. Diving deep I swam across the pool emerging just under the falls. Remaining under the falls I felt it washing away the sweat and grime from my person. The water working miracles toward cooling my anger and frustrations at not getting any answers to my questions.

When I felt something brush against my leg I ignored it, taking it to be merely a fish. I was not prepared when I felt it grab my leg and pull me under the water. Fighting as best one could with an unseen enemy I felt my lungs burning for air. Struggling I fought wishing I had at least kept the small dagger, but all my weapons were on the bank, out of reach. Realizing that we were on the bottom of the pool I searched the ground for any sort of weapon. When my hand found a large rock I grabbed it and swung at my assailant. The surprise in the blow from the rock bringing about my release. Kicking away I swam for the surface as fast as I was able. The weight of my clothing dragging me back. When I broke the surface I gasped for air and then swam for the bank. Climbing out of the water I grabbed my sword and looked back to the water. Except for where the falls entered the pool the water was still. Its blue green color calm, appearing to be peaceful as it hid what ever was underneath.

"What are you looking for?" came a strange voice behind me. Turning quickly I held my sword at the ready. First there appeared to be nothing there. Yet, I knew better. Waiting I made use of all my senses to search the area. Listening to all of the sounds, from the falling water behind me, to the birds passing over head. Somewhere in between, I heard breathing. I watched the area before me. I saw the leaves on the trees slowly move in the soft breeze created by the mists of the fall. I saw a butterfly pass and I saw a ripple, just once, in the air. Then a smell so strong and close that it gagged me. Horrible as it was I held my ground. Fighting to ignore the sickening smell I watched as the ripple opened and a figure stepped out before me. Being the same height as myself I looked it directly in the eyes. Eyes that were the same color as mine, but bore a weary expression. The figure was slight, as if illness or some other horror of life ravaged the body. The smell again assaulted my senses, it was a smell of something dead, something slowly rotting away.

"What are you looking for?" it repeated.

"What ever it was that attacked me in the pool" I answered. My sword still held at the ready.

"What are you looking for?" it again spoke.

"I am looking for what attacked me in the pool." I answered.

"What are you looking for? What are you seeking? What are you looking for?" It stood looking at me, waiting for a response. I realized that if I gave the same answer as before, I would just get the same question again. Searching my mind I tried desperately to come up with the correct response.

A ripple began behind the figure, opening slowly. Before the figure stepped across the opening it spoke once more. "What are you looking for?" Then disappeared as the opening closed between us.

Turning back to the pool I looked across the water's surface, wondering what was underneath while at the same time I pondered what had just taken place. "So many strange things happening", I spoke aloud to myself. Crossing over into the sunlight I sat on a rock to allow myself and my clothing to dry. Yet, where I could easily see the pool before me. The warmth of the sun began to make me drowsy as I sat there. Fighting the sleepy feeling I at first did not realize the moment when I was no longer alone.

"Who are you?" asked the voice

Startled I turned swiftly, unhappy with myself for having been caught napping. Looking at the figure before me I almost laughed, almost. Before me stood a short, rather round figure. Looking somewhat like a man in much smaller form, with a man's face and build, it also appeared as if it really couldn't make up its mind what it was. Sporting large ears like the hare in the wood, the mane of a lion and the tail of a great white stallion. While his face was clean, his neck, arms and hands were covered in a fine fur like hair. His hands resembled that of a man, but his fingers ended with great claws at the moment sheathed carefully. His legs were short and stocky, his feet the hooves of a horse. "Who are you?" I asked.

"I asked first, who are you? What is the name by which you are known?"

"I am called Adwr, now who are you?"

"Adwr?" Turning his head from side to side he looked at me appearing confused.

"Yes, Adwr is what I am called. Now answer my inquiry, who are you?"

Ignoring my question the figure stood looking at me. His eyes moving from the top of my head downward. He took in everything from my appearance to the sword that I held in my hand.

"You look to be a brave young warrior, one that would soon be fit to be a knight in the king's castle. Why then, would you be known as coward? For that is the meaning of the name you profess to be called."

My grip tightened on the sword I held. Taking a deep breath I fought against the anger growing within me. A voice that sounded in a sing song manner rang through my mind, "New name, new name, Adwr is your new name." For several moments I mentally struggled, fighting to remember, and yet fighting to push a memory away. Finally regaining control I turned again to the figure before me.

"What I am called or why is of no concern of yours. I have asked you before, and I will ask you only once again, who are you?"

Grinning broadly the figure before me took a deep sweeping bow. "I am called, Collectif. Obviously because I am a collection of many parts that make up my whole. I am strength, I am wildness, I am laughter. I am the power and the magic of all individually and ahem, collectively. I am, oh brave and noble one, at your service."

Watching Collectif I wondered if I had been under water too long. Before I had time to comment a loud roar was heard coming from beyond the forest. The dragon, MY dragon, was near. This time I would succeed. Gathering up my weapons I turned and began to run in the direction of the sound. Crossing behind the waterfall, against the rock wall and then into the wood.

I could hear Collectif behind me shouting "Hey!! Where are you going?"

"To slay a dragon!" I shouted without looking back.

"Well wait for me, you may need me!"

Before I realized it Collectif was beside me running along without problem. Together we ran through the forest, jumping small gullies and fallen trees. Collectif laughed as if it were a game, while I focused on listening for the dragon. Trying to remain as quiet as possible as we crashed through brush and splashed across small streams. Still we ran. I had to, I was driven by a vow, I was driven by a promise made to myself and to my family even if to them it was unspoken.

When I could run no more I stopped and leaned against a tree, fighting to catch my breath. Collectif had run on ahead but stopped when he realized I was no longer with him. Coming back he looked at me laughing.

"What do you find so funny?" I asked him between gasps for breath.

"You humans look at me as if I am a strange thing, and yet part of my strangeness gives me strength beyond yours."

As I watched him dance around before me, waiting on me to resume our run, I struggled to regain my breath as I sought to ignore his antics. I wanted to shoot him with my crossbow, but I had to save my arrows for the dragon. As my breath returned I stood to continue through the wood when I heard the dragon again. This time it was much closer. Motioning for Collectif to be still and quiet I crept through the trees as low to the ground as I possibly could get. Coming upon a grouping of large boulders I eased up and looked over the top where I was able to see down the hillside to the valley below. I watched as the dragon and a snake larger than any I had ever seen before approached each other. The dragon was much taller in size but the snake was longer in length and as big around as one of the mighty oaks that stand at the edge of the castle grounds.

Collectif had crept up behind me and he too looked over the rocks to the valley floor below.

"Oh, a battle a battle, I love a battle" he spoke almost in song. His glee at the sight annoying to me.

"No, this looks like no fight." I said quietly. "this looks almost as if they are meeting...as if they are talking with one another."

"What is it you are saying? A dragon and a great snake having a friendly chat? Nonsense. It is a battle, I just know it."

"Quiet!" I whispered through clenched teeth. "You are going to give us away with your antics and loud voice. Do you not realize how sound travels? On top of the fact of just how well a dragon can hear?" Collectif reluctantly grew still and quiet as we watched what was going on in the valley below.

The dragon walked slowly up to the snake, its head low and wings folded close to its body. If one could attribute emotions to a dragon this one would give the appearance of being sad. Wisps of smoke trailed from its nostrils to disappear into the air just over its head. The many scales on its back appearing to glitter as they reflected the afternoon sun. Still the dragon walked slowly, almost cautiously toward the snake. The snake's head rose high over the many coils it has wrapped, piling one on top of the other until it stood taller than the trees. This seemingly giving the snake an advantage over the dragon. Even at the distance we were, I could see the tongue of the snake appearing and disappearing, looking like a rope being tossed out in the hopes of capturing something and reeling it back into certain death.

"Looks as if the dragon's not happy about this 'meeting' as you call it." Collectif spoke my very thoughts aloud. I turned to quiet him again only to see the rocks that he was leaning on give way beneath him sending him tumbling down the hillside in the direction of the meeting below.

" Oh no." I spoke aloud as I grabbed my crossbow and made ready to follow him. I could not let him be killed by either or both of the two below. Peering over the rocks I could see the two watching Collectif's tumble down the hillside. When the dragon made a move toward him I charged over the boulders shouting at the top of my lungs.

As if in slow motion I could see the dragon look up and the snake coming uncoiled. I ran best I could down the hill fighting to retain my balance, while all the time watching the beasts before me, mentally and physically preparing for anything. Reaching Collectif I checked on him. He was bruised from his tumble, but otherwise he was well. However, now we were both in trouble as the dragon and the snake approached.

I fought to regain concentration as snake and dragon both drew closer. They were in no hurry as their very movements showed they knew, somehow they knew, they had the advantage. Here I was much smaller than their great size, out in the open with no where to seek protection from their attack. Collectif was of no help as I could feel his trembling through the boots on my feet. His barely audible whimpers just more proof of his fear.

"I thought you said you were coming along in case I needed you." I said as I stood over him, watching the approach. The hand holding my shield in front of me also had a grasp on my crossbow. With the other hand I reached behind me into my bag for an arrow.

"What are you doing? What are you going to do?" Collectif asked as he cowered on the ground.

"If I can only take one with me, it will be the dragon. For it is the dragon that I have sworn to slay."

"You know," Collectif began, "I'm really no good in situations like this."

"What are you saying Collectif?"

"That uh, well..its been nice meeting you and all. I'll tell of your brave deeds to one and all.."

"Collectif..Collectif?" One quick glance down confirmed what I had feared. He was no longer there. I was alone. I was also in trouble. The two were still approaching slowly, it was a game to them. I was the mouse to their cat. Still, I stood my ground, waiting. I could feel the Grandite on the arrow growing warm, I saw a soft light begin to shine from it as its magic grew. In this I took heart, there may be a chance yet.

Once the pair were close the snake slowly began to coil in preparation to strike. It's massive head the size of a wagon, eyes the color of evil glared at me. The dragon stood beside the snake, watching me. Smoke escaped from its nostrils in great streams, rising up to encircle its head. Tendrils of flame licked at the ground before it, setting the dried grasses on fire. The beast was close enough to see the scales on its body. One could see as they moved with the dragon, shifting and protecting it. Each scale glittering like the sunlight reflecting off of ice crystals. This beast would have been beautiful, had it not been so very evil. Still, its golden yellow eyes watched me, almost as if it knew something I did not.

Moments passed, as time itself seemed to stand

still. All of my newly trained senses were on edge. Like the feeling from a bolt of lightning running through me, I trembled in anticipation of what was to come. My fingers tightening around the arrow I held, I waited. I wanted the perfect shot as I knew, I would only get one chance. I had to slay this dragon. Even if the snake were to be my doom, I would be the dragon's. Then those of the castle would never more have to fear leaving the shelter of the rock walls.

As the snake drew back to strike, I moved to stand feet apart, my shield directly in front of my chest. I placed the arrow in my crossbow, drawing it back in preparation. I saw that the dragon too watched the snake more than me. Curious as this was, I knew that today, this dragon would die.

With the first strike of the snake I moved swiftly to the side. The snake missing me by a butterfly's breath. Its movements however had blocked all shots at the dragon. Again I moved my shield before me as the snake coiled itself once again. Watching me, it began to sway side to side. As I watched the snake I felt myself being drawn into its eyes. Caught up in some hypnotizing trap I watched as it swayed. Still gripping my shield, I let it lower slightly, as I watched. The sound like a thousand rattles echoed across the valley as the snake again rose high above me. It bore on its face the look of a grotesque smile. A smile of satisfaction and of evil accomplishment. All but helpless I watched as the great snake drew back, then swiftly struck. From somewhere in the heart of my strength and will came a movement. Raising my shield quickly it lodged in the great snake's mouth, preventing it from closing about me. Saving me from its deadly bite. I moved away from the snake as it fought to dislodge my shield. Its head flailing from side to side in anger and

72

frustration. Seeing my chance I began to raise my crossbow toward the dragon. Just as the snake spat my shield from its mouth. Pure evil glowed from this creature's eyes as it turned to me. I would die this day, that I was sure of.

Just as the snake made ready to strike the dragon attacked. Not me, but the snake. Its great fire holding the snake at bay as it approached. With one swing from its head knocking the snake to the ground. The snake rose swiftly and wrapped its tail around the front legs of the dragon, pulling it off its feet. Raising to strike the snake soared over the dragon, but this dragon was not done yet. With a bite from its sword's edge sharp teeth it wounded the snake, freeing itself and angering the snake even more. I watched momentarily mesmerized by the battle before me. As I watched I realized this was the prefect time to retrieve my shield. Moving slowly and carefully as to not draw attention I eased my way over to where my shield lay. Squatting down carefully behind it I watched the fight before me as it continued. Great clouds of dust and smoke oft times blocking the scene but would clear enough to allow me to see. I watched as finally dust began to settle, I could see the dragon standing over the snake, bloodied and torn. The dragon was missing several of its protective scales. Moving to the side the dragon watched the snake carefully. The snake moved slightly, showing that though not dead, it was deeply wounded. Turning away it moved off across the valley, the grasses swaying as it passed through.

Taking my chance, I raised my crossbow taking careful aim. My hands sweating, trembling from anticipation. I felt satisfaction at the twang of the bow and the hiss of the arrow leaving. Just as the arrow took flight, so did the dragon unfolding its great wings and

moving to lift skyward. Its head turned still watching the
snake it did not see the arrow approaching. As the
dragon left the ground the arrow sank deeply into its leg,
not a mortal wound by any means. The roar of the dragon
was one of great pain as it felt the arrow slice into its skin.
Lifting its massive body into the sky it flew toward the
sun, blinding me of where it went.

"What have you done??" Came Guillaume's voice
behind me, carrying the sound of pain and disbelief.

Surprised I turned, seeing Guillaume, Opsis and
Collectif behind me.

"You do not know what it is that you have done."
Guillaume said as he stood looking in the direction that
the dragon had taken.

Guillaume did not wait for my response to his
question, he had seen. He knew the answer. He turned to
Collectif and began to give him instructions. "It appears
that the dragon has gone to Fire Mountain, there is where
you will find its lair. There is where you should find the
dragon." interrupting himself he turned to me "What arrow
did you use? What was it made of?"

"Grandite." I answered him.

"Only Grandite? Not half steel?"

"Only Grandite. I used all of the steel and had two
pieces of Grandite left. I used both on one arrow. I
thought this was my chance to fulfill my vow and I wanted
a special arrow, so I used the one with solid Grandite."

"This may not be so bad then."Guillaume said as he
turned again to Collectif. "Run as fast as you can to Fire
Mountain. See if the dragon did go there." He handed
Collectif a small cloth pouch. "If you do find the dragon,
open this pouch and toss it inside the lair, taking care not
to inhale any yourself. Wait until it causes the dragon to
sleep. Once the dragon sleeps you can go inside the lair

with no fear. Check to see if you can tell how bad the wound is."

Collectif took the bag from Guillaume and carefully tucked it inside a pocket a his vest. "And then?" he asked Guillaume.

"Then, if the arrow is still embedded in the dragon you must remove it."

At that Collectif appeared concerned. "How will I mange that?"

"Just slowly pull the staff of the arrow toward yourself. All the while you must be saying the words, 'mistake heal; heal mistake. The Grandite will hear you. As long as you repeat the words you will begin to see the glow of the stone begin, growing as it moves closer to the surface of the skin. Glowing brightly once removed."

Nodding silently, Collectif then looked up at Guillaume, "and then? Once I have the arrow out--saying that I do find the dragon, and I do get to use the powder and she does sleep..what is it then you wish for me to do?"

"Once you have the arrow loosed from the dragon's body, hold the arrow as it glows against the wound, once the glow dims break the staff in half. Say one word and one word only, 'lost'. Then drop both halves no less than a foot apart from each other. Once you have done that leave quickly. Find your way back to me as you did before."

Turning again to look in the direction the dragon had gone he crossed his arms and stood in silence. I wasn't sure, but it seemed to me that Guillaume was afraid, of what I wasn't sure. I watched as Collectif disappeared in the distance. Soon it was impossible to see even the dust he raised as he ran.

I turned and looked at Opsis who was also staring

75

off into the distance. "Opsis?"

He looked down at me, this time I could see it, there was a mixture of sadness and even fear in his face. "You do not know, what you have done." was all that he would say. Turning away from me he went again to watching the distance, waiting for Collectif's return. Picking up my shield and crossbow I walked over to the one lone bush growing at the base of the hill. Carefully placing my shield and crossbow beside me I sat in the shade of the bush, watching Guillaume and Opsis, watch the distance

Guillaume stood watching nothing for a long while before turning to Opsis. "Will you look?" he asked.

Opsis nodded and turned to look in the direction that Collectif had taken. His voice, usually loud and strong took on a more quiet tone, one that seemed to come from very far away. Unable to hear him from where I sat, I stood and leaving weaponry where it lay, walked slowly over to stand at his side. It was forbidden for a Cyclops to use their gift of extra sight for anything not of extreme importance. For Guillaume to have asked this, showed his concerns. We waited as Opsis searched for Collectif.

"He has just reached Fire Mountain. He is searching the mountainside quickly. He has great speed still for one that has just ran so far." Guillaume stood silently listening, still looking off into the distance. I wanted to ask why they were trying so hard to find and save this dragon but I did not give voice to the questions raging inside. I simply stood and waited. Guillaume's 'all things will be understood when the time is right' fighting for space among the questions.

Opsis stood in silence for long moments, staring

off into the distance. The sun slowly began to set behind the far mountain bringing cooling to the day, and yet, no one moved. When the evening dusk crept across the sky, wrapping the land in darkness, still we stood. Exhaustion of the day's events threatened my waning strength and I yawned broadly.

"He has found the dragon." Opsis spoke finally. While his voice still held a far away sound, there was a hint of excitement. "He is at the mouth of the dragon's lair, doing as you said, tossing in the bag. I see him, waiting outside. Looking in carefully, waiting for the dragon to sleep. I cannot see the dragon yet, I do not know of its wound." Together Guillaume and I turned to watch Opsis, all hints of sleepiness now gone from my mind.

"Now, he is going in now. Slowly, he is no fool in this. He is placing his hand on the dragon, it does not move, she sleeps. He has found the arrow, it is in the back portion of her front leg. The dragon lost some scales there in the battle with the snake. That is the only way the arrow was able to enter. He is grasping the arrow, slowly pulling it out. The dragon stirs."

Guillaume and I both watched Opsis carefully when he grew silent. I looked past Opsis to see Guillaume, his face an open look of concern and fear. Neither of us spoke as we waited. Long moments passed. I wanted this done, I wanted Collectif back with us telling us whether he had succeeded or failed, but back here and not a night meal for the dragon.

"The dragon still sleeps. He is again slowly pulling on the arrow, removing it. I can see the glow of the Grandite. It is coming free. It is out. He has removed it."

"Is he doing as I instructed?" Guillaume asked, speaking for the first time since this began.

77

"Yes, yes he is holding the arrow against the wound. The glow is fading now, fading, it is gone. He has pulled the arrow away." Opsis stood silent, watching what neither Guillaume or I could see. "He is on his way back, he will be here soon."

"Did he break the arrow? Did he do as I instructed about the arrow?" Guillaume asked Opsis, watching his friend closely.

"I do not know," Opsis answered honestly. "There was a moment that I could not see. It was as if something moved between us, preventing my seeing all that he did."

Finally able to stand it no longer I spoke up. "I still do not understand why it was so important to save this dragon. Why not let it die so that those in the castle would need no longer be afraid?"

"You are right in that you do not understand. There is much that you don't know or don't remember. Those are the things preventing full understanding. When the time is right, when you remember, then...then you will understand why this had to be done. When you remember, then you will know just what it is that you nearly did. Once you understand, then you will be grateful. To the higher power that you pray to, and to us, especially to Collectif for his bravery and willingness to risk so much for your mistake."

When I started to speak Guillaume raised his hand to stop me, 'Collect your weapons, we will head back now. Collectif knows where to come to."

After a very long and quiet trip back through the forest we arrived at Guillaume's home. Entering through the shimmering rock wall I walked across to my cot and waited, mentally preparing for the lecture that was to come. I watched as Opsis exhausted, stumbled to

78

the table and sat down heavily. Propping his elbows on the table he then rested his head in his hands. Guillaume moved across the room to the fire pit, stirring the coals to waken them, building up a fire that seemed to never fully die down. Using the last of the wood that had been stacked near the pit he added it to the fire. When the fire was burning he retrieved his cauldron and began tossing ingredients inside. The only sound in the room was of his movements and the items striking the pot. The silence in the room grew steadily, bringing with it a tension. I knew it was coming.

When Guillaume tossed the last item into the cauldron he dusted his hands together and then turned to Opsis. "Are you well old friend?"

"I am well." Opsis answered, his exhaustion evident in the weakened sound of his voice, muffled by his hands.

Guillaume did not even look at me when he spoke again, "go outside and bring in some firewood. Go nowhere else, just to the woodpile and back."

"Yes, Guillaume." was all I said as I made to follow his instructions. Passing Opsis I saw as he turned his head and smiled at me. It was a tired smile, but a smile just the same and it brought a relief from my fears.

Stepping back out into the darkness I turned toward the woodpile. Listening to the sounds of the night soothing my frustrations. The songs of the crickets and frogs a distraction from thoughts of what was to come. The cool evening air cleared the exhaustion from my mind allowing me to think of what all had happened through out the day. I talked to myself under my breath as I walked, "Just doesn't make any sense.. saving a dragon that has been so much trouble for so long." Reaching the wood I almost tripped over a log out of place. I had forgotten about this mess. Regaining my balance I tried to see. There wasn't enough moonlight filtering through the trees to allow me to see to replace all of the wood so I gathered up what I could safely carry back. I would have to mention this to Guillaume and return tomorrow to clean this up as it should be. Arms loaded I turned to go back. It was as I turned that I ran directly into something causing me to drop the wood. Jumping back from the unseen I reached for a sword I didn't have. I had walked off and left everything inside. Some knight I would make. Looking quickly I grabbed a fair size stick from the ground.

"Oh put that down," said Collectif as he appeared before me, stepping out of the ripple in the air. "it is only I, Collectif, at your service."

Lowering the stick but not dropping it I looked at Collectif. "I see you are back, are you well?"

Collectif stood before me brushing the dust of the valley from his sleeves and vest. Once he felt himself respectfully clean and presentable he looked up at me. "Of course I am well, why is it that I would I not be well?"

"You did just have a close encounter with a wounded dragon."

"Yes, yes, but it slept through the entire thing that I did, there was no problem there. The only problem being the problem you yourself caused in your shooting an arrow into it to begin with. Had you not done as you did then I would not have had to do what I did. There would have been no concern and no worries. But you did, and I did and now it is done." Collectif spoke almost in a dismissive manner. As if he now looked at me as something unworthy of his time.

"Why are you here Collectif? The entrance to Guillaume's place is around the other side."

"Yes, yes I know that, but I uh, I heard a noise as I was approaching and I wanted to make sure that nothing was about that shouldn't be. I, uh, just wanted everyone to be safe, yes, safe.."

Collectif seemed to be acting strangely, but being that we had just met on this day, I wasn't sure if this was how he normally acted or not. Shrugging it off I began to pick up the wood I had dropped. "Since you are here, will you help me carry in more wood? It is scattered about for some reason so be careful as you walk."

"Wood?? You want *me* to carry wood??" Collectif stood, hands on hips, glaring at me for a moment. Suddenly his attitude changed, "Oh, is this wood for Guillaume? I wonder if he is making his rabbit's luck stew? Oh yes, that is good indeed. I will help carry in some wood. Go on ahead, I will be directly behind you, yes behind you directly I will be."

Walking on ahead, arms loaded with wood I couldn't help but feel some confusion at what had just taken place. Why, would Collectif go from indignant to overly excited about carrying wood. While I was sure that Guillaume's stew was good, it didn't make sense to get that excited over a meal. He was hiding something, I could just feel it.

"I'm here, hurry along hurry along. You are much too slow young misguided warrior." Collectif was back to being his annoying self. Especially since he was only carrying a single stick of wood in each hand.

Entering Guillaume's chamber behind Collectif I watched as he reveled in the attention he was getting. I did not hear all that Guillaume had said, only hearing the

word "safe" as I had entered. Collectif was dancing about
the room making all manner of noise with his hooves on
the rock floor. So much that the caTragons in the
room had moved to the area behind my cot, they looked
as if they didn't know whether to attack this odd looking
fellow or leave the room for a quieter location. Opsis had
even raised up and was laughing at Collectif's antics.
Dodging around Collectif's dancing I carried my armload
of wood over to the wall and stacked it in place.

"Oh it was easy, yes easy indeed." Collectif began
telling of his adventure, his arms flailing out as he spoke
in a grand and bold fashion. "Once I found the lair of the
beast I looked inside. There she was, stretched out on
the ground, suffering from the wound inflicted. The
sounds coming from her, from inside that lair was
strange, strange indeed. Between the huffing and puffing
sounds one expects to hear from a fire breathing dragon
there were other sounds. Unusual sounds, sounds that
sounded almost like the sobs and moans of a human in
pain. Strange that." pausing in talking to gain effect he
looked about the room, still dancing and prancing about.

"And?" Guillaume asked. "Go ahead, finish your
tale."

I watched Guillaume, he seemed saddened at the
words he had already heard, why would he need to hear
more? Especially since we knew the dragon would be
well. I jumped as Collectif danced past where I stood,
nearly trampling my feet in the process. Seeing Opsis
motion for me from the corner of my eye I moved over to
the table and joined him there.

"I did just as you instructed Guillaume," Collectif
continued. "I opened the bag and carefully tossed it
inside, directly before the dragon's great head. In its
distress, she didn't notice its presence and after inhaling

the cloud that rose up from the opening, slowly drifted off
into sleep. I watched as the dragon grew silent and still,
and after it had not moved for a while, I entered the lair as
quietly as possible. Approaching the beast I softly placed
my hand on its massive neck. I could feel the
roughness of the scales and see each jewel embedded
with in them. In the dim light of the lair I could still see the
glimmering colors of each stone. When the dragon did
not stir I quickly looked for and found her wound." When
Collectif again paused for effect I sat, staring impatiently
at him. Wishing that he would just finish this and be done
with it. His act, while getting him the attention he wished
from Guillaume and Opsis was growing boring to me.

"Continue, Collectif, what happened then?"
Guillaume asked as if he did not already know.

Bowing in acquiescence he resumed his tale,
"When I found the arrow or what showed of it as it had
sank deeply into the dragon's leg I grasped the shaft
carefully, as carefully as you said that I should do. I
slowly, as slowly as you had instructed me Guillaume,
drew the arrow toward myself. There was one moment
when the dragon stirred, seeming to attempt to raise its
head from the ground, a sound unheard before and
unholy coming from deep inside the beast. A great cry of
pain from the wound inflicted upon it by the misguided
one. I stood as still as if of stone until the dragon's head
again rested on the ground and was quiet. I resumed
slowly pulling the arrow toward myself. Easing it as
carefully as could be done from the leg. I could see the
Grandite's glow while it was still within the beast. Still," he
then paused and looked at each of us in turn. I fighting to
appear interested and not frustrated at his saving the
dragon, while Guillaume seemed to hang on each word,
his concern evident. "still, I fought with myself not to get

83

in a hurry, not to rush this as Guillaume, you had told me plainly to do this with care and caution. I watched the dragon carefully, making sure that the beast was not awakening while I fought to remove the arrow. Once the arrow was free the glow from the Grandite shown brightly. In the purple light cast from the arrowhead the many jewels on the dragon shone and glittered in quite the display. Not only was the dragon encrusted in magnificent stones, they were scattered about the floor as if left there by a child after play. Each one sparkling in its brilliance. Still, I did not allow this to distract me from my mission. Distract me it did not, I carefully and gently placed the Grandite against the wound of the beast and watched as the glow of the stone slowly faded away. The room growing darker, the glittering of the stones disappearing as the wound closed."

I watched Guillaume watch Collectif, waiting obviously for more. When Collectif remained silent Guillaume prompted him yet again with "and?"

"And?? And what?? I removed the arrow. I saved the dragon. I did each as instructed. and I am here.. with you my friends." At which point Collectif took a deep sweeping bow, arms flailing outward, as he moved down on one knee, looking for all the surrounding lands like a king's jester. Yet, the look in his eyes gave proof that he was no fool.

Guillaume for the first time appeared impatient as he approached Collectif. His eyes were drawn in a squint, while his mouth was a tight closed slit across his face. His arms crossed over his chest before him, he took long purposeful steps across the room to where Collectif had begun dancing about again.

"Be still." he commanded Collectif, who immediately obeyed, even if looking unhappy about it.

"Did you break the arrow as instructed? Did you separate the halves as instructed?" Guillaume asked in a tone that allowed for no nonsense on Collectif's part.

"Oh that, the arrow, yes broke it in half I did. I did break it as instructed. You have no worries there." Collectif spoke almost in giddy song as he began dancing again. "I did break the shaft with a snap and a crack, using only my bare hands. I did break the shaft with a crack and a snap dropping it to where it lands. I did enter the lair of dragon bold, removing the arrow as was told. I broke the shaft, making it two. I broke this arrow as I was told to do."

"This is making me want to shoot him with an arrow." I spoke softly to myself. Opsis heard however and placed his hand on my arm. Looking up I saw lurking just behind his look of concern the hint of a smile.

Guillaume relaxed before our eyes. Dropping his arms and guarded stance he turned back to the pot hanging over the fire, the contents now hot and bubbling. As he reached for a large spoon to stir this concoction of his I watched as the caTragons walked over to sit beside him, watching as he absently stirred the stew he was preparing. Opsis again rested his head on his hands as I leaned back at the table, allowing my eyes to close, all but a tiny slit. This allowing me to watch Collectif as he danced about, seeming for all the world about him happy with himself and his accomplishments of the day. When he turned however, allowing me for just a moment to see his face, there was something there, something besides his idiotic behavior and silliness.

I was startled awake by the sound of the bowl being placed on the table before me. Through the anger I felt at myself for falling asleep I heard Guillaume speaking. "You better eat or the caTragons will do it for you." he said as he placed a bowl before Opsis.

"The caTragons would have a fight on their hand this day."Opsis said as he reached across the table for a spoon.

Collectif approached the table carrying his own bowl, taking a place beside Opsis directly across from where I sat. Guillaume taking his place at the head of the table. Bowing my head I offered a silent prayer asking blessing and of thanks for the day. Raising my head I looked to see each one at the table deeply immersed in their own thoughts while they ate. The only sounds in the room was that of spoons scraping against bowl and the occasional huff of the caTragon as they waited for their share of the meal. Reaching across the table for a chunk of bread I tore it in half and dipped it into the bowl before me. Taking a bite of what Collectif called Guillaume's Rabbit's Luck Stew, I found it actually very good. It was no wonder Collectif had acted so excitedly about it. Still, I watched him carefully. Something was warning me, every sense with in me was tingling as if trying to tell me, something was not right with this. Yet it also told me that I had to be silent for now. By all appearances Collectif was an old friend of Guillaume's therefore he would not want to hear or believe anything bad about a friend.

Chewing my food quietly I listened as Collectif began talking with Guillaume. "I am always glad to be here when you have prepared this my friend. I do hope one day to talk you out of the list of ingredients and just how you make this. There is much more in this I know than rabbit."

Guillaume sat watching Collectif actually smiling. The smile even reached his eyes when he responded to Collectif. "There is no rabbit in the stew, that is why it is called Rabbit's Luck."

"Then what?" Collectif looked down at his now empty bowl as if trying to see what was contained within it moments earlier.

"That is for me to know, and you to wonder about."Guillaume answered as he rose and carried his bowl over to the cauldron. Spooning out a large helping he placed the bowl on the floor. When two caTragons appeared ready to battle over the bowl I rose and followed Guillaume's movements. When the second bowl appeared the caTragons, while glaring suspiciously at each other began to eat.

Filling two mugs with Guillaume's hot, bitter brew I carried one over to the table and placed it before Opsis who smiled his appreciation. Guillaume moved to create a place of rest for Collectif. As I drank I watched Collectif as he again began to dance around the room in some odd shuffling step. He was humming a tune I had never heard before as he moved about. His movements gave the appearance of just a random dance, but each time he passed the wall of books, he was always facing the wall, never the center of the room. His steps also slowed when he was there. I looked to Guillaume who was talking with Opsis. Their voices so low that even though I was just across the table, I could not hear what was being said. So deep were they in conversation that neither noticed Collectif's strange actions.

Soon he stopped dancing at all and stood in front of the books, placing his hand on the first book, he touched each book in turn as he looked from title to title. When he reached the last book on the shelf he moved to the shelf above and repeated his actions. By this time Guillaume had noticed and was watching his friend.

"What is it you seek?" Guillaume asked him.

"Only something that would calm my inner

87

excitement, allowing me to sleep this night. As I am still running on the adrenaline of the day and I fear with that, sleep will not come."

Guillaume rose from his seat at the table and crossed the room. Removing a rather large volume from the shelf he handed it to Collectif. "This should do what you wish."

Collectif looked at the book in his hands."Tapestry Weaving: the magic within." Oh Yes, I am sure that this will do exactly what I wish for." Taking the book with him he crossed the room to where Guillaume had placed a mat for his rest. Stretching out on his belly with the book on the floor before him he gave the appearance of reading.

Yawning broadly I stood and carried my mug back to its resting place near the fire. Crossing the room I idly patted a caTragon as I passed it on the way back to my cot. Still yet, my senses screamed at me, something was not right. I wondered as I passed Collectif, just what tomorrow would bring. I knew though, that what ever it was, it would be his doing.

SEVEN

Early the next morning I opened my eyes, seeing a room empty but for Collectif, and he was back at the wall of books. The book that Guillaume had given him the night before discarded on the floor at his mat.

I sat up on the cot and stretched, the creaking and groaning of the frame giving my movements away. "Now what are you searching for?" I asked as I brought my arms back to my side.

"Searching for? Oh no, nothing really, just looking. Only looking at the many, not seeking a one." Collectif was back talking nearly in the same circles that Opsis and Guillaume did.

"Where are Guillaume and Opsis?" I asked as I stood and crossed the room to where Collectif stood.

"Gone."

"I can see that." I said as I stopped beside him. Placing my hands on hips I stood watching Collectif. He began to squirm and wiggle under my gaze. "Just what are you up to?" I asked him, staring at him intently. Collectif looked at me trying his best to get a wounded, injured party look in his eyes. I wasn't falling for it. Standing watching him I didn't speak, just waited.

"I am up to nothing," Collectif insisted, "I am Guillaume's friend, I have read his books many times. From his books, I learn many things."

"Too bad he doesn't have one on how to dance." I said as a parting shot, as I turned away. Crossing the room for a drink of water I stopped and turned back. "You did not tell me where Guillaume and Opsis went."

"That I do not know,"Collectif admitted, "they said

only that they would be back soon."

After getting the drink and replacing the cup I turned again to Collectif as I crossed the room to retrieve my sword and shield. "I am going outside, I will be back in a short time."

"Everyone leaves and leave me with no one. Leaves me alone, so alone I am." turning away from the books for a moment Collectif smiled broadly. "I am accustomed to being alone misguided one.. have no worries. And worry not, I am up to nothing of concern."

Somehow that did not make me feel any better as I stepped through the shimmering wall into the sunlight. It was already late enough in the morning that the sun was well up and all of the previous night's coolness was gone. Tightening my belt another notch I walked around to where the woodpile was. I thought while I waited on the return of Guillaume and Opsis I would clean up the mess and stack all of the wood back as it should be. When I stepped around the side of the wall however I was surprised to find the wood already back in place. Stacked in fact, better than it had been before.

"I did good, did I not?" Collectif asked suddenly appearing beside me.

"When did you do this?" I asked him ignoring the fact he was dancing around me in circles.

"Last night. I did this last night, when you asked me to help carry wood. I gathered it all and piled it here. I did good yes??"

Looking at the pile of wood, glad that I wasn't going to have to stack it after all and yet confused. "Why did you stack it last night in the dark? Why not just wait until morning so that we could make sure it was stacked properly and that nothing was missed?"

"Did I miss any?" He asked, looking around in a

very dramatic fashion, knowing all the while that he had missed none.

"No, you did not miss any of the wood."

"Then, is it stacked wrong, did I not do good? Did I not do right? When I stacked the wood last night?"

"Oh please, no more rhyme. You stacked the wood properly, there is no problem with it."

"Then," Collectif began looking at me with a curious expression, "what is the problem you have, if it is not with the way the wood is stacked?"

I looked silently for a moment at Collectif, he was staring at me, trying to figure out what I was thinking while I was trying to do the same thing.

"I do not know Collectif, I do not know." I walked away from him walking past the woodpile, continuing to walk until I came to the water's edge. Climbing a slight hill I sat down at a place over looking the water. I sat where I was, lost in thought, seeking answers and lost memories, as the sun made its journey across the sky. Finally as the sun made to begin its journey down I leaned over the edge and looked down into the water at my reflection. There seemed to be something different now. There was a leanness, a more serious side where before there had been the soft roundness of youth. But in my eyes, there as still questions. As I stared into the water my very reflection moved on its own, not with the movements and shifts of the ripples, but independently. Looking back at me it asked one question, "What is it you seek?" The words sounded as if they echoed back at me from the trees. Moving back from the edge I grabbed my shield then stood and turned away.

"What is it you seek?" the words came again from behind me.

Turning back and seeing nothing I turned a

complete circle looking to see who was talking. Seeing no one I called out, "Collectif, is that you?" When there was no response I called again, "Collectif, are you there? Is that you I hear?" When Collectif did not respond I started back to Guillaume's place. Walking slowly at first, ignoring the feelings of fear running up my back.

"What is it you seek?" came the question again, this time from in front of me. Almost running now I reached the shimmering wall and all but jumped inside. Guillaume, Opsis and Collectif all turned to look at me as I suddenly appeared, disheveled and pale.

"Our misguided young warrior hurries as if the demons of hell's fires are after him." Collectif spoke, a hint of laughter in his voice.

Ignoring him I walked over to my cot, securing my sword and shield against the wall I stretched out and turned my back to them. This, I did not wish to discuss. I heard Guillaume as he began to say something about needing to discuss what happened the day before, but I also heard Opsis interrupt him with a quietly spoken,'not now.'

Sleep came swiftly, but so did the dreams. I was in the castle, once again running down the corridor. I could hear no words, there was no sound to this dream but a strong sense of urgency. I had to get help. I was desperate to get help. I could feel the agony in my lungs screaming for air as I ran. My legs ached as my bare feet slapped against the stone floor. Tears flowed freely and yet I was unashamed of them. This dream had no color, everything I saw was a strange shade of gray. I ran into the great hall, there was something important going on. While I could still see no color, I could tell that everyone there was dressed in their very best. I rushed among the crowd, almost suffocating among the many coats and wide dresses that I fought to get through. How young I must be, everyone towers over me in this dream.

Breaking through the mass of people I could see an opening in the room, there were only two people standing there, speaking to the person sitting on a throne before them. But no matter who turned to me, no matter who I pushed or shoved or stepped on, when they looked, they bore no face. It was just blank. When I was finally past the last person in the way the two facing the thrones turned in my direction pointing. I could feel someone grab my arm and pull me back. I fought as hard as I could possibly fight. Pulling, struggling against the strength of who ever it was that held me tightly.

"No! No!!" I cried out, the sound more a wail than word as I still fought."let go, let me go I must get help I must!!" I could hear it then, laughter. It began with one and then spread through the gathering.

As I was being pulled away from the room I heard someone whisper "Poor Adwr, I wonder what his crisis is now?" More laughter as I was pulled out the doorway into the corridor.

Still I could not give up, ignoring the laughter I yelled through the closing doors.."Help them please! You must come and help them quickly!" As the doors closed I could not, did not give up. "Please!! If you do not come it will be too late..please!!" I was pounding and kicking at the door as I begged for someone, anyone to come help, to no avail. The sound of my own voice yelling out into the darkness woke me from sleep. Pulling me from the nightmare as I grabbed at my head, screaming out my anguish.

"I did not help them, I tried I tried and I could not help them."

"Who, young warrior, who could you not help?"

93

Guillaume spoke almost gently from just behind me.
    " I don't know, I'm not sure. I only heard their cries. First they were laughing at me, laughing because I don't know..laughing I remember the laughing. Then it changed. They weren't laughing any more. They were afraid. Guillaume they were afraid and I couldn't do anything."Burying my head in my hands I fought the despair. "I couldn't do anything. They wouldn't listen to me, they were laughing at me as I pleaded for help, calling me that name."
Guillaume moved up close enough behind me to place his hand on my shoulder. I felt more than heard his sigh.

    Long after everyone else had gone back to their perspective beds I sat awake on the cot. Memories of the dream haunting me. Usually the dreams would fade away completely leaving only the feelings of loss. I knew I had dreamed, but I could not remember what the dream had been about. This time though, parts remained. I could hear the screams. Again and again ringing in my ears as I ran, I could hear the screams.
    Carefully I rose from the cot trying to keep silent. Stepping quietly around a sleeping Collectif and Opsis I walked to the doorway to the outside. Stepping through the shimmering wall I stood in the night. It was the time just before dawn's first tendrils of light reached out. I walked across the opening to where a tree that the dragon had pushed over lay at an odd angle. Climbing up onto the trunk of the tree, I leaned back against a large branch and waited for the dawn. I listened to the silence around me, finding a peace in it. It wrapped around me like the arm of a comforting friend. Crossing my arms before me I sat and watched as night began its retreat from the sun.

94

Just as I was feeling sleep tugging at me a voice whispered to me from the dark, "What are you seeking?"

"Who asks me this question?" I spoke into the darkness as I sat up quickly, looking around.

"What are you seeking?" came the whisper again.

"Why do you ask me this question?" I asked the voice.

"What are you seeking?"

I stepped down from my place on the tree and stood in the slowly fading darkness. Using all the skills that Guillaume had taught me so far I tried to find who ever, or what ever was speaking to me. Try as I might, I could feel no other presence. Closing my eyes, I allowed my mind to search the area. I mentally remembered the area surrounding this place. In my mind, I walked this ground. I could see no one there. Allowing my senses reign, I reached out, nothing. I could feel no one. Opening my eyes I turned to see Opsis watching me.

"Are you well young warrior?"

"I am well Opsis, the dream is fading and taking the feelings with it."

Opsis walked over to where I stood, together we watched the morning appear. Finally he asked me, "What is it, that you were doing when I first approached?"

"I heard a voice, speaking to me." I turned to look at Opsis, hoping that maybe he could explain. " I heard the voice, but could see no one. When I spoke to this voice, asking who they were, asking why they kept asking me the same question, I got no response. I was trying to find them. I was trying to use what Guillaume has taught me, to find who or what was speaking."

Opsis stood silent for a moment before speaking, "What was the question this voice is asking?"

"Over and over it is asking me, What are you

seeking?"

"How does it ask this?"

I looked away from Opsis for a moment then turned back. "At times it speaks as you and I are, at times, it shouts loudly. Just this moment, it was a whisper."

"And in your search?" Opsis asked as he watched me carefully.

"No, I had no luck. There was no one here. Which I do not understand. I know I hear this voice. I know it is real. Someone is here. But yet, there is no one here."

Opsis reached out and put his hands on my shoulders, watching me, "No one, but- you." He watched as first the expression of surprise and then understanding moved across my face. I looked out into the brightening light, the first hint of any understanding growing just as the light grew before me.

Removing his hands from my shoulders Opsis turned away. "You are fast becoming a man Young Warrior. You are fast, growing into your name. Come, Guillaume will have a meal ready for us. There is plenty of time to face what you have learned just now."

EIGHT

The aroma of food greeted us upon entering Guillaume's chamber. Walking across the room Opsis and I each took a seat at the table. Collectif was already deep into his bowl, food dripping from his chin onto the table. Using his arm to wipe his mouth he looked up at me. Shoveling more food into his mouth with a spoon running over, he then used it to point in my direction.

"Warriors don't cry. Warriors don't scream in the night and wake other people."

I sat watching Collectif, I knew what was coming.

"Warriors, brave and noble don't cry for help, Co..."

"Enough Collectif." Guillaume stopped him. "I have seen many brave warriors that have wept unashamed. Wept when facing an unbearable loss, wept when wounded, wept even in moments of great joy. That makes them no less a warrior."

Collectif bobbed his head up and down repeatedly like a mad squirrel as he backed down from his attack on me trying to placate Guillaume. "Of course, of course, you are right of course." Taking his spoon he scrapped around the edges of his bowl making sure he missed no crumbs. Dropping the spoon onto the table splattering remnants of his meal he made to rise.

"I will take my leave of you now Guillaume, Opsis, Young....Warrior, I have things that await my attention and I have put them off too long. Yes, too long have they waited and I must get to them." Taking the deep sweeping bow that he had perfected he spun quickly around to face the entrance to the outside world.

"What things await you my friend?" Opsis asked him. "Since you have been so kind as to help us in our need, perhaps we could return the favor and help you in your responsibilities."

"Yes, that would only be fair." Guillaume agreed readily. "What is it that we can do to assist you Collectif?"

I watched the many expressions cross Collectif's face as I continued to eat. The expression that seemed so close to remaining was one of panic. But what had this annoying little creature to be afraid of?

"Oh my no, I could not ask anything of you. You are my friends, it was my great pleasure to be of assistance in your moment of need." Collectif was speaking quickly. I watched as he seemed to search the room for something, but what? While his head never turned, his eyes darted about, seeking inspiration, answers, excuses. Holding his arms out before him almost in a supplicating manner, he bowed deeply yet again. "There is no need for you to feel as if you are obligated to do anything for me. My errands are of mundane sort and easily handled."

"Ah, then, "Guillaume spoke, "you will be returning your company to us in quick manner?"

"Oh yes of course, of course. I will return once the completion of my errands is accomplished." Collectif spoke, repeating himself over and over as he all but ran through the shimmering wall.

"Nasty little beast." I spoke under my breath. Opsis however heard me and nearly choked on his food. I glanced up guiltily only to see Opsis fighting laughter. A quick look in Guillaume's direction proved that he too had heard my comment and was momentarily choosing to ignore it.

"All is ready?" Opsis asked Guillaume.

"All is ready." Guillaume answered.

Having no idea what they were discussing I stood and crossed the room to the cauldron. Filling my bowl I turned to feed the caTragons. None of the beasts were to be seen. Turning in a circle where I stood I looked about the entire room. The place beside Guillaume's bed where they normally rested was empty. Neither were they near Guillaume himself.

"Guillaume, where are the caTragons?" I asked confused at their disappearance.

"Busy." he answered still sitting at the table. He looked from the entrance to Opsis and back once again to the entrance.

I placed the full bowl on the floor in its usual place, then made sure the water container was full. Seeing that neither had moved from the table I filled three mugs with Guillaume's bitter brew and carried them to the table. Placing a mug in front of each one I watched as they ignored them. Opsis was the first to pick up his mug while absently brushing at the mess Collectif had left behind. Both seemed far away, lost in thoughts of things I knew nothing of.

After a while Opsis finally spoke. "He will not succeed, the caTragons will see to that."

Guillaume reached for his cooling brew and looked across at me. There was a look of worry in his expression. Turning to Opsis he finally spoke. "I do hope that you are right. This is just one more thing we do not need."

I sat there at the table for a while, waiting as they waited. Impatience soon got the better of me and I could sit no longer. Standing I carried my mug back to its place beside the fire. Turning I watched as Guillaume and Opsis both merely stared at the shimmering wall before them. Moving away from the fire, I made my way down the corridor. Torches would come to life at my approach, lighting my way to the Great Chamber. Entering the room I stopped just inside and looked around. It was once again empty but for the table containing the weapons that Guillaume had told me I was not ready for, and the table of crystals in the center of the room.

Leaning back against the wall I folded my arms across my chest. Looking down at my boots I sighed deeply. Lost in thought I at first did not hear the whisper.

"What do you seek?"

Raising my head I looked around the room. As I suspected I was alone.

"What do you seek?"

Stretching my arms out before me, palms up, I looked out into the empty room. "I seek answers."

"Do you know the questions?" returned the whisper.

"I have questions, but I am not sure, that I know the right questions."

"One has to know what questions to ask, and in what order to ask them, before answers can be given."

Stepping away from the wall and standing straighter, I lowered one arm while reaching outward with the other. "That doesn't seem fair. What difference does it make what order I ask?"

I heard only silence in return. "Well now that's good. I made myself mad." It was then that I noticed a glow coming from the crystals on the table. Walking over I watched as the glow brightened and the cloudy appearance cleared. Inside the crystal I could see

Collectif. Confused I watched as he ran through the forest clutching something in his hand. As I stood there I began to see things I remembered. Another of the crystals came to life, in it I could see the dragon's lair, I could see the many precious stones littering the floor. Hundreds and hundreds of stones reflecting the light, glittering and brilliant in color.

"He's going back to the dragon's lair." I spoke aloud to no one in particular. "He's going back to.." I could see then what he carried..the arrow, he had the arrow. I had to stop him. I didn't know why, but I knew I had to stop him and stop him now. Running down the corridor I could hear my boots as they pounded on the rock floor. Torches flared to life before me, dying instantly as I passed. The corridor taking on an odd gray cast in the on again gone again lights of the torches. I ran, feeling the pain growing in my chest as my lungs screamed for air. Bursting into Guillaume's chamber I ran for my weapons. Shouting at Guillaume and Opsis, "He's gone to the dragon's lair. He wants the stones. We have to stop him, we have to."

"We know where he has gone." Guillaume said.

"Do you also know that he has the arrow?" I had not slowed in my movements as I grabbed my shield, sword and crossbow. Turning quickly I almost ran into Opsis.

"We know where he has gone." Opsis told me

"And you just let him go? Knowing what he plans?" my voice growing louder and more impatient as I tried to get around Opsis. "There is no more magic in the Grandite. It was used up when Collectif removed the arrow from the dragon's leg. If he should use that arrow on the dragon now, what would happen?"

"If he strikes the dragon in the right place with the

arrow , he will kill it." Guillaume answered my question. "It is his greed that drives him to this, it is, as you said, the stones he desires. He would be quite content to collect the stones while the dragon is gone. However.." Guillaume hesitated before continuing, "I am sure that if the dragon is there, or appears while he is there, he would not hesitate to use the arrow."

"I know that. That is why we must stop him. We can not allow him to do this!" I tried again to get around Opsis only for him to reach out and place his hand on my shoulder holding me in place.

"What matters it to you, if he kill the dragon? I thought you wanted to see it dead."

Opsis question stopped me momentarily. I looked up at him slowly, trying to answer as honestly as I could "I do not know, but I know that I can not allow him to kill the dragon. It may be that it is not yet the dragon's time. It may be that I want that privilege myself being that it is my vow. Or, it may be that this dragon is to live. Something is telling me that I just cannot allow Collectif to bring harm to the dragon" before Opsis could react I slipped out from under his hand and hurried through the shimmering wall to the outside.

Running through the trees I realized I was at the disadvantage. I knew how long Collectif had been gone, and I knew just how fast and well he could run. There was also that walking through ripples of reality thing he could do. I knew though, that I had to try. With all that I was, I knew if I didn't try I would never forgive myself. Tree branches tore at my face and arms as I ran without watching. Jumping those same gullies and fallen trees as I had once before, when on an entirely different mission.

My shield caught on a limb causing me to spin nearly
completely around and lose my balance. Yet I kept
upright and pulling the shield free began to run again.

"Why am I always running?" I spoke to no one but
myself as another small branch raked across my face.
When my lungs could take the lack of air no more and felt
as if they would burst I stopped. Leaning against a tree
for support I held my side and took great breaths. If I had
not known better, I would have thought this any other day.
Everything seemed as normal. The sun was bright, the
sky was blue, the birds sang, the squirrel searched
for missing nuts. "Just like me." I mumbled to myself as I
pushed away from the tree and began to run again.
Sweat ran down my face into the many scratches and
into my eyes, blinding me with the pain and still I ran. I
could taste its saltiness as it ran unchecked into my
mouth. I tried using my shield to protect me from the
branches that tore at my face, but its very weight worked
against me. Growing heavier and more awkward the
longer I tried to hold it up. Giving up I dropped my arm
back lower and just ran, ignoring the painful slaps from
the branches as best I could.

Running along a pathway created by the forest
animals, in my haste I did not see the root that grew
above ground. Tripping over it I slid headfirst into some
low growing brush. Rolling over onto my back, groaning
from the pain I heard another noise. A noise that had me
grow still and try to breathe as silently as possible.

Again I heard the noise. The roar of the dragon as
it passed over head. I could not see it through the canopy
of leaves, but I heard the hiss of its breathing, the sounds
of its flame as it singed the tops of the trees in passing. I
watched as the leaves directly above me swayed crazily
in the winds created by the dragon's wings. From my

103

position on the ground I watched the leaves above me as they danced, giving evidence of the dragon's direction. It was returning to its lair. And Collectif was there.

Jumping to my feet I again began to run. My thoughts running wild inside my head. I had to get there, I wasn't going to make it, but I had to make it. When did this forest grow so wide? Time and my mortality was my enemy here. With no magic I could only run. Trying with only the physical strength that I had, to get there as quickly as it allowed. I thought of the many prize stallions in the castle stables and how I longed for one of them so very far away. Not allowing my wishful thinking to deter me I ran still. The forest around me not as bright as before, the day was passing and the sun would soon be going down. I could no longer hear the dragon's roar and the leaves overhead had long stilled. Still, I ran, if my heart burst in my chest, so be it. I would have at least tried.

As the pains in my sides and chest grew so did my fears and frustrations. My anger at my inability to reach the dragon in time was threatening to overwhelm me. Forced to stop yet again to ease the pain in my chest from lack of air I yelled into the air around me. "Somebody help me! Do something. Give me something to help me!"

At a sound in the darkening woods near me I stepped back. Out from the trees stepped a large caTragon. Glaring at me with its cat like eyes it approached. "Getting eaten wasn't exactly my idea of help." I muttered as the beast approached. I watched as when it was within reach, it lowered its body to the ground as if waiting. I stood watching it warily for a moment before I realized what it was offering. Stepping over to the caTragon I climbed onto its back and grabbed hold to its mane. I watched amazed as wings that I had not noticed before opened, spreading widely away from its body. With a look back at me it began to move those great wings and we were swiftly moving into the sky. Leaning down close to the beast's body I held on tightly, refusing to look down. Yet overjoyed that I was going to make it after all.

Holding tightly to the caTragon's mane, my face against its back with my eyes closed, I felt the wind blowing across my own back. Tugging at my tunic and shield. How fast could this beast fly? Opening my eyes just a slit I peered over its back to the ground far below. The caTragon's wings barely moved and yet the ground beneath us passed in a confusion of color and shapes. As we moved above the trees I could feel what was left of the afternoon sun as it made its final descent to the horizon. I watched the ground grow closer as the caTragon started down toward the earth. Landing lightly it folded its wings tightly to its side and waited for me to move. Stepping off the beast I stood on trembling legs. As my strength returned the caTragon turned away, looking off into the distance. It looked back once at me and then began to lope off toward Fire Mountain. I knew where it was going, I recalled the conversation between Guillaume and Opsis. The caTragons were to protect the dragon, but I intended if not to protect it myself, to play a part in its safety.

For its size and shape the caTragon moved swiftly and silently through the trees. It was all I could do to keep the beast in sight. Finally, fighting my way through low growing brush I stood once again beside the caTragon. This time however it was not alone. It appeared that every caTragon I had seen at or around Guillaume's place was here. Watching the lair, and waiting. I slipped up to the front of the tribe and looked up the hillside at the opening of the dragon's lair.

Slipping my arm further through the strap on my shield I slung it over my back and began to climb. Huge boulders lay scattered about the hillside making my climb difficult. With no cracks or crevice to use as secure foothold I could only jump and grab, hoping to be able to hold on while pulling myself over the biggest of the boulders. After what seemed like an eternity, just as the last rays of the sun disappeared, I reached the mouth of the dragon's lair.

Waiting just long enough for my strength, energy and wind to catch up with me, I took my crossbow from its bag and carefully loaded an arrow into place. I then leaned around to look into the dark cavern. Just as I moved I heard the dragon's roar and it did not sound happy. Easing my way into the dark of the cave I stayed close to the wall. Cold and dampness seeped into my tunic chilling me. This surprised me seeing that I was in a fire breathing dragon's lair, but then as Guillaume loves to say 'All is not always as it seems." Creeping ever so slowly along I could hear the sound of something entering the cave behind me. Guessing it to be one or more of the caTragons I continued on. Again I heard the dragon's roar, much closer and must more angry sounding. This time, immediately after the roar, I heard Collectif yelling at the dragon.

"Foul beast! I will have these stones!"

Pushing myself away from the wall I moved around the turn in the cave to see the battle taking place before me. Collectif stood behind a shield of his own making, the size of it hiding all of him but his head and the tips of his hoofed feet. In his hand I could see the half of the arrow that he had hidden, now firmly attacked to a

long pole turning it into a potentially deadly spear.
Scattered around his feet were dozens of precious stones
spilling from a cloth bag that he had dropped. "I will have
these stones, they are mine, mine do you understand foul
beast?! I will have them even if it means your death. But,
your death would be better, for then, I would have even
the stones that are shining from your very hide."

As he jabbed at the dragon with his weapon, the
dragon in turn lowered its massive head and exhaled
large plumes of smoke and flames. The flames
surrounding and overflowing Collectif's shield like a rush
of flooding water. Collectif was undeterred, fazed not by
the flames.

Moving forward he attempted to strike the dragon
with the spear. Missing as it moved away. The dragon
swung its spiked tail in Collectif's direction only to bounce
off of his shield. I watched as Collectif staggered briefly
then regained his balance. He then once again made to
take a stab at the dragon, this time at an unprotected
area of its belly. The one thing in the dragon's favor was
that Collectif's fear was obviously as great as his greed.
His hands trembled causing his grip to not be a strong as
need be to do damage.

"Collectif!" I shouted, startling him into almost
dropping his spear. "Leave this place! Leave the dragon's
stones and leave this dragon unharmed."

Not taking his eyes off of the dragon he began to
laugh. "Do not hurt this beast? YOU of all people telling
me not to hurt this beast?? YOU, yourself shot this
creature with this arrow and now You dare to tell.. no no..
ORDER.. me not to hurt the creature??"

The dragon hearing my voice turned on me,
lowering its head I feared I was about to become ashes.
Before the flames erupted from the dragon's mouth I was

surrounded by caTragons. Standing around me like the king's guards. The dragon lifted its head and turned its attention back to Collectif who had used that unguarded moment to not only grab up the bag and stones he had dropped but moved closer to the dragon. Drawing his home made spear back he made to strike.

Moving my crossbow quickly into position, I fired without hesitation. The arrow struck its mark sinking deeply into Collectif's shoulder. His cry was one of pain and of anger. Grabbing the shaft of the arrow he pulled it from his shoulder in one move. Blood flowed down his chest from the wound.

"I do not wish to kill you Collectif." I spoke as I slowly drew my sword from its sheath. "but if you insist on this, I will do what I must to protect the dragon."

Collectif turned on me in anger, drawing his good arm back he made to strike me with the spear he had made. Holding my shield before me I stepped out away from the caTragons and waited for his move. Fighting to hold onto enough strength to win this he dropped his shield. Blood flowed down his arm, as anger flared deep in his eyes. While I could hear the caTragons moving behind me, drawing closer, I watched Collectif closely. Out of the corner of my eye I could see the dragon watching the entire proceedings just as closely as I watched Collectif. The smoke and sulfur smell of the dragon filled my senses. I ignored it as best I could while I waited for Collectif's decision. With a yell he made it.

"I will kill you and then the dragon! I will have these stones! They are mine... mine... mine." His shouts growing louder as he lunged in my direction.

I realized now that his greed had driven him to a strange form of madness. Using my shield I deflected his spear easily. Falling away from me he still managed to keep his balance and prepared for another attack.

The caTragons behind me began to roar. One after another they alternated back and forth. The sound disconcerting to Collectif. It wasn't a loud angry sound, instead it was as if they were calling one to another. The sound grew as each and every caTragon began to growl and roar. I watched Collectif as he looked at the caTragons standing behind me.

"You need them to protect you, ADWR??" Collectif spoke in a sneering manner. "Can you not fight me, a wounded enemy, without them?"

"I do not wish to fight you at all, Collectif."I spoke trying to reason with him. "I only do so because you refuse to hear me. You have allowed rocks to become your god and master and do not listen to anyone but them." I stepped away from the caTragons as I spoke, watching his reaction to my moves.

Staggering now, he slowly raised the spear that seemed to have grown too heavy to lift. As I watched him fight with the spear I did not at first see the movement of his wounded arm. Reaching into his belt, using the last of his strength he pulled a dagger from his vest and threw it at me. As the dagger sliced into my arm I made a move of my own. Driving my sword deeply into Collectif's chest. Hearing the sound of his life's breath pushed from his lungs with the blow. Falling to the ground he slid off the sword as blood pooled about his body. His eyes growing dim as life left them.

I stood for long moments staring at Collectif's body as his blood dripped from my sword. Mixed emotions ran through my mind. Finally taking a deep breath I turned to the closest caTragon. "We cannot leave him here. He was Guillaume's friend, he deserves to be treated with respect for that."

The dragon did not move from where it stood as I pulled Collectif's body across a caTragon's back and secured it in place with his own belt. Walking along side the caTragons I left the dragon's lair. Once outside the same beast that I had ridden before lowered itself before me, offering me a ride once again. Gratefully I accepted the offer, climbing onto its great back and taking hold of the mane once more. Fighting against the exhaustion and darkness that tried to claim me.

Somewhere in the haze between awake and asleep I could feel the cool night air pulling at my hair and person as the caTragon flew through the darkness. I could feel its muscles as they shifted, hear the almost silent sounds of its wings as they moved. I could smell the musky odor of the animal I rode. Draped over the beast's back like a discarded cloak I held on as we made our way back to Guillaume's place on the far side of the forest. Forcing my eyes open I looked to the sides and saw other caTragons flying with us. Including the one that carried Collectif's body. Below us the black of night hid everything from my sight, but for an occasional spot of light that was there and then gone. I did not bother to look up. I did not want to see the stars and moon, continuing on as if nothing had happened on this day. The weight of my sword lay against my leg, growing heavier by the moment. Thoughts of the day's events ran through my head, pictures of what had happened chased them, running and crashing together like a bad horse race. Colliding in confusion only to jump and run again. At some point, the exhaustion and loss of blood fully claimed me and I knew no more.

It was when the caTragon lightly stepped from the sky to the ground, walking a few steps to slow that I awoke somewhat. I heard the sound of Guillaume and

Opsis talking as they approached. I felt hands gripping my shoulders and I tried lifting my head. Opening my eyes just enough to see Guillaume I whispered, "Collectif,,,,,Guillaume, Collectif.."

"I know , we know..rest now. Tomorrow is another day."

Some where in my half conscious state I felt myself half walking -half being carried. I could tell when we were inside, the coolness of the night air was replaced by the warmth of a fire. I fumbled with the tie to my belt, feeling the weight of the sword falling away, hearing the clank of metal on the stone floor and not caring if I mistreated my weapon. Dropping the bag that contained my crossbow and arrows as I stumbled across the room, I felt the weight of my shield as it was lifted from my back. Feeling the edge of the cot against my leg I turned and nearly fell onto it. The last I remember was feeling the cot beneath me as I stretched out upon it, turning my face to the wall. Then the sleep of the wounded claimed me.

The dreams that haunted me this night were different. Again and again I found myself in the dragon's lair. Each time I was facing Collectif, every one ended with the sound of his last breath as my sword pierced his body. All during the night I tossed and turned, hanging onto or over the edge of the cot as I fought battle after battle. While in the dreams I knew the caTragons were near, I could hear them moving behind me, they were not seen. I knew the dragon was there, I could smell the smoke and sulfur, but it was just out of sight in the darkness. In my dreams, all I saw was Collectif, and every now and again, I could see myself, as if I were a third party watching this battle. I could see the glint of the steel, hear the sounds of metal against metal as we fought. Yet time and again, as each dream came and

111

went, they ended the same. Collectif falling to the floor, bleeding because of the mortal wound inflicted by me.

Dragging myself from deep sleep into wakefulness , I struggled to leave the memories of the dreams and all the senses they had touched. I fought in my conscious state the feelings of fear and despair I had fought while asleep. Swinging my legs over the edge of the cot I rested my elbows on my knees, placing my head in my hands. Silently I stared at the white bandage wrapped securely around my arm. The hint of a dark stain showing just under the top layers of cloth. Shifting my position just a little I sat staring at the floor, finally I allowed my hands to drop as I dared to look across the room for the first time.

CaTragons lay stretched out about the room like contented house cats. Yawning and stretching they watched Guillaume and Opsis as they sat at the table eating.

"You are awake," Opsis spoke the moment he noticed my movements. "come Young Warrior and eat. We have saved some for you." Motioning with his outstretched arm and hand to my usual position at the table, where a bowl waited. I could see the steam still rising from the bowl. I could also see Guillaume as he sat at the table, watching me.

"Thank you Opsis, but I am not hungry." I looked away, unable to bear seeing Guillaume's watching me. Guilt eating at me for what I had done.

"Come Young Warrior and eat," Guillaume spoke, "we will discuss or not what happened after you have eaten and are stronger."

"Guillaume, I tried, really tried to reason with Collectif..." my words stumbled to a stop as I looked to the floor before I continued, "I did not wish to harm him. I

112

told him so, but he refused to hear me."

"Do not worry yourself over what happened." Guillaume spoke calmly. I finally found the inner strength to look directly at him. His face held no sign of anger, just an expression of calm acceptance, not even a hint of sadness lurking anywhere. Standing I looked about the room. My weapons were placed carefully in their positions against the wall. Reaching over I picked up my sword and slowly pulled it from its sheath. There was no sign of blood anywhere. Shoving the sword back into the sheath I reached for my bag. Carefully counting the arrows I saw there was indeed one missing. Placing my hand on the bandage on my arm I knew that it had all happened. Yet, there was something playing at the edges of my mind. I felt that even with all the thinking and dreaming I have done on this, I was missing something. Guillaume called to me again, "Your wound was deep, you lost a lot of blood and have been asleep for several days. You need to eat to regain your strength."

Shaking off the momentary confusion I crossed the room to the table. Stepping around caTragons as I went. I sat down and reached for a spoon. The low growl of hunger in my belly stopping me for the moment from asking any more questions.

After I finished eating I rose to feed the caTragons but Guillaume took my bowl from me. "I'll do that. You need to rest."

I looked at Guillaume for a moment, he was acting oddly. I decided to save my questions for later and turned to walk away. Not wanting to rest I wandered down the corridor toward the Great Chamber. I watched, counting to myself how many steps between the torches

113

and when they would flare to life. Entering the Great
Chamber I walked around the outer edge of the
room. Dragging my hand along the wall idly as I walked.
By the time I was on my third trip around I had a couple
caTragons for company. Tagging along behind me they
didn't seem to mind that we were going no where. It was
on this third trip that I noticed there was one place in the
wall that felt differently. It sank in just the slightest amount
and then a feet steps away it came back outward.
Shrugging it off I continued to walk. In the center of the
room the crystals began to glow softly. I kept walking
along the wall, ignoring the glow.

"The crystals call you." Opsis spoke from the
entrance way.

I shrugged dismissively "I see them."

"You are not going to go over there?"

"I wasn't planning on it, no." I said, still walking
as a third caTragon joined us as we passed Opsis.

"What are your thoughts Young Warrior?" Opsis
asked as he too fell in beside me.

"I'm not sure. I know that I am not happy about
what happened. I tried to talk him out of what he was
doing, what he planned." a sigh escaped from
somewhere deep within me, "I tried to talk to him. He just
seemed lost somehow, different."

"Greed can do that to a person. Cause them to
focus solely on one thing. Cause them to not listen, to
refuse to hear reason."Opsis was watching me as we
walked. "Greed isn't the only thing that can do that. We
can get so wrapped up in ideas and plans, goals and
promises that we refuse to listen to the voice of reason
around us."

Keeping my eyes focused on what was in front
of me I still listened to what Opsis was saying. "I've been

114

listening to Guillaume when he speaks." I said without slowing.

"Yes, but are you really, fully, hearing him?" Opsis asked, stopping when we reached the doorway to the corridor. "Are you hearing him, and understanding what he's trying to teach you?"

Leaning back against the wall I crossed my arms and legs in front of me. Hanging my head down for a quiet moment I then looked off toward the still glowing crystals. "Understanding is one thing that I seek in all of this." I said almost to myself. When I turned back Opsis was gone. "I hate when they do that." I said to the nearest caTragon which looked for all the lands to be bored.

Crossing the room I walked over to the table holding the crystals. The glow had grown to where it encircled the table, casting shadows and light along the floor. Placing my hands on the table I watched as a strange light appeared in front of me. In that light I could see what appeared to be a wall, on that wall was a tapestry that I had never seen before. As I watched the image cleared, becoming sharp and easy to see right before my eyes. Woven in the fabric was the picture of a man standing over a fallen form. What appeared to be blood dripping from a sword in the hand of the conqueror. In the background stood a large dragon- my dragon- watching what was going on. The tapestry was beautiful and colorful. All around the two figures and the dragon were the precious stones. I was beginning to shake when I dared to look closer at the conqueror. It was me. Spinning away from the image I ran right into Guillaume who was standing behind me. In my surprise and concentration on the image I had not heard him enter.

"I don't understand," I nearly shouted.

"Come and see." Guillaume said as he turned and walked toward the place in the wall I had noticed earlier. Placing his hand high on the wall it began to move slowly, creating an opening. "Come and see." he said again, when I had not moved. Then he stepped through the opening out of sight.

Looking down at the caTragon at my feet I moved around it and followed Guillaume. Stepping through the opening I stood looking at the very same tapestry I had just seen the image of. Looking at it I could tell that it was very old. The edges were frayed by time, but the tapestry as a whole was magnificent. Standing in front of where it hung on the wall I looked at it, from top to bottom it had to be fifteen feet in length, then width of it was no less than twelve feet. It was the pattern of the tapestry that had me catching my breath and my eyes widening in surprise. The tapestry contained a woven picture of the exact thing that had happened. It was of Collectif's death.

"I still don't understand. I need to understand Guillaume."

Guillaume stood looking at the tapestry for a few more moments before looking down at me. "Some things are fore told. They are meant to be. All of us, have a destiny. It is just that the destiny of some, is greater than that of others."

"I do, and yet I don't understand Guillaume." I turned from looking at the tapestry to looking at Guillaume, "I just wish I understood all of this." Turning back to look one more time at the tapestry I turned to follow Guillaume when he made to leave the room.

"What do you seek?" came the whispered question.

"I seek, to understand." I whispered, turning to watch the rock as it slid back into place, sealing away the room and the tapestry within.

Opsis was waiting when we entered Guillaume's chamber. Taking a seat at the table I sat staring at where Collectif's mat had been on the floor. Gone now, leaving no sign of having ever been there. I moved back when a mug of hot brew was placed before me. When Guillaume and Opsis also sat at the table I turned to Guillaume.

"Was Collectif a good friend of yours? Did you know him long?" I asked turning to look at Guillaume.

"Collectif was someone who would appear and disappear quickly. He never was still for long. One could only know as much about Collectif as he allowed."

"But he was a friend?"

"Yes, Young Warrior, he was a friend." Guillaume looked away, his eyes taking on a far away look as he remembered. "I have been told that he was different once. Young, brave, not the frittering fool that you saw. Something out there changed him. He seemed lost."

When Guillaume grew silent I looked to Opsis. "Did you know him as a friend as well?"

"For a time, not as long as Guillaume did, but still, we were friends for a time."

Opsis took a swallow from his drink before speaking again. "We may never know, what brought on the changes within Collectif. I, too, remember hearing word of him as different. Whether it was the greed growing with in him, or something else. None of it matters now."

"What matters," Guillaume interrupted, "is how you are doing. You have never taken a life before. How does that sit on your heart?"

I sat staring down at the mug before me. My hands were wrapped around it absorbing the warmth from the hot brew within. "I told you, I did not wish to kill him. I tried to talk to him, but ..."

"One can not talk to a mad man Young Warrior.."
Opsis spoke quietly, reassuringly.

Nodding without looking up I took a swallow of the drink, giving myself time to collect my thoughts. "I knew, I just knew I could not let him do what was in his heart. He could not kill the dragon or even take the stones. Something inside kept telling me, he could not have the stones. But the stones, his desire to own them, drove him beyond reason. Drove him to a battle that ..." taking another long drink I set the mug on the table and looked to Guillaume. "I did not wish to kill Collectif. As annoying as he was, he was your friend, he was becoming my friend. But I had to stop him. If it meant, and it did, taking his life, then so be it. How do I feel? Saddened, but strong in feeling I did what was right. I stayed true to what was right in my heart and did not allow friendship to prevent my doing that very thing."

I stood and moved to rinse my mug and place it on its shelf. "I do not know why, I do not understand, why. The dragon is alive and safe- for now."

"Understanding will come, when the time is right." Guillaume spoke from his position at the table.

I stared into the fire, not acknowledging his comment. I was tired, so tired of hearing that and wondering when the time would be right. Turning back from the fire I made to return to the table, absently rubbing the head of a caTragon as I passed it.

Guillaume watched my approach, "How did you enjoy your ride on the back of a caTragon?"

Stopping in the middle of the room I looked back to where the caTragon sat. "I don't remember much at all of the return ride. The ride to the dragon's lair I remember more of. There is a different feeling when one is flying."

"One that you would enjoy again?"

Shrugging, I turned to face Guillaume. "Possibly, Yet I do not know that the caTragons would care to just fly me about idly, without cause."

It was Guillaume's turn to shrug. "One never knows what is possible, unless one seeks to find out."

Watching Guillaume I noticed there was a hint of a smile lurking in his expression. Turning around to face the caTragon I watched it, as it watched me, looking as if it were waiting for something. Taking a quick look back at Guillaume and Opsis I turned to the caTragon. "Would you," I hesitated, somewhat uncomfortable taking to the beast before me. "Would you, take me flying again?"

Without hesitation the caTragon turned to walk toward the shimmering wall, looking back to see if I were following. With a quick glance toward Guillaume he waved me on my way. Running to catch up with the caTragon we walked through the wall together.

NINE

Walking out into the sunlight with the caTragon I felt a bolt of excitement moving through me. Having left all of my weapons leaning up against the wall in Guillaume's chamber, there was going to be nothing to slow us down. It was going to be me and the caTragon soaring. I couldn't wait to see if it really was flying as fast as I thought, or if I simply imagined it all. The caTragon settled low to the ground watching me as he waited. He slowly edged forward just a bit, his muscles twitching in anticipation. As I climbed onto its back his wings unfolded from his body. Within moments we were airborne. Clutching the caTragon's mane I looked over its shoulder to the ground below. We were flying just over the tops of the trees, sending the branches and leaves into a frenzy of shaking in our wake. Diving downward we skimmed over the top of the pond and then shooting almost straight up the caTragon decided to see how well I could hold on as it began to fly in a looping pattern. If a caTragon could smile, that was exactly what this one was doing as we played through the sky. For a while I clung to the caTragon as we flew over the forest. For a while I laughed and enjoyed the moment, forgetting everything that had happened and all that had me questioning past, present and future.

At one point the caTragon began chasing birds that had been lazily flying in circles watching the ground beneath them. When the caTragon flew through the center they scattered to various areas of the forest below. I could hear them, from where they hid in the trees raising quite a ruckus over the interruption. Leaning over to look to the forest below I noticed a burnt spot in the ground through a clearing in the trees. As we flew over a small hill I noticed another such place on the ground. Curiosity got the better of me and I signaled for the caTragon to land. Touching down lightly we walked over to one of the places I had spotted from the air.

Some one or some thing had a camp fire here. It was long cold now, with only this burned circle as proof that it had happened. That, and a vague memory of the spots of light in the dark. Today from the sky I had noticed two through the trees, but I remembered seeing many that night. Walking together the caTragon and I made an ever widening search around the cold circle, I had no idea what I was looking for, anything that would give a hint of who or what had been here. The area looked too clean, like someone had scoured the grounds making sure not to leave anything at all behind. Crossing through the trees I could see what looked like another circle. The grounds around it were cleared the same as the first. There was nothing here other than the burned circle in the ground.

"Strange, so very strange." I spoke aloud as I stood near the darkened place looking around. The caTragon stood watching me. "I wonder if Guillaume and Opsis know of this?" Standing in quiet contemplation I decided that we needed to find out.

Climbing onto the caTragon's back I felt its muscles flex and move beneath me as it began walking across the ground to where there was an opening in the trees. As we approached the opening I watched the caTragon's wings as they unfolded once again from its body. I could feel every one of its muscles as it moved, sleek and powerful, preparing to take flight. Lifting off the ground we again took to the skies.

If this beast could think, I would have sworn that it decided to show off a bit before we got back. Within moments of being back in the sky we were moving at an incredible speed. The winds tearing at my face forcing my eyes closed. Holding my head down, buried almost against the caTragon's shoulders I was able to force open my eyes enough to see. The trees below me were nothing more than a blur of green color. I closed my eyes and merely enjoyed the flight. Feeling the wind against and across my body. Those same winds had my hair blowing madly about, slapping at my face. The strength of the wind tearing at my clothing. The mane of the caTragon wrapping around me, hiding my face as I held it down closer to its shoulders. The soft sounds made by the movement of its wings a music in my ears. All too soon we were touching down gently in front of Guillaume's place. Climbing from the caTragon's back I stood for a moment watching as its wings folded tightly against its body. Placing my hand on its head I hesitated only briefly and then said simply, "Thank you." Again I thought, if the beast could smile, this one did. Together we walked back through the shimmering wall into Guillaume's chamber.

Entering the chamber we found it empty. The fire, however, was burning high so Guillaume, was either not far away or had not been gone long. Walking to the entrance of the corridor to the Great Chamber I saw that the torches were lit. The caTragon was close behind me as I headed down toward the Great Chamber and hopefully Guillaume and Opsis. I had to find out if they knew of the campfires. Hearing their voices I knew I had found them. Entering I saw them standing at the table in the center, watching several of the crystals as they glowed brightly.

I started speaking as soon as I entered the room. "Guillaume, the caTragon and I found several campfires in the forest that had grown cold. Do you know of this?"

Guillaume and Opsis looked solemnly at each other and then Guillaume motioned for me to move closer. "Yes, Young Warrior, we know of the cold fires."

Moving to the table as Guillaume had motioned for me to do I could see the crystals and the images showing within them. "That is the castle. That is Dragon's Doom." I exclaimed when it came up and then disappeared. "Why is it showing the castle?"

"Watch the images Young Warrior, it is not good."

I stood transfixed as the images appeared before me in the crystals. I watched as the castle appeared, on the turret stood several of the best knights firing arrows from their crossbows toward something on the ground. I could hear shouts of anger and pain. When the images moved it showed the grounds surrounding the castle. There looked to be hundreds of campfires burning, even though it appeared to be mid day in the image. Spears were stacked by the dozens, stone spearheads pointing toward the sky. Creatures in odd uniform fired on the castle with burning arrow and spear. It was impossible to tell their number as they filled the crystal and more.

"Who is this that is laying siege to the castle?" I asked Guillaume, outrage in my voice, yet it was Opsis that answered.

"They are Molditians. They are thought to be related in some form to Trolls or possibly to Ogres, neither of which they will admit or lay claim to. Nor will the Trolls or Ogres lay claim to them. Ordinarily they live underground in the many caves and tunnels in the side of Fire Mountain. I do not know what has stirred them to this. They are an evil race of quite vile and ugly creatures, Young Warrior and if they succeed in taking the castle, there is no hope for those inside."

"We must do something. We can not sit here and simply watch this happen." Desperation and fear drove me to impatience, Leaning over the table attempting to move closer to the crystals, as if that would help me aid my family within the castle walls. "Guillaume, my family is in that castle."

"I know Young Warrior, I know." was all that Guillaume said, as he stood watching the crystal.

"I'm going!" I said as I swung away from the table."I believe the caTragon will take me there." As I started away from the table Guillaume placed his hand on my shoulder. I stopped and turned in his direction.

"We can not run into this without thought or plans, Young Warrior. If we are to succeed in helping them and find a way to defeat this vast army, we must plan first."

"Guillaume is right," Opsis said, "we must prepare carefully, or all is indeed lost."

"Guillaume you have magic, can you not use that?" I asked bluntly.

"I have magic yes." Guillaume spoke with a look of great sadness in his eyes. "I have been commanded to never use it in or around the castle ever again. Not in this life or any other."

"Why?" my one word came out more as a demand than a question.

"It is all a part of the past you do not yet remember. It is a part of why my name is whispered and not spoken within the castle walls."

Frustration welled up within me. Exploding in a rage I slammed my fists down on the table causing the crystals to jump and bang together. "Have you never broken a command?" I spoke harshly without thought.

"Yes, Young Warrior, I have. And that time, has caused me a sorrow that has lasted all these many years. That one time, has brought you here to me, in the hopes that we can correct that mistake."

"But first," Interrupted Opsis, "we have this to deal with, and I have an idea that just may work."

Guillaume looked at Opsis, turning slowly to fully face him. Placing his hands on the table before him, he waited, appearing to gather his thoughts before speaking. "What is this idea of yours Opsis?"

"I will tell you, once you give me your word to hear me out."

"To start with a condition does not bode well for your idea my friend."

"Possibly, but do you agree?" Opsis asked as he watched Guillaume.

After several long moments Guillaume relented. "I do not like it, but, yes, I agree."

Opsis looked at me to where I had moved across the room, then turned back to Guillaume, "You can not use any of your magic around the castle, but our young warrior here can."

"NO." Guillaume cut Opsis off.

"You said you would listen..."

"NO."

"Guillaume.. hear me.." Opsis began.

"Opsis, you of all people should know and understand why I can not even consider this that you suggest."

"This would be different."

"It would be no different. It can not happen."

"Guillaume..."

Guillaume slammed his hands down on the table

in a rare display of anger. The look in his eyes one of pure agony. "No, Opsis, No. I refuse to even consider it."

"Guillaume, hear me, this could actually be an answer to even that. First we must do this, otherwise, nothing matters. Not even the past."

I had been leaning back against the wall, arms and legs crossed in front of me. Watching Guillaume and Opsis, I couldn't help but smile slightly even in my impatience. I had never witnessed such a polite argument before. Even though their voices got loud in turn, they still for the most part held control over their emotions. All the while this was going on the crystals glowed, screams of anger and pain could be heard along with sounds of battle.

"Guillaume,"Opsis spoke, his voice softening, "I know this is difficult, but it has to be. It is our best chance."

Guillaume had been standing with head bowed, staring at the crystals on the table while Opsis talked. When he turned to look at me, he looked as if he had aged a hundred years. His eyes held a sadness even greater than what I had witnessed moments earlier. It was obvious even to me, that he did not want to do this. You could see in his eyes that he hoped in the depths of all that he was for some miracle out of it.

"It is the only way Guillaume." Opsis spoke gently as he placed Guillaume's book on the table.

Guillaume slowly reached out and placed his hand on the over sized book resting before him. There was something familiar about this book, something- a memory perhaps- kept playing around the edges of my thoughts. Obviously very old, its cover faded with edges worn and bent. The center of the cover was embossed with several designs that I could not make out due to the positioning of Guillaume's hand. I could see the edges of the pages inside had a yellowed cast to them. Guillaume gently caressed the book, a far away look in his eyes. Eyes that still held that tormented look. When his shoulders sagged, he hung his head, the determination to fight this gone. I watched as he closed his eyes, hiding the emotions running unbidden and unwanted in them. When I was beginning to grow weary of the wait, his hand slowly closed around the spine of the book. When I straightened and started to speak I saw Opsis motioning for me to remain silent. Lifting the book from the table Guillaume turned to me.

"What we are about to do, I promised, no I *swore* would never happen." hesitating he looked to Opsis and then back to me, "however, Opsis is correct in that we have no choice if the castle is to stand and the people inside survive. Follow me." Carrying the book he quickly crossed the room and walked down the corridor away from the Great Chamber. Falling behind Guillaume I heard Opsis as he moved in behind me and followed us from the chamber.

Entering his personal chamber Guillaume pointed in the direction of my cot. "Collect your weapons, you will need them- and much more."

Without a word I quickly gathered everything together and stepped back to Guillaume's side. Watching me for several long moments he finally turned and stepped through the shimmering wall to the outside. I looked to Opsis who silently nodded. I too then walked through the wall.

Guillaume was standing several feet from the wall. In one hand he held the now open book, the other hand was raised toward the sky with his palm turned upward, his fingers slightly bent inward. Looking toward the sky I saw that dark clouds were gathering, lightning streaked from cloud to cloud as thunder shook the ground around us.

Opsis stepped up beside me, he too looked to the sky. "We or rather you, are about to storm the enemy attacking the castle."

Hearing a familiar sound I turned to see the caTragon I had ridden earlier approaching. He walked without hesitation to my side and stood as if waiting. The scent of sulfur and smoke, that was such a part of him, drifting on the wind that was rising. Dust was picked up and swirled madly as it crossed the ground before us. I could feel the sting as it struck my face and arms like thousands of needles. Still watching the sky and the gathering storms I heard as Guillaume called to me. "Come and hear this." Walking over close I waited.

"I am going to show you one page of this book. You will read the words on that one page only. Do you understand me?"

"Yes Guillaume, I do understand."

"Commit these words to memory. The caTragon will take you to the castle. As you cross over the top of the hillside at the edge of the forest, just before the fields of the castle you will speak the words. You will recite the words exactly as they are written. You will change nothing, not the way they are pronounced, not the order in which they are written. You will not say them more than once."Guillaume was watching me intently, "do you understand this?"

"Yes, Guillaume, I do understand."

"Do you understand Young Warrior, that if you change the words in even the least of ways, it could bring disaster on us all?"

Gripping my sword tighter, the only evidence of my

nerves, I nodded, "Yes, Guillaume, I do understand."

Accepting my answer he moved the open book around to where I could see the page. Read these words, do not say them aloud until the time instructed. Read them until you know them Young Warrior, for everything depends on your memory."

"Guillaume, when the time comes, and I say the words, what will happen?" I asked him once I was sure I knew the words perfectly.

"That, my brave and noble warrior, you will only believe when you see it. Do not be surprised or afraid of what it is you see. Accept it, and use it." Guillaume placed his hand on my shoulder, something that I had grown accustomed to finally. "Go now, go in grace and save those that need you. Once you have defeated this enemy, it will then be your decision as to whether you stay at the castle, or return here."

Carefully securing my shield and bag on my back I then checked to make sure my belt was tightened. My sword secure, I then climbed onto the waiting caTragon's back. Settled in place I turned to Guillaume, "I will return."

Guillaume nodded as the caTragon's wings unfolded from its body with a whisper of sound. With only a single step forward we were airborne. I leaned down close to the beast's back to ease any resistance. I didn't bother to look down, I could feel how swiftly we were moving. On this trip, the caTragon flew straight and true to our destination. There were no playful moves meant to excite or frighten, the beast knew the importance of what we were doing.

I felt a difference in the movement of the caTragon's muscles beneath me. The feeling of the wind tearing against me was less, causing me to straighten and look to see where we were. The hillside Guillaume had spoke of was just before us. One look back told me that the storm Guillaume had created was over taking us. The clouds now so thick as to appear black. I could hear the sound of the lightning as it crackled and popped, streaking among the clouds. I could smell the storm, the sulfur in the lightning, the air full of moisture and I felt the charge that only the lightning brought.

Reaching the top of the hill I hesitated, I could see the castle still surrounded by the hoards. Fires burned high and bright. I sat patting the caTragon on its muscular shoulder, more as an excuse to clear my head than anything else. With a bowed head and a whispered prayer to the Higher Power I began. Taking a deep breath I mentally pictured the page of the book and began to recite the words. Carefully, very carefully I spoke them as Guillaume had instructed.

Raindrops began to fall around me hard and fast. As they fell they began to change. I watched as before my eyes each raindrop became a copy of me and the caTragon I rode. Every one waiting, watching me. CaTragons of rain, excited and impatient bearing soldiers of the same shuffled in the air, eager to attack.

"Yeah! We can do this!" Turning to the castle I drew my sword, hearing around me the sound of a thousand swords being pulled from their sheaths. The roar of an army of caTragons filled the air like thunder as we made for the castle. Lightning tore through the clouds around me as the rain fell harder, quickly changing, transforming, creating an ever growing army. As we bore down on the Molditians they turned and watched our approach. I had hoped to see fear. I had hoped that they would run. They did neither. Drawing weapons of enormous size they awaited our arrival.

Eyes the color of hot coal glared at us. The size of the Molditians was almost of giant proportions. They stood head and shoulders over the tallest knight I knew. Dark skinned with a leathery appearance they were covered with a layer of short, dark hair. They wore a tunic of chain mail tied in place with a belt of spikes. The helmets on their head also bore a smaller circle of spikes. The boots that laced up over their legs almost to their knees held daggers. Some Molditians held swords that reflected each flash of lightning while others carried a double sided ax. Not a single one carried a shield. It was obvious by their stance, they did not think they needed one. The look in their eyes told me they felt as if no one nor no thing could stop them in their desire for blood and death.

In one great wave we swooped down on the Molditians. The battle that raged went long into the night. The Molditians rarely contacting a member of my *army,* when they did, the warrior would disintegrate before their eyes, only to gather together again to fight once more. The fire from the caTragons setting tents and stock piles a blaze. The clank of steel against steel ringing out across the fields echoing back to us from the castle walls. The scream of death rang out continuously through the night. The roar of the caTragons loud and powerful, meaning to bring fear to the Molditians while at the same time proving they remained strong and fierce. The moon rose, enormous and orange in hue. It crossed the night sky, turning a blinding white, as still the battle raged. As the night progressed the screams and shouts grew fewer. The sounds of steel against steel or steel against flesh growing less frequent. As dawn broke, it was a gruesome sight that was exposed on the grounds around the castle. Bodies of Molditians lay covering the ground, not a one showing any sign of life. The fires they had lit to intimidate, now merely smoldered, slight wisps of smoke drifting upward in the growing light.

Sitting on the caTragon I raised my sword in victory, hearing a shout rise up from the castle. As the loud cheering rang out, echoing across the field my army suddenly returned to their original form, falling to the ground as the raindrops from which they had been created.

I sat, still mounted on the caTragon listening to the cheering and shouting coming from the castle. Leaning over the beast's shoulders I spoke to it. "Do you hear that?" I asked, "that is for me. Can you believe it? They are actually cheering for me."

Sitting back upright on its back I turned to look at the castle. All along the walls of the turrets I could see people standing and waving. Flags and banners hung from windows. All the while I could hear shouting. I watched as the drawbridge began to lower, I could hear the angry creaking of the crank and pulley as the chain moved through it. Almost before the bridge hit the ground with an audible thud I could see the knights on horses thundering in my direction. "It is tempting." I spoke again to the caTragon. I could feel it growing restless beneath me. Muscles shifted and twitched. I could tell that it was uncomfortable with the approach of the knights. Snorting short burst of flames it watched the approaching group.

"My vow is not yet accomplished." I spoke to the caTragon. "I can not stay here, not today, not yet. Let us return to Guillaume as I promised." The words barely spoken when the caTragon turned and streaked into the sky. Its wings spreading wide it carried us ever higher. I could not help but laugh at the feeling of giddiness and freedom I felt soaring so high above the world. The knights shouted from below, but I could not make out their words as we left them far behind. Nor did I even try.

The caTragon must have felt the same feelings of freedom and giddiness as it played and danced its way across the sky. I held on tightly as the caTragon did strange loops and spirals through the air. I laughed dizzily as sky and ground alternated in my sight. As we made our way back other caTragons joined us, creating a line across the sky one moment, other patterns the next. It was almost a dance the way they carried on.

Still, I was glad when Guillaume's place came into view and we lightly touched down onto the ground. Guillaume and Opsis stood waiting just outside the shimmering wall.

"I see Young Warrior, that you decided to return." Guillaume spoke the obvious.

Dismounting from the caTragon I turned to face Guillaume, "My vow has not yet been fulfilled. I can not go back until I have done what I swore to do."

Guillaume merely crossed his arms across his chest and watched me as I approached.

"You should have seen it Guillaume! It was amazing!" I began to speak quickly, reaching out I caught hold of his arm. "I did exactly as you said. I spoke the words and the rain became me. Hundreds and hundreds of me on caTragons." Turning to Opsis I continued. "Together we dove down into the enemy's camp, swarming among them striking them with our sword, causing them to strike each other with their own weapons. The caTragon's fire burning their tents and supplies, leaving them with nothing to fight with or survive on."

"Young Warrior..." Opsis began to speak, but I interrupted..

133

"And cheering, at dawn's light when it was obvious that we had defeated the attacking enemy, when they were all dead or had run off, all of the cheering, all of the shouting that was going on was for me. Guillaume, they were cheering for me. Not in ridicule, not in sarcasm, but honestly cheering for me. And they sent out the knights to receive us, but I knew we had to return here. As tempting as it was to go with them back to the castle, I knew I had to return here. I had promised."

"We saw Young Warrior and we heard." Opsis told me, not able to hide his smile. "We kept up with you and the battle using the crystals. You did well."

When I turned to look at Guillaume, he too was smiling, albeit one that was still tinged with a sadness because of his hidden reason.

"Yes, Young Warrior, you did do well." was all he said as he turned to go back inside.

"Coming?" Opsis asked as he made to follow Guillaume.

"Yes, I will be there." I answered, "as soon as I get some wood for the fire."

As I entered Guillaume's Chamber with the wood I heard Opsis speaking.

"..it all turned out well, there was no need to worry."

"There was plenty of need my friend, the what ifs were great." Guillaume watched me enter the room yet continued speaking. "if he had gotten struck.."

"Which he didn't." Opsis seemed ready to argue his point.

"There was no threat to me." I spoke up getting the attention of both, "the caTragon I rode made certain to keep me out of the worst of it. We were only low a couple of times, the rest I used my crossbow from above. While the army of warriors were a likeness of me, they worked independently of me. Able to fight and move on their own, no need to copy my every action." I crossed the room and carefully stacked the wood. "It was amazing to see really. So many of me being brave and storming right in there to fight even at the threats present."

Guillaume watched me as I spoke. There was a look of pride in his eyes, but then his demeanor changed. "You did do well Young Warrior, but now you must forget the words used. You must forget that I even allowed you to see the book, much more so the page within."

"But why Guillaume?" I turned to ask, feeling very confused at the instruction.

"Because I have instructed it. That is all you need to know."

I looked to Opsis but he merely shook his head and shrugged.

"Well I do apparently have the ability to forget things I don't want to remember, so may be I can just do as you instruct." I dropped the last piece of wood onto the stack and walked away. Opsis reached for my arm but I shrugged him off as I all but stomped through the ripple to the outside. Leaning against a solid section of the wall I watched the sun as it began its slow descent to the far horizon. The forest night life was waking as the area darkened. I could hear the sound of frogs singing loudly in the pond, while an owl called from a nearby tree. Crickets joined in the chorus and off in the distance I heard the roar of a caTragon on the hunt. In my mind, I heard the cheers. In my mind, I did not hear the hated name, Adwr. It was something else they shouted, but the distance I was from the castle prevented my hearing. So I held onto the cheers and shouts of joy. I let the pictures of the day play through my mind, flags and banners waving in my honor. The knights approaching. Me, leading an

135

army and defeating a strong foe.

Closing my eyes I allowed my thoughts to be carried away. I smelled the caTragon before I heard it. That musky cat smell mixed with the burning sulfur- smoke odor had me opening my eyes and turning my head to look to the beast. Huffing loudly it stretched out at my feet, seemingly content.

"Looks as if you have made a friend." Guillaume spoke as he approached.

"Looks like." I agreed without moving.

Guillaume stood before me for a while, waiting on me to speak. I chose instead to ignore his presence.

"There are reasons Young Warrior that I gave you the instruction that I did."

"I'm sure there are Guillaume." I leaned back against the rock wall, drawing my foot up behind me, resting my weight on the other as I looked to the sky. Guillaume stood where he was for a long while, waiting on me to say more. I, however chose again to ignore his presence. I stood watching the sky grow dark and the moon and stars appear. I began trying to find the constellations that hung in the sky at the will and instruction of the Higher Power. The trees around me giving me only a limited view so I gave up and closed my eyes once more. Guillaume waited for some time before he turned and walked away. I remained where I was, leaning against the wall, watching nothing.

After much time had passed Opsis approached. "I do not wish to discuss it Opsis." I spoke without turning from my pretense at watching the night sky.

"No matter what you wish, discuss it we will."

"Opsis, it makes no sense. Why does he not trust me? I followed his instructions. I did exactly as he said, when he said. Everything worked perfectly. When it was finished, the army created, disappeared. Gone. Yet, instead of being happy for me, glad that I did as told, exactly as told, proving that I could follow instruction and be trusted, he acts as if I am a child unable to handle anything other than childish toys." During my tirade I had turned to face Opsis. My movements startling the caTragon causing it to move a few feet away and sit waiting.

"You do not have all the facts." Opsis began.

"You are right, I do not have all the facts. I do not remember the 'facts' so I do not wish to discuss it any longer." I turned and started to walk away.

"Then listen only." Opsis said, the tightness in his voice giving away his own anger. At that, I stopped and turned back. "You do not understand the pain he carries. You do not know, the suffering and the guilt, that eats at his soul like some disease. Slowly destroying him a little at a time."

"No, you are right, I do not know. If he would but tell me, I could understand."

"He can not tell you his pain. For it is also yours. You do not know, Young Warrior, because you do not remember. You do not remember, because the pain you suffered was just as great as his in different ways. Your loss, is what took your memory because your heart could not bear the pain. Only when your heart feels that it is strong enough, when your spirit brave enough, then, only then, will you remember."

"I am strong. I have gone into battle, I have wounded and even though I am not proud of it, I have killed. I am strong."

"Yes, I agree. But Young Warrior, strength of body and will, is different than strength of heart." With that Opsis turned and walked back through the wall into

Guillaume's chamber. I turned back to looking at the stars in the night sky. My thoughts wandering lost among the constellations above me.

I stood leaning against the rock wall until the night chill began to seep through my tunic making me aware that the hour was late. Still, I was in no hurry to move from where I stood. There as something about standing in the night, watching the stars. From somewhere in the back of my mind a memory stirred. I could feel strong hands on my shoulders and a voice explaining each constellation as we found them. He knew all of the legends with each one. What they were, how they came to be. A voice so familiar. I watched a light streak across the sky, Pegasus in flight. While I stood watching the sky was filled with many lights crossing the night sky. All the time, a memory lurked, just as the edge of remembrance. A voice so familiar.

"Pegasus has company tonight."

"Opsis." I turned and stood looking at him, "Opsis, it was you so long ago was it not? Showing me the stars, explaining all about how they came to be hung in the night sky. That was you."

"Yes, Young Warrior, that was me. You were very young, and very intelligent, even then."

I turned to look back at the night sky, watching as the lights multiplied in number and then slowed, until there was no more. All the while I fought to remember more, but nothing more came. Nothing more teased at my memory. Frustration welled up inside of me and threatened to overwhelm my self control. In my anger I began hammering my fists back against the wall behind me. Closing my eyes I gritted my teeth to hold back the wails that threatened to escape.

"It will come,"Opsis spoke calmly, "it will come, in its time. Just as you remembered this one piece, each one will come to you as you are ready for it. In time, when the time is right, your heart will see, and understand what your eyes can not. Then, you will remember."

I fought back the tears of sheer frustration that threatened, as warriors do not cry. I could not allow any sign of weakness if I were to continue this. I refused to allow it.

"The proof that one is becoming a man,"Opsis began as he watched me closely, "is that they learn there is no bad emotion. As long as they control it, and do not allow it to control them. To laugh, to be angry, to weep, is human. To try and act as though you do not feel one emotion or another is against all that one is. To deny feeling, is to deny self."

Turning my head away I quickly scrubbed my eyes with the back of my hand. "You are incredibly wise Opsis. How did you learn so much?"

"It comes with age Young Warrior."Opsis smiled as he placed his hand on my shoulder and turned me back toward Guillaume's entrance. "It comes with age, and experiences, good and bad."

Just before we stepped through the shimmering wall Opsis stopped and looked down at me. "You were rather rude to Guillaume earlier." was all he said before he turned and stepped through. Sighing, knowing that no matter what meal may have earlier been prepared, I was first going to have to eat a few of my words and offer an apology.

Stepping through the wall I looked around the room, Guillaume was no where to be seen. I looked to Opsis who motioned in the direction of the corridor to the

139

Great Chamber. Nothing like dragging out the inevitable I thought as I headed off in the direction Guillaume had gone. Walking down the corridor I tried to think of what I was going to say to Guillaume. How could I apologize as I knew I needed to, and not look too much like a child and nothing like a warrior. The corridor seemed to grow in length and still, it seemed to end much too soon. As I entered the Great Chamber I saw immediately that the hidden room on the far side was open. Crossing to the doorway I stepped quietly inside. Guillaume was placing his book carefully back on a shelf. Hanging near the shelf was the tapestry that I had seen earlier. As he brought down his arm the tapestry moved. There was another behind it. Curious now I walked up beside Guillaume, wanting to see, but nervous at what was there. Guillaume looked at me for a moment and then reaching up pushed the first tapestry aside. With a quick indrawn breath I stared. It was as I thought.

Guillaume looked at the second tapestry, just as old as the first, showing the same signs of age in the slight wear along the edges, the yellowed tinge of time dulling the vibrant colors of the threads around the edge along with a single frayed corner. "Some of us, have a destiny." he said, his voice low, as he and I looked at the tapestry quietly.

There woven into this one was a portrait of me. I was on the back of the caTragon, holding my sword high as all around me lay a slain enemy. In the background was the castle, complete with banners hanging from windows.

Without thought I reached for the tapestry, I wanted to see if anything was behind it, but Guillaume stopped me. "To see the future Young Warrior, one must first understand the past. You have not gained that as of yet."

140

Dropping my hand back to my side without argument I stood looking at the tapestry before us. "Guillaume," I tried to speak, but his name came out more a garbled croak that a word. Clearing my throat I tried again, "Guillaume," I hesitated and then took a deep breath. The words rushing out almost as one. "I have come to offer you my humble apology for my rudeness earlier on this evening." Stopping, I turned from the tapestry and looked directly at Guillaume. "I was wrong."

Guillaume had turned to watch me as I spoke. Quietly waiting until the last words were said. "You are indeed growing Young Warrior. It takes a man to admit when a mistake has been made. It takes a man, to admit when they are the one that has made it. Your apology is accepted." As he spoke the words he placed his hands on my shoulders, just as I had remembered Opsis doing so long ago and yet so recently.

"Guillaume, I remembered something earlier. I remembered a time when Opsis taught me about the constellations. It was only a small thing, but it was very clear."

"Your heart grows stronger Young Warrior, the time is coming for understanding. For now, a meal awaits you, and then rest, for tomorrow your lessons resume."

Sighing, I looked at Guillaume, "More lessons?"

"More lessons. You are not yet ready for what waits you."

"And what is that Guillaume?"

"All things will be understood when the time is right."

I watched as Guillaume dared to smile as he turned and left the room, waiting for me just outside the door. Placing my hands on my hips I watched Guillaume then looked once more at the tapestry before I too left the

141

room.

My night was a restless one. There were no dreams that I remembered, just vague flashes of thoughts and emotions. Possible memories that lurked at the edges of understanding, taunting me with their presence. Hiding just far enough from clear sight that I could not grasp what they were. All this left me tossing and turning in my cot.

Dawn's first light found me back sitting on the ground outside of Guillaume's place, leaning once again against the rock wall. The quiet coolness better than the heat of the chamber. The caTragon I had ridden into battle sat beside me looking like one of the contented castle cats as it yawned and stretched, then made itself comfortable on the ground beside me.

"You need a name." I told the caTragon, "but what is a good name for something that cannot decide exactly what it wants to look like?"
I sat there leaned back against the wall watching the caTragon as it played games. Changing back and forth with an occasional look back to make sure I was watching.

"All right, I shall call you, Sir Switch." Hearing a noise beside me I looked to see Opsis approaching.

"Sir Switch?"

"Sure, because about the time you think he's going to stay one way, he switches to the other."

Opsis said no more about the name, but I didn't miss the thoughtful expression that crossed his face. Finally beginning to turn away he motioned with his hand for me to follow him, "The meal is ready and Guillaume is waiting for you."

Sighing I rose from my seat, "Ah yes, more lessons. No fighting the dragon, no fulfilling my vow, just more lessons."

Opsis smiled at my mild grumbling, "The lessons are to make sure that when you set out to fulfill that vow, you will return."

Accepting the truth in that comment I caught up with Opsis and walked into the chamber beside him. Crossing the room I saw that Guillaume had already filled the bowls and had them waiting on the table. Taking my usual place I made ready to eat when the caTragon suddenly decided that it wasn't going to wait and wanted what was in my bowl right then.

"Go lay down Switch, you'll get yours in a few minutes."

"What?"

I turned to look at Guillaume at the sound of his voice.

"What did you just say?" he asked carefully.

"I just told the caTragon to go and lay down, I'd feed it soon."

"But what is it that you called it?"

"Oh, that..I decided that it needed a name if it were going to hang around like that. And since it couldn't make up its mind whether it wanted the dragon's head or the lion's I gave him the name of Sir Switch."

"That's what I thought. Interesting indeed."

"Is there a problem Guillaume? Does it already have a name and I didn't know it?"

"No, it had not been called by any name." Guillaume answered. Then as he turned away from the table, I heard him in a barely audible level say,"not for a very long time."

Bringing his own bowl to the table he motioned for me to eat, "We must begin your lessons soon. Time grows short."

TEN

After finishing eating and feeding Sir Switch I walked over to gather my weapons in preparation for Guillaume's next lesson.

"Leave those here." Guillaume said as he made for the corridor.

"Leave them?"

"Yes, leave them and follow me, time is short." Guillaume said as he disappeared down the corridor.

Leaning my sword back up against the wall I hesitated. I wanted to take it with me anyway.

"Guillaume said to leave them." Opsis said from his seat at the table.

Nodding to acknowledge that I had heard I dropped my hand and turned to the corridor. Not looking back I walked away from the weapons that were almost a part of me. I pointedly ignored the chuckle I heard coming from Opsis.

Running I managed to catch up with Guillaume before he reached the Great Chamber. When we entered the room remained dark. The torches had lit in the corridor as we walked, but here they did not. Even the crystals on the table were dark.

"Guillaume?" I began to question but with a raised hand from Guillaume I stopped.

"Trust me." was all he said before he stepped into the darkness.

"Trust you? I can't even see you." I mumbled to myself as I peered into the dark, trying to see where he had gone.

"Come into the room." Guillaume instructed from somewhere in the darkness. When I still hesitated leaving the dimly lit end of the corridor, every torch in the corridor went dark.

"Trust me Young Warrior and come into the room." came Guillaume's voice from a different area of the room.

"Think think think.." I quietly instructed myself. "There is a table in the center of the room, there is one table on the wall opposite from this entrance..other than that, there is nothing to run into or trip over..yes, all right.." inhaling and exhaling quickly I stepped into the room.

The moment my foot hit the floor with my first step a loud roar came from immediately to my right. Jumping to the left I waited, footsteps followed me, loud and heavy. I crouched waiting. Was it real? Or was it just a test? When the steps drew closer I stood my ground. I could hear the snuffling sounds of breathing, like an animal tracking its prey. Still, I remained where I was. The strong smell of smoke and sulfur assaulted my nose. The sound of movement stopped, every sense I had in me screamed out warnings. I stood my ground waiting for something, I didn't know what, yet I waited.

"Move!" came Guillaume's shout from the dark. At his command I jumped backwards and to my left, falling to the ground and rolling away. Mere moments after I obeyed, even as I rolled, I saw the burst of flame that exploded right where I had been standing.

Then all was quiet again.

Taking slow deep breaths, trying to be as silent as possible I waited. Suddenly it felt as if dozens of spiders were crawling on my skin. Frantically I slapped at them.

"Be still." came Guillaume's words from the dark.

Be still?? Be still? There are thousands of bugs on

me..be still?? The thoughts ran madly through my mind, but I gave them no voice. With strength of will alone I forced myself to stop and be still. I could feel them still. The eerie sense of something walking across your face. I closed my eyes, placing my hand over my nose and waited for what seemed an eternity before finally it stopped.

I moved to a crouched position in the dark. I was not laying on that floor any more. It was silent. You could hear the smallest of noise if there was any to hear. Nothing moved, the only sound, was of my breathing and of my heartbeat pounding in my ears.

Without warning the floor gave way beneath me. Clinging to the edge of the floor that was left I felt the rising heat of the lava flow under me. The glow brought an eerie light to the room. Sweat broke out on my brow and ran down my face. My fingers were losing their grip on the floor I held onto.

"Guillaume!"

"Let go." came his response from the darkness.

His instruction of 'trust me' whispered through my mind. "I can't. I can't." I whispered back.

"Trust me, Young Warrior." his voice a thought more than a sound.

Closing my eyes to what was below, I let go, and the floor was there. Trembling now I was ready for this lesson to be done, but it wasn't. I could hear the hiss behind me. I stiffened in response. Then, the sound came from before me. My hand reached for a weapon that wasn't there. I felt the rough scales of the snake as it crossed over my arm. I was still on the floor, I hadn't moved. Now the snake moved across my chest, I could actually hear the tongue flickering back and forth from its mouth.

146

"This is a test," I spoke to myself, "It is a test, nothing more."

I reached to push the snake from my chest to only hear Guillaume's voice, "Remain still."

From the snake came a voice, "Adwr, Adwr, your name is Adwr."

Clenching my fists I fought the urge to grab the creature. I felt it move across my chest, slowly creeping, the scales moving individually as it slid along. Still speaking in a sing song voice. Repeating the same words over and over. Still, I lay there, fighting every urge to grab the beast as it moved down my stomach and across my legs. When the weight of the snake was finally gone from my body, I slowly turned to get up. Every muscle trembling as I fought the sick feeling in my stomach that had come with the snake.

Out of nowhere came the voice, giggling and laughing, "Sir Switch is a silly name for a caTragon. You can't name it that." I wasn't in the Great Chamber any longer, I was in the castle. I was standing in one of the many corridors looking into a room. A room I didn't recall. I was standing beside a young caTragon, even though it was taller than I appeared to be here. I could feel myself reaching up to place my hands on its back.

"It is not a silly name! It is a noble and brave name! You are just jealous because you didn't get to name him. Guillaume told me I could name him and I have named him Sir Switch." I could hear more giggling coming from the room, I listened as I spoke to the caTragon at my side. "Come with me Sir Switch. I'm sure that Guillaume will like your new name."

"Its a noble and brave name...its a noble and brave name.." I whispered between the heaves from my stomach. I struggled to stand upright. Slowly a couple of

147

the torches began to light around the room, growing brighter gradually. I staggered slightly as I turned in the direction of the sound of Guillaume's approach. He was watching me closely as he drew near.

"Is that the same caTragon?" I asked him.

"It is." Guillaume answered, "He was protective of you then. He is protective of you now." When I turned to look down the corridor, slowly regaining control of muscle and emotion Guillaume spoke.

"That's enough for this day, lets go back."

Tired in many ways, this time I did not argue.

Walking down the corridor as tired as I was after Guillaume's latest lesson I realized it was still early. I did not want to sit in Guillaume's chamber listening to him and Opsis talk about things I knew nothing of. I did not wish to do chores and I definitely was not ready to sleep. My mind wandered over possibilities as I walked. Entering Guillaume's chamber a few steps behind him I looked to see he already had mugs of that bitter brew of his.

"If you have no need for me at present, I would like to go back to the pool and swim a while. Perhaps catch a few fish for our dinner." I said, hoping for no disagreement from Guillaume.

"Take care of your surroundings at all times," was all he said as he waved me on my way.

As I turned to head for the doorway I motioned for Sir Switch, who quickly rose and followed me outside. Watching the caTragon at my side I tried to remember more. I tried to recall this strange and wonderful beast from times before. Strange how when I tried so hard to remember, I could almost actually hear a door slamming closed. The sound carrying through my mind, echoing again and again. As if that sound alone should mean something.

Upon reaching the edge of the pool I made ready for my swim while the caTragon found a comfortable place to stretch out in the sun. I couldn't help but notice his comfortable place also gave him an unobstructed view of the pool. With a shake of my head and a short laugh at over protective beasts I dove into the water. As I swam I noticed something odd, causing me to swim back and forth across the pool several times. On one side, the side that I dove into, the water was cold enough to take your breath. As I swam, it began to grow warm until finally the water became near to the point of being too hot to bear. Swimming under the surface searching I could find no reason for the difference. I could not recall Guillaume saying anything about a lava flow beneath the pool, in fact, I didn't recall it feeling this way the first time I was here. Returning to the surface I then swam to the bank and climbed out of the water. I wasn't far from the waterfall so I crossed behind it, climbing over and around the boulders on the other side. Finally getting past those obstacles I began to explore the shoreline of the hot side of the pool. I hoped to find the cause of the heat. As I walked I wasn't surprised when the caTragon was suddenly at my side.

"You're quick and quiet aren't you?" I said looking down at the beast, smiling as I said it. Resting my hand on its massive head I continued to walk, carefully searching as I went. In the back of my mind I regretted the fact that I had left all of my weapons leaning against the wall back in Guillaume's chamber.

As I made my way around the pool I carefully pushed aside a branch from one of the many bushes growing along the banks. Before I could move it far, I was grabbed around the wrist and dragged through the brush to the other side. I struggled to free myself from the grip that held me but it only grew tighter, painfully so. I heard the roar from the caTragon as it followed. The speed of which I was being dragged only increased at the sound. Rocks and roots tore at my legs still bare from my swim. How I wished I had at least lashed on my boots, but I had not, and now I suffered from that mistake. Dust kicked up by what-ever or who-ever it was that held me choked me, leaving me fighting for breath. Low growing branches and thorns tore at my face, the pain driving me to fight even harder to free myself. The sound of my captors footsteps as they ran sounded in my ears so close that it hid almost every other sound from me. All but the sound of the caTragon as it caught up with us and pounced from the brush.

At the sight of the caTragon the grip on my arm was released. I heard a sword being drawn, the metal of the steel sliding against the metal of the sheath holding it. Rolling away from the fight I finally saw who or what had held me. One of the Molditians that had ran from the fight at the castle. Now it stood in battle with my caTragon. I watched from a distance, desperate to help but having no weaponry to do so. I watched as the Molditian held a shield before him, deflecting the caTragon's flames. The sword he held glowing hot from the absorbed heat. The caTragon slowly moved around his enemy, searching for weakness, any weakness. The Molditian turned with him, waiting, watching for his chance to strike a mortal blow. I knew that a caTragon could not change its appearance in battle, the time in the transition leaving them vulnerable. How I wished that this time the caTragon had the body of a dragon, it would have offered it more protection than the one of the lion it now moved in.

150

The caTragon roared angrily in its frustration at not being able to move in. It circled, continuously watching its enemy. Thinking to help I yelled out, hoping to distract the Molditian. Instead, the caTragon looked, and the Molditian struck. His sword going deep into the caTragon's body. The roar of pain just before it collapsed onto the ground tore at me. My fault. it was my fault. Then, the Molditian, turned to me.

I didn't even realize when the Molditian once more grabbed my arm, I was frozen, staring at the body of Sir Switch, laying so still in the blood soaked dust. Jerked to my feet I ignored the point of the sword up against my side. It could have been driven into my body, and the pain would have not been as great as it already was. Shoved forward I attempted to look back one more time, in hopes that I was wrong. Hoping to see something, a breath, a twitch, something that told me that he was not in fact dead. Realizing what I was doing the Molditian dared to laugh. Laughing at my pain and the death he had caused. No, the death I had caused by yelling as I had. Any anger I felt was only at myself, but it was buried so deep beneath the pain I could not act on it.

Shoving me away the Molditian turned to go back to where the caTragon lay. Still laughing cruelly he raised his sword in a manner meant to behead it. Looking back to me, an assurance to himself and his monstrous ego that his actions were being watched, he drew the sword back further. His laughter was abruptly cut short as the caTragon attacked. Its bite catching the Molditian in his exposed chest, crushing it. Blood flowed from the many deep punctures in his chest and back. Staggering backward he looked from the wounds in his body to the caTragon. Slowly the caTragon, limping but very much alive, stalked the Molditian, making sure that the direction he moved was far from where I stood. Forcing him backward through the brush. Staggering, tripping over the very roots he had just dragged me across he backed away. The caTragon never slowed. It followed him through the wood, never taking his eyes from him. Weakening the Molditian dropped his sword, turning as if to flee he fell face first into the boiling water of the pond. The smell of his death rising with the steam around him.

When the Molditian moved no more I crossed hurriedly to where Sir Switch stood. Checking his wound I saw that it was as deep as I feared and that he had lost a great amount of blood. Collapsing on the ground he looked up at me, in his eyes an expression of trust. Too weak to travel even the short distance to Guillaume's chamber I knew I had to leave him. I could not however leave him in the open as since there had been one Molditian close, I knew there had to be others. Some how I felt they were responsible for the heat of the water. How or why I wasn't concerned with at the moment. I had to get Guillaume and Opsis. Finding two sturdy poles I managed after much struggling to get the caTragon across them and drag him slowly out of the clearing and into heavy brush. This time I did not feel the pain as the branches raked across my face. Concealing the caTragon carefully, I then used a branch to brush away any tracks other than the ones that appeared to move away from the body toward the pond, making it appear as if the caTragon had fled in that direction. Once that was done I turned and ran, tossing the branch away as I did so. I did not even care at this point if I appeared childish and less the warrior. My caTragon needed help and it trusted me to get it for him. He had saved my life, I could do no less for him.

I retraced my steps as quickly as one could in bare feet, ignoring the pain from the stones I stepped on. Ignoring the pain of the thorns tearing at my legs. I could feel my chest and leg muscles complaining, but I ignored it. Jumping from boulder to boulder I climbed across and ran blindly behind the waterfall. I found no solace in the roar of the thundering water as I passed through. Once on the other side I ran as if the Dragon of Death itself chased me. All but falling through the shimmering wall I called to Guillaume.

Jumping from where they had been seated Guillaume and Opsis both caught me before I fell covered in blood to the floor.

Gasping for breath, fighting to get the words out I leaned against the table. Between the gasps I managed to get the words out, "Molditian...attacked... dead.... caTragon hurt badly."

"Where is he?"Guillaume asked.

"Hidden... in.. the.. brush, on the far side of the pond." I was finally getting my wind back. I had help, now we must go back. Rising from the table I started across the room for my weapons as Guillaume moved in the other direction.

"What are you thinking Young Warrior?" Opsis asked.

"I'm going back for him. He saved me, I will do the same for him."

"You are not going back, there is no need." Guillaume spoke from the doorway to the outside.

"What are you saying?" I demanded. "He is not.."

"No, he is not," Guillaume answered. "What he is,

153

however, is here."

I watched amazed and overjoyed as several of the other caTragons that I had seen earlier entered the chamber, Sir Switch across their many backs. Walking over to a place near the fire one by one they carefully stepped aside, allowing Sir Switch to slide slowly and gently to the floor. Once they had all moved away Guillaume approached, kneeling down he examined the wound. The caTragon made no sounds nor opened his eyes as Guillaume poked and prodded the injury.

"He is very weak. He has lost a great deal of blood in his battle." Guillaume stood and turned to the wall of shelves that held countless containers of various sizes. With no hesitation or thought he walked purposely across the room. I watched as he reached for one container, bringing it down he opened the top and poured some of what ever was inside into a bowl. Into that he added just enough hot water to make a poultice. That he packed inside and around the caTragon's wound. Bandaging it best one could an animal he moved to straighten the mess that had been made. I stood watching, waiting for some miracle of magic.

Opsis walked over to where I stood. "It has to heal naturally Young Warrior. Otherwise it would be too easy for the injury to open again. But remember, caTragons are magic in themselves. Their healing takes much less time that ours would." Nodding to acknowledge I had heard I stood and watched Sir Switch, not looking when I heard Opsis moving away.

I don't know how much time had passed as I stood there before I felt the mug being pressed into my hands. The aroma of Guillaume's bitter brew drifting up, catching my attention and making me realize how tired I was.

"We must talk," Guillaume spoke from beside me.

"Turning I followed him as he crossed the room to sit once again at the table.

"Tell us what happened, leave out no details."

Nodding, I raised the mug to my lips to take a drink as I thought back to that time earlier in the day.

Sitting at the table with Guillaume and Opsis I looked off into the distance, trying to remember it all.

"We arrived at the pool and I made ready to go swimming while the caTragon found a place to lay in the sun. As I was swimming I noticed that the water changed temperatures drastically from one side to the other. I remembered it wasn't that way before. The longer I swam the more curious I became and decided to see if I could find out why. I swam to the bank and climbed out of the pool and started around to the other side."

"Why did you not just swim to the hot side and climb out there?" Opsis asked me.

"The water got hotter the closer you got to the shore. From just over two-thirds of the way across all the way to the bank the water actually boiled. You could see the steam rising above the surface."

Opsis silently nodded and waited for me to continue.

"I went around the other side and was trying to search quietly when I was attacked by the Molditian. It was dragging me through the brush when the caTragon appeared and attacked." Looking down I took a deep breath before admitting the next part. "Sir Switch would not have been injured if I had not yelled as I did. I distracted him and when I did, the Molditian struck. I was trying to distract the Molditian not the caTragon."

"One thing you need to know," Guillaume spoke up,

155

"Molditians that are in battle, any battle, are never distracted from their target. Only by their death can they be stopped once they have a victim in sight."

I nodded my understanding and continued, "when the Molditian went back to try to cut off Sir Switch's head the caTragon attacked and killed him. I hid the caTragon and came for you."

Guillaume stood as soon as I finished talking and made directly for the corridor. Opsis watched him go and then stood himself. "He will expect us to be right behind him."

I stood and looked back at Sir Switch, 'I'll be there in a moment, I want to check on the caTragon."

Opsis nodded and followed Guillaume down the corridor.

Checking on Sir Switch I found him to be sleeping so I did not disturb him. Instead I turned and followed Guillaume and Opsis down the corridor. I knew I would find them using the crystals. Entering the Great Chamber I saw that I was right. The glow from the crystals on the table lit the entire room. Guillaume and Opsis stood in front of the table watching closely what the crystals were showing them. Walking across the room I stepped up beside them and looked to see what the crystals displayed.

In the first crystal I could see tent after tent lined up, hidden among the trees. No where around them was there any movement. Even with no one there, campfires all over the area burned brightly.. But for the fires the campsite appeared abandoned, but I had learned long ago how appearances can be deceiving. Looking into the other crystal I saw movement of some sort. Figures were moving about stealthily through the forest. I could see the flash of light as sunlight was briefly reflected off of steel. I could also see the area where they were. It was just on the other side of the pond. We were about to be attacked.

"Guillaume.."I spoke up

"The rain army would not work this time." Guillaume said stopping my question, "They know your importance, that was why they tried to take you today. Your escape from them is something that has never happened before, just as they have never been defeated in true battle, you can imagine that they are very angry. The most of that anger is going to be directed at you."

"How did they find us?" I asked Guillaume.

"Molditians could track a flea on a caTragon." Guillaume answered thoughtfully. "If they find any type of evidence, any clue at all that can lead them to what they are seeking they will use it fully and they will be successful in their search."

"So, what do we do?" I asked not taking my eyes off what the crystals were showing.

" The doorway to outside will be sealed, they will not be able to enter and we will be safe."

"Hide? You want to hide and hope that they will just go away?" I was now staring at Guillaume, not believing what I had heard.

"It will only be until plans can be made Young Warrior to face them in battle." Opsis spoke up, trying to calm my growing anger. "If they get in, none of us will have a chance. We need time to decide the best way to not only fight them, but to defeat them."

Accepting his words as truth I turned back to the crystals. More and more of the figures were gathering on the far side of the pool. As I looked into the crystal I noticed that now almost the entire surface boiled.

"Why is the pool boiling?" I asked to which ever

one would answer.

Guillaume looked into the crystal at the images of steam rising above the water. He began speaking, from all appearances reciting what one would learn in their studies, "Molditians live in the caves and tunnels in the side of and under Fire Mountain. They are accustomed to and need that extreme heat."

Opsis spoke up then,"Without the heat, they cannot function. They most likely could not survive."

"How can we cool the pool?" I asked Opsis.

Guillaume grew still, silently watching the images. Slowly his eyes brightened and a slight smile crossed his face. "We can cool the pool, put out their fires and defeat them all with one action."

I stood waiting, realizing that Guillaume would answer when he was ready. Instead he walked over to the hidden room and opened the door. Going in he took his book from the shelf and walked across the room. Without a word to either of us he walked up the corridor. I turned and looked to Opsis, unasked questions in my expression.

"He has to be outside to do what he has planned."Opsis said.

"But that's where the Molditians are." I spoke rather loudly, " I have to be there with him." Without giving Opsis a chance to respond I hurried away and down the corridor trying to catch up with Guillaume.

"Guillaume can sure move fast when he wishes." I mumbled audibly as I crossed his chamber. I could see him just outside the doorway, holding his book and looking to the sky. Making a quick side step I grabbed my shield and sword and hurried to the way outside. Crashing into the wall I staggered backwards before catching my balance. It was then I noticed that the wall wasn't shimmering.

"NO!" I shouted angrily, slamming my fist into the solid wall. "Guillaume! Guillaume! Let me out there..!" Running my hands along the wall I searched for any weakness. I watched it closely for any sign of a shimmer. All the while I could see Guillaume just outside. He was speaking out loud, but I could not hear what he was saying. Pounding on the wall I tried to get Guillaume's attention.

Opsis stepped to my side, calmly and quietly watching Guillaume.

"It appears that he wanted to protect us, to protect you, Young Warrior." Reaching out he placed his hand on the wall. "We can see out, but no one out there, can see in. Out there, this appears just another part of the hillside."

"I need to be out there helping him." I was not giving in easily, there had to be a way out there. "What if the Molditians attack?"

"He has the caTragons with him, He has his magic as well."

Standing at the doorway I watched Guillaume. I could only see a minute section of the sky through the trees if I leaned to one side and concentrated. It had became a dark gray. The winds had picked up and the trees swayed crazily. CaTragons stood around Guillaume, the winds blowing their manes wildly in every direction. They seemed to be huddled together to protect each other from the wind. Guillaume's cloak twisted around his legs looking as if it would trip him should he try to move. Wrapping like a white clinging vine, similar to the ones that grow along the castle walls. I watched as it began to snow. Flakes the size of the serving platters in the castle fell to the ground. One at a time at first,

159

scattered about the clearing. Soon it was falling harder and faster. The ground was beginning to turn white.

"This is not good." Opsis muttered when something moving caught his attention. The caTragons had seen it as well. A line of Molditians moved as one from out of the woods approaching where Guillaume stood. Guillaume never moved, standing stone still with arm and face raised to the sky. I could see the only thing about him moving was his mouth as he recited words repeatedly.

"Guillaume!!" I shouted to him again and again, trying to warn him. Trying to get him to allow me outside. Pounding on the wall with my fist I tried to break free of his protection.

The snow outside began to fall at a rate that you could not see through. Looking out the sealed doorway all I could see was a solid white. Guillaume blending in with the blinding snow. Opsis and I watched as the snow piled up along the outside of the wall. I watched as it swiftly grew deeper, with no sign of slowing. All the while wondering what was going on just outside the doorway.

Time seemed to come to a halt as we stood, trapped in a protective cocoon of Guillaume's making. Even though we had added no wood to the fire, it burned just as strongly, warming the room and all within it. Occasionally somewhere in the back of my conscious mind I would hear a piece of real wood popping as it burned with the magic. All the while, the snow continued to accumulate, piling higher against the wall outside. Opsis and I stood rooted to the spot, not moving, having no plans to move as we stared out into the white world beyond the wall. Both of us attempting to spot

160

movement. Concentrating on the area just past the wall, the last place we had actually seen Guillaume.

"How much longer can he remain out there in that?" I finally dared to ask after what seemed like an eternity had passed.

"You forget one thing Young Warrior."

"And that is?"

"Just wait, you will see."

"What, Opsis, what will I see?" I asked, almost demanding, as I turned away from the wall to look up at Opsis, hoping he would give me an answer, a reassurance. He simply smiled a smug and secure looking smile and continued to watch the snow piling up outside. All through the evening and into the night it snowed. Still Opsis and I remained at the wall, waiting, trying to look out into the mass of white that was now reaching the height of my waist. Leaning against the wall I noticed that even with the snow storm blowing on the other side of the wall, just out of reach, the wall on this side was warm to touch. Without realizing it I closed my eyes and dozed, still standing on my feet. It was the hand on my shoulder that brought me quickly awake.

Opsis was looking down at me, "Go and get some sleep.."

"No, I will wait here for Guillaume." I interrupted.

Opsis ignored my outburst, "Go and rest, I will stand watch for Guillaume. When he returns I will wake you. If he does not return after a while, I will wake you so that you may take a turn at watch and I may rest."

Argument with Opsis was futile, I knew that. I took one last look at the snow just outside. It was now past the height of my chest and still falling. Turning away I crossed the room to my cot. Stretching out I lay facing the doorway, watching until sleep claimed me.

161

It was a hand on my shoulder that woke me from troubled sleep. As I struggled to come fully awake memories of the dreams slipped one last time across my mind. An unseen enemy, laughing madly echoed through dark dreams. Pages in a book blowing in a cold wind, turning, flipping back and forth, from beginning to end and back again. I heard footsteps sounding against stone floors realizing they were mine as I approached the book. I had to see what book it was, what page was wanting to be seen.

Raking my fingers through tangled and sweat dampened hair I looked up at Opsis. "Is he back?"

Opsis shook his head, "No, not yet."

Standing I looked to the doorway, all that was visible was a solid wall of white. The snow reached all the way to the top of the doorway and possibly beyond. Opsis handed me a mug of Guillaume's bitter brew. "The fire still burns."

As I took the mug from Opsis I looked from him to the fire, that as he said, was still burning strong and warm. "So?"

"If he were not well, the fire would have gone out." At my look of confusion Opsis shook his head in an exasperated manner. "Think Young Warrior, think..the fire is obviously magic, no wood has been added to it since yesterday and yet it burns."

"Yes, so?" I looked from the fire back to Opsis, "How does a burning fire prove anything?"

"For a moment, forget your concern for Guillaume, you are allowing that to prevent understanding." Opsis stood towering over me now, looking at me for a long moment making sure he had my full attention.

"Think back to your rain army. It was created with

162

magic. As long as you lived, it existed. As long as you were unhurt, it fought strongly. You were the strength of the magic." As understanding came to me Opsis continued, "The fire burning was created by Guillaume's magic. As long as he lives, it burns. As long as he is unhurt, the fire burns bright and hot."

"As it does now." I finished for Opsis, finally fully understanding. "But what keeps him outside, and how can he not be suffering from the cold of such a great amount of snow?"

"As I said earlier Young Warrior, you have forgotten one very important thing, which," he held up his hand to prevent my interrupting as I began to do.."you will find out soon enough. I will rest now, it is your turn to watch for Guillaume's return."

I listened to the sounds of Opsis settling in to rest, creaks and groans from his cot and the sigh of one giving in to sleep. I listened to the sound of Sir Switch as he snored nearby. Mostly, I listened to the silence. Carrying my sword and shield along with the steaming mug over to the wall, I sat in a chair that Opsis had moved there. Placing the mug on the floor beside me I prepared for how ever long I had to wait.

I had no way of telling what time of day or night it was. The light from the fire and the torches around the room reflected off the wall of white, giving it a brightness almost surreal in nature. I did not move from where I sat. I did not take my eyes from the wall before me. Time moved and yet it did not. Even when Opsis awakened and came to stand beside me, I watched the wall.

"Why is it taking so long?" I asked Opsis. When he did not answer I looked up at him, repeating my question.

163

"Opsis, why is it taking so long?"

"I do not know Young Warrior. I have tried, and I can not see beyond this wall no more than you can."

"He has prevented you from seeing?"

"He has, "Opsis answered. "I think, it was on the chance that he did not win this, I would not see his death."

Standing so quickly the chair beneath me toppled over. "I'm tired of waiting!" I nearly shouted as I slammed my fist against the wall holding us in. It shattered into a thousand shimmering pieces before my eyes. For the first time the cold of the snow made itself felt. Grabbing my weapons I rushed out into the wall of white that crumpled away before me. Outside finally, I found myself standing in snow that only reached my knees. Momentarily confused I looked to the snow and then dismissing it, quickly began to search for Guillaume. With Opsis at my side we hurried in the direction of the pool, knowing that was the place the crystals had shown the Molditians to be.

It was there in a clear place on the bank of the pool where Guillaume stood. Head down and shoulders drooping it was obvious he was exhausted. He was turned away from us, facing the water before him. I noticed immediately what Opsis had been hinting at as to how Guillaume could be outside for so long. To make it that he could concentrate all of his magic on the battle and not his own comfort and safety the caTragons had formed a circle around him. Every other one faced Guillaume, the ones that did had been keeping him warm with their fiery breath. Creating a large clear area free of any snow. Along the perimeter of this clearing were the others. These were the protectors, guarding securely, watching every possible route of approach. They made a fierce looking opponent, as some had chosen to appear as dragons their lions heads emitting angry snarls, while those whose body held the head of a dragon spew flames out far into the snow turning it instantly to steam. When the caTragons saw our approach they each lay down in turn, accepting their job was almost done.

Entering the circle Opsis and I approached Guillaume. His eyes were dull and held a distant look as if he were far away. His stance so still as if to not even be breathing. Taking a deep breath he slowly came back to himself, Blinking several times quickly he took another deep breath and turned to look at us.

"And they are defeated?" Opsis asked.

"They are defeated." Guillaume answered as he turned to walk back to his chamber.
When I myself turned to follow I noticed that the last of the snow was disappearing. The ground beneath where it had been, showed no signs of it having ever existed.

Walking along behind Guillaume, Opsis, and a collection of caTragons I looked around. There was no sign of a battle anywhere. The ground was undisturbed, there was no blood, no damaged shrubbery, there were no bodies anywhere. This had to have been an interesting battle. I was fighting to keep silent as we walked. Entering Guillaume's chamber I watched as he crossed the room and without saying a word sat on his cot. His book still held tightly in his hand. As I stood watching he looked down at the book, seeming to realize for the first time that he still held it. I could see Opsis out of the corner of my eye where he had crossed the room and was stirring what ever it was that was bubbling in the cauldron.

Guillaume started to stand once again, staggering

from his exhaustion.

Stepping forward I reached out to help Guillaume steady himself. "Guillaume? where are you going?"

"The book needs to be returned to its place in the room."

"I will take it for you. You need to rest." I said offering my help.

Guillaume first shook his head, refusing my assistance. "I must do it." he said taking a shaky step forward.

Opsis approached with a bowl in his hands. "Let him help you Guillaume. Follow your own lesson on trust."

Guillaume stood looking intently at me, as if judging whether or not to listen to Opsis. Finally he relented and held out the book to me. As I reached for it he spoke to me, his voice weak in his need for rest.

"Take the book directly back to the room. Do not try to open the book, do not try to read the words within. Carry it straight back to the room and place it on the shelf where it belongs. Do not forget to close the door behind you."

As I took the book from him and turned to go I heard him speak in an almost whisper, "I am trusting you Young Warrior." I looked once at Opsis who nodded as I walked away.

ELEVEN

     Moving down the corridor I watched the torches come to life before me. I kept up my pace, refusing to acknowledge the curiosity about the book I carried. Holding it down to my side as if to pretend I didn't have it. Yet watching for evil lurking in every shadow hoping to take it from me. "I'm going mad." I said aloud looking down at the book in my hand. Continuing on I entered the Great Chamber. The torches around the wall flared to life, lighting my way. When I crossed the room near the table the crystals began to glow. "oh not now." I muttered beneath my breath, still I walked over to see why they too, had come to life. Standing in front of the table I watched the pieces of my dream play out before my eyes. Frustrating for me was that it was no different in the crystals than it was in my dream. Vague images appeared and floated across to disappear. The image that lasted the longest was of the book. I watched as the pages flipped madly as they had in my dream, the one difference is this time the book slammed closed. On the cover there was an embossed design. A large golden dragon was entwined with a giant snake in silver. Looking at this image I could not tell if they were fighting or joining forces. As I looked at the image in the crystal I started to get a nervous feeling. Trembling I looked down at the book I held. The way I held it I could only see the spine of the book, but I could feel something against the palm of my hand. Slowly I turned the book over to where I could see the cover. In the center of the book was a golden dragon intertwined with a silver snake. All manner of emotions crossed my mind from opening this book and seeing why it haunted my dreams, to throwing it just as far and as hard as I could away from me. Instead I stood where I was following Guillaume's example and took several deep breaths. Then resolutely I walked away from the table to the not so hidden room. Entering the room I placed the book on the shelf I had seen it taken from and began to back away. It was then that the tapestry hanging beside it caught my attention. It was different than before. Now it was woven with the same dragon and snake design.

Backing out of the room I did not take my eyes from the tapestry. Once I was outside the room I imitated what I had seen Guillaume do and watched as the door moved into place. Turning away full of questions I walked back down the corridor to Guillaume's chamber.

As I walked I heard that now familiar giggle, teasing me from somewhere in my memory. "Guess what?" it whispered in the voice of someone young. I kept walking, ignoring it.

"Guess what?" came the whisper again, still filled with the sound of giggles and muffled laughter. I kept walking, determined to keep looking straight ahead.

"Adwr..Adwr, guess what??" this time the whisper was even more hushed, bare of laughter. As if wanting to share a wonderful secret. Stopping I turned and leaned back against the wall of the corridor.

"What?" I asked the memory.

"Dragons live forever."

"Where did you hear such a thing?"

"He told me. He said dragons live forever."

Fear gripped my heart as I swallowed the bile threatening to come from a stomach churning. "Who? Who is it that told you dragons live forever?"

"Guillaume. Guillaume told me."

"Who are you? Who are you that haunts my

dreams and now my very sanity?" There was no answer. Silence again reigned in the corridor. But my heart was so very cold with the fear of the dawning understanding.

Walking the rest of the way down the corridor my emotions swung from confused to angry. Part of me thought that I was supposed to be angry with Guillaume, but the other side said no. I still couldn't figure out whose voice I was hearing that haunted me. Entering Guillaume's chamber I saw that he was asleep. Crossing the room to the fire I took my mug and poured myself a serving of the bitter brew I was growing accustomed to. Carrying it back to the table I sat looking at, but yet not seeing Guillaume.

"Problems Young Warrior?" Opsis asked taking a seat across from me.

"Why do you ask me that?" I asked turning my attention to Opsis.

"You seem very far away."

"I guess maybe I was at that."

Waiting for a few moments Opsis gave me time to say more, when I didn't he continued. "And just where were you?"

Still I did not respond. I wasn't trying to be rude to Opsis, I just wasn't sure what to say. That, and I wanted what ever answers I got to first come from Guillaume. Being that it was him that the whispers named.

"Did something happen between here and the hidden room?" Opsis was determined to get an answer himself.

"Yes Opsis, something did happen. No I did not

open the book or even attempt to open it. I followed Guillaume's instructions and put the book back where it belonged just as he told me."

At that Opsis visibly relaxed, but still watched me, waiting for more of an explanation.

"The crystals lit up when I entered the room. They showed me pieces of the dreams that haunt me. And I heard the voice as well. Still, I do not have answers. I do not remember who or what or why."

"And this I know bothers you, the not knowing. It will come Young Warrior, it will come." With that said Opsis stood and crossed the room leaving me to my thoughts. There was only a brief moment of guilt for not saying more. Still, I did not lie, not really. I just gave him a very brief version of what happened. Crossing the room to put away my mug I checked on Sir Switch. He raised his head to look at me and then tried to stand.

"Stay down there, stay. " I instructed this great beast. Running my hands across its head and mane it relaxed and stretched back out on the floor. Standing I looked to Opsis, "I am going for firewood." Opsis looked up at the sound of my voice and then nodded his acknowledgment at my words. Passing through the shimmering doorway I stepped outside. Looking around I placed my hand on the hilt of my sword out of habit. When nothing set off any instinctive alarms I walked along the wall toward the wood pile. I half expected to hear giggles or voices at some point but didn't. I did hear the dragon. Moving as close to the wall as I could and still be able to see I watched as it flew past where I stood. It was there, and then it was quickly out of sight. I could hear its roar long after I could no longer see it. I stayed where I was, leaned back against the wall for a long while.

170

"I came out here to slay a dragon. I've made friends, I've killed a friend, I've fought in a battle. And still that dragon lives." I stood talking to no one, watching the skies waiting to see if it would return. After a while when it didn't I walked on around to the woodpile and gathered an arm load. When I carried it into Guillaume's chamber I saw that he was awake and sitting at the table with Opsis.

"There you are," Opsis said as soon as I entered, "Guillaume was just about to tell me all about his battle with the Molditians. Come and join us, that way he will only have to tell it once."

Stacking the wood in its place I walked over and sat at the table and watched Guillaume prepare to tell how he and a handful of caTragons beat an entire army. When I had sat down and gotten still Guillaume began to tell his tale of the battle.

"As I stepped out of the chamber I knew that you would both attempt to follow me. To prevent that I sealed the door. I knew that I could not keep you safe out there, and do what I had to do to win the battle. My full attention had to be on the Molditians, if I were watching you as well, it would not have been."

"We're not children in need of caretakers Guillaume." the sound of my sarcasm drew a disproving look from Opsis but Guillaume looked up at me, responding. "There are times, when everyone needs a caretaker Young Warrior. You were attempting to get out of here to be mine were you not?"

I could do nothing but nod in acknowledgment at his comment. With that, he continued his recounting.

"Once I knew the doorway was sealed I stepped away from it and into the clearing. Bringing up a storm of the proportions that I needed takes a little time. Unfortunately, time is not what I had as I could see the

171

Molditians moving in the trees. What was on my side was that the Molditians know of me, and from what I have gathered have heard strange and amazing tales of what I can do and what I have done to my enemies."

"And just where would they have heard these tales?" Opsis asked trying but not managing to hide an odd grin.

Guillaume looked first at Opsis, and then to me, "Collectif himself helped to spread exaggerated rumors of my expertise. He could get into areas that most people could not. His actions led others to believe him not fully of sound mind and therefore harmless. Still, they believed his tales, which kept us safe here for these many years."

I stared at Guillaume as I fought the emotions that threatened to surface at the mention of Collectif. He had annoyed me to great measure, but I still had not wished him harm. Yet harm is what I myself personally caused him. After a moment of watching me Guillaume continued his tale.

"The Molditians hesitated, trying to get what was left of their army together near where I stood. In the time that it took I was able to get the first signs of the storm to form. The clouds thickened with winds that were sharp from the cold of the ice building inside them. The winds began to blow and to swirl in patterns that confused the Molditians when the dust was picked up and carried skyward. All the while it grew steadily colder. The winds formed a line of twisting, spinning cyclones that stood between me and them. Slowly the winds advanced on the Molditians, causing them to back away. It was then that the snow began to fall."

Opsis who had risen moments before from the table returned with mugs of brew for everyone. Guillaume took his with an expression of gratitude. I wrapped my

172

hands around the hot mug, warming hands that had grown cold.

"When the snow first began to fall the Molditians ignored it. If you remember we told you Young Warrior that once a Molditian has a victim in sight and mind they do not give up until that victim is deceased. I was their target, and they had no plans of giving up. Forming something resembling a line, they waited on the cyclones. Hunkering down in low areas, holding tightly to trees they held their ground as the cyclones reached them. The strong winds tearing some away from the trees when their grip failed, while lifting others easily from their hiding place in the ground. Even over the winds I could hear their screams as they were carried away. But the winds did not take them all, a great many were left standing their ground as the winds rose into the skies and disappeared into the clouds from which they had come. Once the winds and dust stopped swirling madly the Molditians prepared to advance. I had tried to rush the storm and almost made a grave error. I thought for a moment the snow was stopping. There was not much on the ground and there didn't seem to be any more falling. The caTragons moved close and formed a supposed protective circle around me. I knew though that the Molditians have little fear of the caTragons and no matter how many of them may have died in the process, they would have kept fighting until all of the caTragons were dead or I was. In the end, their goal was to see me dead. They were not leaving without that being accomplished."

Guillaume stopped for a moment, watching me. In his look I could see more than he was saying, he knew something. And what he knew, had nothing to do with what he was telling.

He took a long swallow of his brew and resumed

173

speaking. " I could not hear your calls through the wall Young Warrior. What I could however, was feel it every time you struck it. Your emotions are strong, stronger than your physical abilities. Each time you struck the wall a vibration of those feelings crossed to where I stood. It was a distraction I could not permit. I began to walk away from here, I had to get far enough away that if the vibrations reached where I stopped, they would not be strong enough to distract me from what I had to do. When I and the caTragons began to advance on them it confused the Molditians and they moved back into the trees. As I walked I could feel them closing in, forming a circle around us. I could feel their hatred growing stronger. The evil that surrounded them was a dark cloud in itself. I reached the banks of the pool and stopped. Even though the temperatures had dropped so drastically and it was still snowing slightly the water still boiled and steamed. I added my magic to theirs and used it against them. The steam from the pool froze as it rose up into the sky and fell back as snow. This time it fell fast and hard."

"But," I interrupted," how could you stop their magic? Since the Molditians were alive and well, their magic should have still been strong..right?"

Guillaume smiled at this, "You are indeed learning. I did not stop their magic. Theirs was to make the water hot and boil to keep them warm. Their magic stopped there. They cared not about the water after it was warm, whether it stayed in the pool, rose or sank into the ground as long as it was warm. I did not attempt to change that. All I did was change the water after it had boiled and risen from the surface. I made it so that once the water rose out of the pool, it would freeze quickly and fall back to the land as snow and ice."

174

Looking from me to Opsis he then continued. "The Molditians are not a stupid race. They used my own caTragons against me. As the snow fell they quickly advanced. The caTragons in their attempt to protect me were using their fiery breath to fight the Molditians. This was keeping the Molditians warm and able to fight. As they drew closer I could hear their grunts and growls of battle over the winds. It was the sounds of a hunter stalking their prey. I had to find a way to stop the caTragons and also stop the Molditians."

Pausing Guillaume watched me. The look in his eyes seeking something. I looked away, not sure what he knew, and if he knew, I was not ready to discuss what had happened in the corridor.

"Emotions are a strong tool," Guillaume continued, "when we focus those emotions, channel them together into one purpose they become a great weapon. Even though I had deliberately moved away from the reach of your emotions I now used them. Every time you called out, every time you struck the wall, there were vibrations. You could see them cause the snow to tremble ever so slightly in their wake. It took only a slight addition of magic to cause that wake to grow. When it flowed over the caTragons it was just diversion enough to get their attention. Their battle angry stance changed as they looked to me. With one hand signal they stopped using that fiery breath on the Molditians and every other one turned to warm the area around me. The ones still facing the Molditians crouched, claws and fangs extended, ready to attack if given the command. By this time the snow reached my knees and was still falling. It just did not seem to be slowing the Molditians down any at all. I knew, with all that I am, was and will ever be, that I could not allow doubt to enter my mind. I had to trust and

175

believe I would succeed. The fire I had left burning inside, burns on the magic of hope, I had to believe and not lose sight of that hope. When I saw the briefest glint of light reflecting off of steel I had an idea. Concentrating on the cold I sent some of it directly to the metal of their weapons. Sword and shield swiftly became too cold and painful to hold onto. The sounds that were being made as the extremely cold metal was dropped onto frozen ground was not pleasant. Grunts of the hunter had become words of great vulgarity. They were not happy, but they were not giving up. I had to come up with a way to hold them off longer, to get them to hesitate, to be still long enough that they felt the cold rather than the hatred that was compelling them."

"But without weapons, how could they attack?" I asked Guillaume.

"Molditians are a driven race. Once they are in battle, they will fight with weapons of any sort, even if it is only their bare hands. They will not stop until they are themselves dead or have succeeded in their battle plans, defeating their victims."

"Yet, some did ran away from the battle at the castle." I said, remembering.

Guillaume nodded, acknowledging my comment. "That memory entered my mind as well. When that happened I wondered about it and spent much time at the table of crystals attempting to find out why that was. From my experience and knowledge of Molditians I know that they hold a certain respect for one considered to have any form of madness. They believe the magic of the mad to be stronger than that of anyone else, even their own. The only thing they have a grain of fear of, is the spirit of the dead that has not gone on to the land of rest. One that lurks here, possibly trapped, possibly being punished for some wrong, possibly just lost and having not found their way yet. If they think one of these spirits is among them, or against them, they will flee, seeking the protection of their caves. Standing before the crystals, watching again your battle, there was something, someone else there. Dancing among the Molditians, appearing and disappearing at will."

I had been sitting at the table, leaning forward propped on my elbows that rested on the table. As I listened to Guillaume words, however I leaned back quickly, shaking my head from side to side. "No, I don't believe it."

Opsis reached out to me but I moved back away from him.

"I killed him, why would he help me?"

"It may be that he felt that he had to make amends for things he did, before he can move on." Opsis spoke up.

"Or, it may be that he so loved annoying the Molditians that he couldn't resist one more time." Guillaume added, obviously remembering something from a time long past.

Standing, I moved away from the table putting distance between me and Guillaume. I had to think. I didn't believe in ghosts and repentant spirits did I? Spirits simply did not become trapped or lost, did they? Could they actually return and help, even if the one they were helping is the one that sent them into this other realm that they found themselves in? I stood staring into the fire as the quiet in the room grew.

"There is more isn't there? Something that you haven't said yet." I asked still looking into the flames.

"It could be," Guillaume said, "that he is not dead as we know it."

177

Turning away from the fire I faced Guillaume."I saw him die, I killed him. I watched my sword pierce his body and the blood flow. I lashed his body onto a caTragon and brought it back here. I know he was dead."

"Indeed a mortal man would have died with that wound," Opsis spoke to me, "Collectif was not mortal, he was and is a creature of magic and madness. He once said that he was created out of left over parts, and then on another occasion said that he had angered someone powerful and been changed from mortal man to the collection of creatures we see. However he came to be, the fact that he is magic, leaves him in many ways, invulnerable to mortal ways."

"But what of his body? Did you not bury his body?" I thought frantically, thinking, trying to remember, but I could not recall seeing a grave anywhere near the chamber.

"We saw to you, Young Warrior." Guillaume answered. "when we returned to see to Collectif's body, it was gone. Only his blood soaked cloak remained lashed to the back of the caTragon."

"Why did you not tell me this?" I asked them, looking from one to the other.

"You were upset enough over his death. Since we did not fully understand ourselves what had happened we remained silent." Guillaume answered, watching my reaction.

"I've spent all this time thinking I killed someone, some thing, that I may not have actually killed. Or, killed, but that did not remain dead. And you didn't tell me." Guillaume watched quietly, waiting.

I stood glaring at Guillaume, wanting to confront him with the accusations of the whispers, yet a fear of his answer kept me silent. Not ready to face that particular demon yet I walked back over to the table, standing with arms crossed looking down at Guillaume. He and Opsis both sat watching me, waiting for me to come to an understanding of what they were saying.

Finally I spoke, "So, Collectif may or may not actually be dead. You may or may not have seen him, yet you believe that you saw him helping me in the battle. That his presence was what caused some of the Molditians to run away. It was those same Molditians that survived, that gathered here to attack us. Why?"

"My guess,"Guillaume began,"is that they still want to over run the castle, but that to do so, they have to defeat you. They searched until they found you, and planned their attack."

"Would they not have feared Collectif's being here, being that he was a friend of yours?" I asked.

"Molditians, while not an ignorant race, put strange restrictions on their superstitions. If they indeed saw Collectif, thinking it was his lost spirit, they will believe that it is trapped there near the castle. They believe that where a spirit is first seen, that is where they remain." Opsis volunteered.

"The castle they still want to over run."

"It is their belief that if they kill you, his spirit will no longer be bound here and can move on to the next realm." Guillaume answered.

"Why would they believe that?"

"Because it is you that he returned to help."

"So, how does all of this fit with your battle?" I asked Guillaume, trying to move on as I once again took my seat at the table.

"I thought,"Guillaume began, "that if I could get them to believe Collectif was here, that he wasn't bound to the castle that would, if not frighten them, at least make them pause. The problem was that meant dividing my concentration on the storm. It was a chance I had to take however. As the snow reached a point that was near waist deep I created a disturbance in the air. It looked like his form, and yet it had the appearance of a something that could not hold form, even as it tried. Moving and shifting it danced through the snow. The Molditians when they saw this stopped in their advance. They seemed transfixed and unsure as to what it was, watching it as it moved before them. All the while the snow fell, not as fast, but it fell steadily on. The shape moved about in the air, just a few feet above the ground, moving around the outside of the circle formed by the caTragons. I could hear the sound of mutterings coming from the Molditians, while I could not make out the words, I could understand the emotions behind them. They did not like this 'spirit' and even more so, they were feeling fear, an emotion that they despise as they believe it gives them the appearance of weakness. When I thought they were going to turn and run, they decided instead to attack. By all appearances thinking they could destroy me and what ever was dancing in the winds. As they drew close, moving slower due to fighting the deepening snow, the caTragons made ready to fight, then suddenly moved back toward me. I heard a laughter, just for a moment in the air. The Molditians heard it as well and stopped in their advance. Confused they looked to each other for some form of answer. When the laugh did not come again they started to move forward. That was when the snow that had been falling downward, suddenly exploded up and outward in a large burst covering the Molditians fully. In the center of that burst, laughing, was Collectif. He hung in the air six feet above the top of the snow just laughing, nothing else. Taking my eyes from him to the

Molditians I saw that they were frozen solid, as stiff as the statues in the castle. Collectif seeing this, turned to me and took one of those deep over exaggerated bows of his and disappeared back into the snow he had appeared from. Logic tells you that when something that is frozen warms, it melts. Taking that logic I stopped the snow from falling and with the help of the caTragons began to warm the area. As the snow melted, so did the Molditians. Being magical, does have its bad side."

Taking a deep breath Guillaume looked around the table, "Just as the snow melted, that was when you came rushing onto the scene."

"You had decided that the danger was past and you could release us from your protection." Opsis stated as a matter of fact.

"So, Collectif lives?" I asked Guillaume.

"In some form, Collectif is still here." Guillaume answered. "whether he is alive, I do not know."

I sat at the table silently for a few more moments and then rose, crossing the room to sit on the floor beside Sir Switch. Raising his head from the floor he looked at me for a moment and then lay back as he had been. Seeing that he was improving, and too restless to sit still I stood and paced the room. There were too many thoughts and questions fighting for attention racing through my mind. How to accept that someone that was dead, may not be dead. Did I, or did I not kill him? Who was whispering to me, and did Guillaume really tell them that dragons live forever? With clenched fists I paced, gritting my teeth until the ache in my jaw forced me to relax them. Still I walked, circling the room, lost in the thoughts that tormented me.

I lost all track of time as I paced. I wanted to ask the questions, but I did not want to hear the answers. A part of me wanted to know who called to me, but another did not. Did Guillaume have a part in what I could not remember? If he did, could I accept and forgive?

"You are making me tired with all of that pacing Young Warrior." Opsis said as I passed the table yet again. The smile on his face not hiding the look of concern that also resided there. "Come sit down and tell us what has you putting so much wear on your boots."

Making a decision I returned to the table, standing before Guillaume I asked without preamble, "Did you tell someone that dragons live forever?" I watched as the color fled his face and he grew deathly pale right before my eyes. His expression was one of great sadness.

The look on Guillaume's face was the only confirmation that I needed. "Who, Guillaume, who did you tell that to?"

"To have the answer to that, you must remember on your own." Guillaume answered.

"Why? Why must I remember myself? What difference does it make should I remember or that it come from you?"

"It matters greatly Young Warrior, for in the remembering, you will also find an understanding that you would not take time to get from me."

"Why, then, would you tell someone such a thing?"

Guillaume simply shook his head, refusing to discuss it further. When I looked to Opsis, he merely shook his head, remaining silent.

With a cry of pure anguish and frustration I slammed my fist onto the table and then turning away walked through the shimmering door to the outside. Even in my frustration I realized that I did not have any of my weapons so I remained close, walking only as far as the wall I had rested against before. Leaning back against it now, staring up into the small area of visible sky I slammed my fists repeatedly against the rock behind me.

"I know that it is hard Young Warrior." Opsis spoke from nearby.

"Opsis, you have no idea how difficult it is. To have dreams and I don't know, visions of some sort haunting you, tormenting you, but not letting you see them. To hear the voices of someone that is familiar, but yet unknown. Pieces of many things but all of nothing, teasing but not allowing understanding." I spoke to him, but did not look. Instead keeping my eyes on the sky. "To try so hard to remember, to catch and hold onto a thought or image, only to have it fade away just outside my grasp."

"You cannot force it, the answers will come.."

"I know I know," I interrupted, "When the time is right, when my heart is ready to remember..I know that, but it doesn't help." This time I did turn to Opsis, on his face I saw the same pain that flowed through me.

"The one thing I ask of you, is as the memories return, allow them all to return before you come to conclusions or make decisions." When I looked somewhat annoyed Opsis continued, "There are more feelings at stake here than just yours Young Warrior, remember that."

Accepting his wisdom I moved away from the wall and walked with him back inside. Guillaume still sat at the table, judging from the expression on his face he was lost in his own painful memories. Walking over I sat down at the table and waited until he looked at me.

"It is a difficult journey we must take at times in this life," Guillaume said quietly, "there are moments of joy but then, there are times of anger, pain, frustration. When things happen that we wish did not, that we wish we could go back and prevent or change. Things get put into motion and cannot be stopped until they have reached their set conclusion. No matter what our wishes are." I sat quietly watching him, wondering just what or how much he was about to tell me. "This that you fight to remember, is one of those things. Innocent things that were combined with the less than innocent. Something that was told one way only to be taken and used for another. Along with an act of negligence. All together it became what it is, and only in its set time can it be changed."

"When is the set time Guillaume?" I asked him. My voice quiet, holding my hands out across the table in a near pleading manner.

Shaking his head he looked at me with an open honesty. "When the time is right. That is all I know."

I watched Guillaume for a moment as his head dropped and he stared at the table, lost again in his own haunted memories. "True Dragons, do live forever." he whispered to someone who was not here to hear.

TWELVE

Leaving Guillaume sitting at the table I wandered down the corridor to the Great Chamber. I felt badly for Guillaume, he appeared so haunted by what ever it was that had happened. What ever this thing was that everyone was waiting on me to remember, even me.

Entering the chamber I sat down leaning back against the wall facing the door to the hidden room. The torches around the chamber had lit up as they always did when someone entered. Other than knowing the room was no longer dark, I gave them no thought. As I sat there the crystals on the table began to glow softly. I chose to ignore them, sitting where I was watching a door to a room that held more questions than answers. Leaning forward resting my arms on my knees I sat, watching the door. Hearing a soft noise I turned and watched Sir Switch as he walked toward me. Drawing up beside me he sat down facing the door, watching it right along with me.

"So what do I do Switch? Do I sit here watching a door do nothing? Do I enter the room and take a book that in some way had something to do with this, hoping it will open to answers? Do I get up and go over there and see why those crystals are glowing yet again? Or do I just leave it for today hoping tomorrow will be better?" Switch merely looked at me and then settled in for however long I planned to sit where I was. Sighing, I shook my head looking back to the door, "You're no help."

I don't know how long I sat there lost in thought

before the sound got my attention. Giggles, coming from, where? Sitting as still as I could, I looked about the room trying not to turn my head for fear the sound would stop. The longer I listened the more it seemed that the sound was not coming from one place but was coming from every where, but mostly it sounded inside my head. Listening I realized that I recognized that laugh from somewhere, I had heard this before, I knew I had heard this before. Before my eyes a long corridor appeared. Was this real? Was it another of Guillaume's lessons? If I stood up would it remain or disappear?

"There is only one way to find out." I mumbled as I slowly stood. The corridor remained before me. As I stepped forward the sound of laughter returned. Walking down the corridor the sound grew louder. Cold chills crawled up my spine, as fear churned like bile in my belly. Sweat beaded on my forehead, then ran in rivulets down my face. Ahead of me, at the far end of the corridor was a doorway, light spilled out from it, bathing the floor . Inside that room, waited my answers. I just knew it, but was I ready? Could I handle what I found out? There is no turning back now. I told myself sternly. I would have the knowledge I needed of what happened. I would finally know, what has lead me to this place and time. Slowly I walked the corridor, listening to the giggles and laughter of youth. Placing my hand on the frame of the doorway I took a deep breath. Closing my eyes I stepped forward in front of the doorway and opening my eyes looked into the room.

The bright light in the room blinded me momentarily. I wondered just for a moment if it was a last effort on my mind's part to prevent what was about to happen. As my eyes adjusted I could see figures moving about in the room. One was Guillaume seated on a chair much too small for his size. His head was bare of the hat that he always wears causing his long hair to hang down over his shoulders. Its dark coloring surprised me for a moment until he raised his head to look at something and I could see just how much younger he was here. And he was laughing, not in a ridiculing manner, but in a happy almost carefree way. This was a Guillaume that I had not seen, at least not since his appearance rescuing me from the dragon.

At his feet were two other figures much smaller than he. When I heard the now familiar giggles I knew they were also much younger than he was, even here. The figures were seated in the floor at Guillaume's feet facing him, their backs were to the door hiding their identity from my view. The light that had blinded me was slowly fading away, allowing me to better see the room and its occupants. I remembered this room, the familiar feeling growing in intensity and yet, causing the fear of what was about to happen to grow as well. Over in the corner, across from a huge fireplace was a canopy bed, someone was laughing along as they made the bed. I could hear them telling the figures not to bother Guillaume any more.

Guillaume was still smiling as he looked from the speaker to the figures before him. There was an expression of something different on his face. A look I was surprised to see. There was a look of tolerance there, but also of love. He smiled as he looked back,"There are some things, that are not a bother." he said, the smile on his face growing.

"Just one more, please Guillaume, just one more story." spoke one of those in front of him.

A sick feeling grew in the pit of my stomach. I knew

that voice. In my heart, I knew that voice.

"Yes Guillaume, please, oh please just one more." these words coming from the second figure. I gripped the doorway tighter. I knew these voices. Somewhere in the back of my mind a memory called to me. Remember, remember. I did not want to remember this. The cold sweat of fear formed, running into my eyes and down my back. My hands trembling uncontrollably as I swallowed again and again fighting back the bile that threatened. Closing my eyes to this I stepped back a half step, I wanted desperately to back away, to turn from the doorway, leaving it to fade back to where ever it had been. I wanted to run far away, but I knew I couldn't. I could not leave this now. I had to finish this. Even as that sick, cold fear grew, even as I could smell it growing in my heart and soul. I could not leave this.

Turning back I looked into the room again. Seated on the floor before Guillaume sat two young girls. Blond hair pulled back into caps yet still managing to spill down their backs. One with an unruly curl that would not be tamed, Guillaume's hat was perched crazily on top of her cap. The others hair held in check by the thickness of the braid it was woven into. Ribbons peeking in and out of the braids. Their dresses were long and elaborate, evidence of their station. As I stood in the doorway watching, one leaned forward, reaching out in a pleading manner, asking again, "Please Guillaume, just one more." My heart lurched in my chest at the sound.

I felt the caTragon as it walked up pressing against me, standing beside me in the doorway. Making snuffling noises that seemed to fit in with the emerging scene perfectly. One of the young girls at Guillaume's feet also seemed to hear it as she turned and spoke to me,"There you are, I knew that would be you and your caTragon. Come, Guillaume has told us some wonderful stories and you can help us talk him into another. I'm sure he will tell another with you here now."

Everything around me seemed to go dark at once. Sick I was so sick, sick of heart, sick of mind, sick of soul. My grip on the doorway tightened as I fought to remain standing and not give in to what reached for me. "No oh no." two small words drawn out into a wail of pain that escaped even as I fought it. Sliding downward, falling to my knees I rocked forward. Covering my eyes, hiding them behind trembling hands I took deep breaths. Fighting the pain that tore at my heart. Over and over the words escaped into the empty air around me, "no, oh no, no no. It isn't so, can't be so." but I knew, it was.

As the tears I could not prevent flowed from behind hands still pressed tightly to my face, I watched between my fingers the images progress. Guillaume motioning for me to come in and join them. I watched, seeing the room around me as I walked in and sat down facing him. The caTragon stretched out by my side. I leaned over, resting my head on its back as I heard Guillaume begin to talk. Glancing over I saw the look of adoration and rapt attention in the eyes of the two girls. They hung on every word and movement of Guillaume's. I saw myself as I rolled my eyes at the sight, thinking that girls were so silly.

"Across Fire Mountain, on the other side of the land, is a special place. It is the place of Dragons." Guillaume's words interrupted my musings of disgust over the actions of girls. "It is here that they live undisturbed. They fly over the treetops, happily doing tricks to amuse themselves as they fly. Chasing and disturbing the flocks of birds that dare to cross their path."

Guillaume watched his audience, smiling as they leaned forward as if to catch every sound he made. "Don't listen so closely", I whispered desperately, wishing they could hear, knowing they couldn't.

"It is in this place that they are allowed to play uninterrupted, they have no enemies here. There are rivers and lakes that offer not just water to drink, but somewhere to swim and chase the many fish that live there."

"Like they do with the birds." came a young voice.

"Oh how wonderful." came the voice of the one with braided hair.

"It is here," Guillaume continued, "that dragons live forever. With nothing or no one to bother them as they spend their time happily ever after."

"Do any people live in this place Guillaume? Do people there live forever?" asked the girl with braids.

"No, my young one, there are no people there. People only live forever in our hearts. Only dragons live in this land, and only there, do they live forever." Standing he started to cross the room, removing his hat from the young girl's head as he passed. "I must go now, it is time for your studies and I have work to do."

Oh, Please Guillaume, one more.."

"No", he smiles as he shook his head, "no more stories, I will tell you more later, for now, your teacher waits, and I will not have her angry with me." With that, he left the room, the sound of his footsteps on the stone floor fading away.

I could hear the pleading continuing along with the sighs and giggles. Girls. I thought then with a hint of disgust. My sisters. I thought now, suffering a pain worse than any battle injury could produce. Could I really bear what was about to come?

I heard the whisper calling me, "Come look."

" What do you want now?" was that me, sounding so disgusted? Maybe bored at girlish interruptions?

"Come and see what we found."

I had been passing their room. I remembered I was going to climb up the tower to watch for dragons. I wanted to show one to my caTragon so he would know what he was related to. This was just an interruption of the worst part. I looked down at Sir Switch walking beside me, "The world would be better off without girls. You know that Switch?"

"Ohhhhhhh is that you, Adwr, afraid to come and see?" came the taunting voice from inside the room.

" My name is *not* Adwr!" I was so angry at her. How could she keep calling me that name? Just because I refused to bow down to her wishes. Just because I wouldn't break the same rules that she did. She wasn't braver than me. She just thought she was. Angry as I was I turned and walked into the room. I was going to tell her she couldn't call me that any more. Or I'd find a name just for her. I didn't care if she was my sister.

"I demand that you stop calling me that."

"Oh hush and look at this." Turning around to face me, ignoring my anger she held out what she wanted me to see.

"That is Guillaume's book... how did you get it?"

"He was writing something in it and when he was called away he left it on the table."

"What are you doing with it? You know he told us never to bother his things." Her attitude was making me nervous.

"You are such a silly coward. We're not going

191

to hurt Guillaume's book. We are just going to borrow a few words."

"How do you borrow words and what for? What are you planning on doing Delwen?" I felt the fear growing in my belly. She was my sister, but she was stubborn and had strange ideas sometimes. At my question and obvious suspicion she smiled, licking her lips as if anticipating something sweet. All the while, reminding me of a snake.

"Delyth," she said motioning toward our other sister who sat behind her, "and I have been talking and decided that we want to live forever."

"But you know you can't do that, people don't live forever, Guillaume told you that." the fear was growing stronger.

"Yes, I know all that."Delwen said waving her hand in the air in a dismissive manner. "He also said that dragons do live forever."

"So? You are not a dragon, what does that have to do with you?" I asked her, not wanting to hear her answer.

"We have decided to try being dragons for a while. If we like it, we shall remain dragons and live forever. If we don't, then we will return to being human again." Delwen answered in a rather self assured and overly smug tone.

"Don't be silly." was all I could think to say, and it was the wrong thing.

"I am *not* being silly. You *Adwr* are proving the coward that you are. You refuse to see how wonderful this really is. Its flying, its playing, its not having to do studies."

"You don't know what words to borrow. You need to give Guillaume back his book. I can not let you do this." I was feeling more and more desperate. I wasn't really there, this was a memory, but I was there. I was seeing this all over again. The panic filled my heart, the fear fed on my soul and I knew, with all I could, that something terrible was about to take place and I wanted desperately to find a way to stop it. Knowing, all the same, that I couldn't.

"I do know the words. Look, "Delwen turned the book to face me, "there is a picture right here of a dragon..all we have to do is repeat the words under this picture and we will become dragons. It says so- see?"

I saw that it did say exactly what Delwen was going on and on about, but there was more. Her hand covered it, I needed to see that but couldn't. "You are wrong, you shouldn't do this. Delyth, don't do this." I was pleading with them now.

"Join us brother, become a dragon with us." Delyth pleaded with me.

"No, I won't and you shouldn't either."

"Then your name will forever be Adwr." Delwen said, the sneer in her voice impossible to miss.

"I'm going for Guillaume." I almost shouted at her as I ran from the room. I could hear them starting to read the words. Hurry, I have to hurry. I had not gotten far when I heard the screams. Screams of fear and of pain. Screams that seemed to go on forever. I stopped in the corridor only for a moment, looking back toward the room, hearing the screams, not knowing whether to go back or continue on for help. I chose to get help and began to run again. All the while knowing, I was too late.

I burst into Guillaume's chamber like a crazed animal causing him to turn and look at me oddly. "Guillaume, you must come you must!" I was shouting over and over.

"What is wrong..."

"Delwen and Delyth got your book," I was fighting to get the words out as I tried to breathe.

"My book, what are they doing with my book?" Guillaume asked as he made to leave the room.

"They want to be dragons. I think they have already turned themselves into dragons." I was clinging to Guillaume by now.

"Where are they?" He asked and demanded at the same time.

"In Delwen's room"

Pushing away from me he ran from the room, disappearing down the corridor. I followed him, returning the way I had just came. Finally turning the corner I saw Guillaume standing outside the door, looking in with an expression of horror and disbelief. He did not realize when I stepped up beside him. Stepping under the arm he had across the doorway, tightly gripping the post to hold himself up, I too looked into the room. The room was destroyed, everything that had lined shelves, adorned table tops or hung across windows was broken in some way. In the center of the room lay two figures caught in the middle of transformation. A shapeless gray mass, reminding me somewhat of a worm's cocoon trembled on the floor, a sound caught between a cry and a moan sounded from one, or maybe both. At that point I couldn't tell. When I started to speak Guillaume kept me quiet me with a motion of his hand. Silently we stood in the doorway and watched. Some how I knew that he couldn't stop this now that it had started.

Time seemed to stop as we stood there. There was no sound from anywhere but from the shapes in front of us. Groaning now, slowly and continuously. Suddenly one mass and then the other began to glow as an odd light shown from within. The room grew warmer by the minute. A tear began in each cocoon moving from one end to the other. Slowly the head of a dragon emerged from the first. Struggling to rise it flopped about, reminding me of the fish I had caught just days before. Seeming to finally gain strength it managed to hold its massive head up as it fought to emerge from the thin membrane covering it. I could hear that membrane tearing as the dragon's body came out, wet and glittering in the sunlight coming in the broken window behind it. I backed up at the sight of it. Seeing that it barely fit into the room, and still the other was just fighting to get free.

When it did begin to appear I looked to Guillaume confused. When I took a breath, preparing to speak he again stopped me as he watched the scene before us.

Out of this cocoon emerged the biggest snake I had ever seen in my life. I stepped back to a position halfway behind Guillaume, still watching. The snake pushed its way free, rising up above the floor hissing in a way I would have sworn showed a great anger. Slamming its head back against the dragon they appeared to be preparing to fight. Instead the dragon turned and using fire and brute strength broke through the wall by enlarging the window there. Grabbing the snake in its talons it pushed its way through the window, stretching wings outward it rose into the sky, unsteady at first but then quickly getting its balance and disappearing into the distance. Moving in the direction of Fire Mountain.

I watched as Guillaume crossed the room and stood staring out the opening at the disappearing figures. In the center of the room, laying open in the floor was Guillaume's book, the pages flapping madly in the wind entering through the broken wall.

I don't know how long I sat there against the wall,

195

lost. My face was soaked with shed tears while my hands ached where I had pounded the floor leaving them cut and bloodied. My stomach sore from heaving, the bile rising leaving me sick, still. But the guilt in my heart hurt the worst. I had attempted to murder my own sister, and hadn't realized it. The memory of all this locked away as too horrible and painful to bear, had almost allowed me to do the unthinkable. Now I understood why they posted a guard at the castle to warn of the dragon's approach but never tried to kill it. I wondered how much if anything she remembered of being human, and if it was the lack of memory that caused her to attack. Or if it was something else, something I didn't know or understand. There was so much I didn't understand about this. I heard the steps approaching but didn't turn to look. Using the back of my hand to scrub across my face hoping to hide my tears I sat and waited.

Guillaume sat on the floor beside me, leaning back against the wall, looking off across the room. He didn't say a word, just sat there, waiting. I could see him at the edge of my vision as he stared off into the distance. He had aged so much since the change. Now I understood that part. All of those whispers about 'the change'.

Drawing my knees up I draped my arms across them. "I do not blame you Guillaume." When he did not respond I continued, "I understand how you could feel at least partly to blame because Delwen got your book when you left it on the table. But I think that she would have found a way to get it even if she had to sneak into your chambers to do so." I felt more than heard his sigh of relief. Still he did not speak. He remained sitting watching the far wall and letting me talk.

"I understand a lot of things now. All that stuff that I

196

didn't before. The hushed, sad feelings in the castle.
Whispers that stopped when I entered a room. People
looking at me so funny. I think that at times they all
believed I could have done something different, stopped
them in some way. That instead of trying, I just ran away
and that was why they all continued to call me that
name. I think that my own sister actually cursed me with it
in a way. I think that, I cursed myself with it because in
my own heart, I felt as if I should have, could have done
something to prevent it, and didn't. In my heart, I felt the
coward." I leaned forward, resting my chin on my arms,
ignoring the blood on my hands as I stared off into the
memory that was now so clear.

"I remember watching from a corner unseen, as they
made you leave. My father yelling and crying and
threatening to send you to the guillotine. I think that all
the while he was hoping that you could do something,
change them back. That at any moment you would walk
into the Great Hall with them back as themselves and all
would be wonderful again. When days and weeks passed
and that didn't happen things just changed. I watched as
Father had them seal the doorways to their rooms, and
then eventually they sealed off the corridor. No one was
permitted to speak of them. Happiness and magic left the
castle. No one laughed any more. Switch disappeared
one night. I feared that they had destroyed him, I wanted
to be angry with them, but it was easier to just forget. To
hide somewhere inside and pretend that nothing was
real. There had been no change, there had been no
horrors happening before me. Then, it just became, I
don't know, normal, every day just moving, going from
one day to the next day. At some point my father grew
tired of my silence and hiding away, he placed me in the
care of Raimond and I began my knight's training. By

197

then, everything was locked securely away by a mind that did not wish to remember." The room was quiet when I fell silent, lost in what was.

"If I could have changed anything," Guillaume finally spoke, "I would have. I would have done anything, even given my own life for them, if it would have changed things, brought them back. However there was nothing that I could do. The ignorance in their choice of spell sealed their fate."

"Guillaume, why, "I hesitated in my question then continued. "why did one become a dragon like they planned, and one a snake?"

"One of them, spoke the words wrong. Remember how I told you that the words must be said correctly and in the correct order? Nothing could be changed, nothing." I nodded quietly, acknowledging his comment while waiting, hoping for more.

"One of your sisters said something wrong. Doing that, it changed the spell and instead of a dragon, she became a snake."

Together we sat there in silence. Me with a question I was afraid to ask, while Guillaume kept glancing in my direction as if he knew and waited. Not looking at him, I took a deep breath trying to gain strength, and asked him, "Is there anything that can be done? Can they be changed back?"

"Yes, Young Warrior there is, but only you can bring it about."

THIRTEEN

I sat there for a few moments trying to understand what Guillaume meant and how it was that getting my sisters back was up to me. Giving up I turned to ask Guillaume to explain. Before I got the words out Opsis appeared in the doorway.

"There you are Opsis," Guillaume began, "Our Young Warrior here has remembered. We can now move forward."

Opsis watched Guillaume stand and move across to the hidden room before looking to me. I, too, watched Guillaume, thinking he was acting strange. He was moving quicker, almost as if he were lighter, younger, but that made no sense.

"The weight of this pain, is beginning to lift from him." Opsis said, watching me, "He has born this agony and guilt for all this time. Knowing, that if you never came, he would bear it to his grave."

"But, did Guillaume not say that some of us have a set destiny? And that this is mine? How would I have not come?"

"There are those who do not recognize things that they must do. There are those, who see the things, and do not want them. They turn and run in a different direction to try and escape what is asked of them. One is never forced to do something, it is asked, and it is up to them to accept or not."

"In this, I accepted, without understanding. I only knew that I had to go, but I thought I was to kill the dragon, not save it."

"It is not unusual for people to become confused or set off without full understanding. At least in this,

199

Guillaume was expecting you, hoping for you to accept and then when he saw that all the times and signs were right, he began watching for you."

"Which is how he knew to come rescue me, or maybe it was my sister from me, when I came to the forest." I watched Guillaume as he came out of the room, his arms laden with many items, some I had seen, others I had not.

"Opsis, how do we know if my sisters even want to be changed back? What if they are happy as they are?" I hesitated for a moment, dreading the next question but having to ask it, "Opsis, do they, I mean, what if they don't even remember being human?"

Opsis watched me, understanding my concerns. "Come over here," was all he said. Motioning for me to follow him he walked over to the table of crystals. Looking over I saw that Guillaume was busy at the table along the wall sorting and arranging the items he had placed there, so I stood and followed Opsis. As we approached, the crystals began to glow, coming to life as if they had awaited us. After all this time I was still not accustomed to it.

Reaching the table Opsis glanced only briefly in my direction before turning back to the crystals. "Let us see if we can find the answers to your questions."

Turning to look at the crystals I was confused, they glowed, but one was dark. There was nothing to be seen for the blackness. "I don't understand this." I told Opsis still staring at the crystal, 'why is it so dark?"

"The one it has found is underground somehow. She is either in a cave or tunnel and there is no light there."

Guillaume joined us at the table and silently looked at the crystal. With a single word spoken and a motion of his hand in the direction of the crystals we could then hear sounds. It was the sound of something large sliding across the ground, crossing whatever was in their path in a great hurry. We had found the one that was a snake. The crystal began to lighten quickly as the snake obviously approached the opening. Reaching the end of the tunnel the snake stopped. Through this crystal we could see what the snake saw. Stretching out before it was the almost desert like field were I had first saw the snake and dragon together. Rocks lay scattered about before it as if tossed there during a giant child's tantrum. A couple of stones were resting precariously on top if each other. There were no trees to be seen, so the light from the sun beat down relentlessly, the air moving in waves from the heat. From this viewpoint, and from what I remembered, there was no water anywhere near this place. This was the exact opposite of the lands around the castle.

Opsis touched my shoulder to get my attention, when I looked he motioned to another crystal. In that one the face of the snake was visible as it looked out. Dirt and debris clung to it's head, partly covering one eye. If it were not for the dirt coating the scales it would have been near to a silver color, just as on the book. The snake remained motionless for long moments, not even its tongue was seen as it lay in the same place. Suddenly moving, turning its head in a way that made it appear to be looking directly at us. Through the crystal I could see into the snake's eye, feeling almost as if I were looking into its very soul, if snakes have a soul. But, this is my sister, so surely it must. My mental ramblings came to a halt when I realized what it was I could see. The image of one of my sisters, at the age I remembered her. Her face hidden, yet I could see her hand reaching out to me.

Then the snake turned away and it was gone. Sliding out into the light and across the barren ground, for something so large, it quickly disappeared.

"This one has some memory still. From that image, I would think that she is not happy." Opsis said softly.

He was guessing I thought, or was he?

"What of the other?" I ask, impatient now to know.

"There is your answer." Guillaume said, as he pointed at a glowing crystal.

I could tell immediately that it was showing the dragon's lair. It was almost as dark as the snake's underground tunnel, but there was some light that reached   inside. All the way to where the dragon rested. All along the walls I could see the precious stones that Collectif had wanted so badly. The ones that the light managed to reach glittered and sparkled casting off a multitude of colors across the walls of the cave. The image of the dragon filled the crystal. It did not look well. Laying on the floor of the cave, its head lay to one side. Only a bare trace of smoke was seen slipping out and upward. Its breathing was shallow and appeared to be labored. Its eyes were only partially open, yet did not appear to be actually seeing anything. As the image changed in the crystal I was able to see deep into the dragon's eye as I had the snake's. In this I could see what appeared to be my other sister, laying down, arms outstretched but appearing lifeless.

"Guillaume? Is she..."I swallowed hard, then turned to look at Guillaume, the look of fear and desperation filling my own eyes. "Guillaume, Opsis, is she alive?"

Guillaume turned away from the crystals, "She is

alive, but her sadness will kill her if we do not do something quickly."

"Being a dragon is not as she thought it would be is it?" I wasn't really expecting an answer but Opsis volunteered one.

"They thought they would be dragons together. That they would play forever." Opsis looked from the image to me, "they did not expect to be different from each other, and the instinctual urgings of the creatures they became have gone against everything that they knew as humans. All this time it has been a constant battle for them. Seeing them here, in these images, no, Young Warrior, it is not what they thought."

Turning to look for Guillaume I saw that he had again crossed the room to the far table. His back was to me but I could see he was once again fussing with some of the things he had placed there. Turning to see me watching him he motioned for me to come over. When I reached the table I looked down at the array of items he had spread out. Some of it I remembered as the weapons I had seen the first time I entered the Great Chamber. They each glowed now, as they had glowed then. The sword that I had reached for on that first day was the nearest item to me. A sword that I still ached to hold. Beside it a shield of large proportions, oddly enough in the center of the shield was the embossed emblem of the intertwined snake and dragon. On one end of the table Guillaume's book rested on top of a deep crimson cloak. Beside the cloak were a pair of boots, the laces the same crimson color. Near this was a large chain and leather halter imbedded with crystals alternating with Grandite. The reigns of this halter glittered brightly in the light of the torches. At the far end of the table was a carefully folded net beside a two sided hammer that I did not need to pick up to know was heavy. I looked to Guillaume and waited for the explanations and instructions that I knew were to come.

Guillaume stood staring at the table as if checking to make sure there was nothing missing before he finally spoke. "Your lessons were interrupted before you could learn everything that you need to know. Your own high spirited nature mixed with Collectif, and then the battle with the Molditians trying to take the castle and then us, prevented us from completing them."

"Which I still do not understand." I interrupted. "Why did they want the castle when they live underground?"

"We have no time for that now, Young Warrior, we must take care of your sisters." Guillaume answered, by not answering.

At my look of frustration Opsis spoke up, "The Molditians did not want the castle. They did not want you to follow your destiny as it was written. They did not know where you were, but they knew if they attacked the castle you would show up. Whether it was from inside the castle or outside."

"What difference did it make to them whether I followed my destiny or not?"

Guillaume joined in the conversation. Whether to hurry it up or because he felt he knew the answer better I did not know. "They were no better than Collectif as they suffered the same greed as he. Every time the dragon left its lair they would enter and remove large quantities of the precious stones. Stones exposed or created by the dragon's fiery breath. Stones that were simply and readily created by the magic that surrounded the dragon. If you killed the dragon, as they assumed you were out to do, then their supply of precious stones would cease to be."

"But you defeated them in your battle right? There are no more Molditians?" I asked hoping I did not have them to still worry about in this.

"I defeated the ones that were here."Guillaume answered truthfully. He watched me intently as I thought over what he had shared.

"So I may end up facing them yet again?" Neither answered, but I knew without either of them saying anything. Yes, I could end up facing them again.

"Explain all these things to me Guillaume." I told him, turning my attention back to the table. "As you said, time is short."

As he prepared to explain I reached across the table. Picking up the sword, finally holding it in my hands, I was once again awestruck at its beauty. The craftsmanship in the making could have no equal. I turned it just in time to catch the reflection of Guillaume and Opsis as a look passed between them. There was more to the Molditians than what Guillaume was telling me, but for now I was going to let it pass. For now, I had to worry about saving my sisters, before it was too late. Turning the sword in my hands the light of the torches reflected off the steel. The smoothness of the metal shone, almost glowing with a blue hue. Other than the single fuller running its length there was not a mark on it. The glow I had noticed earlier was coming from the sword's hilt. Embedded inside was a large Grandite stone surrounded by small precious stones forming an oval shape. Silver and golden cord wrapped around the hilt. Along the cross guard were markings that I did not recognize, yet for now did not question. Holding this sword in my hands, wrapping my fingers around the grip, just felt right.   Tightening my hold on it, I closed my eyes and took a deep breath.

"You have fought in battle, and you have killed. You are no longer a child, you are a man. In that truth, you know now that it is a weapon. It is something to be handled with respect and trust. You know it, and it knows you." Guillaume spoke quietly, almost reverently from my right side. "It will do you well in any battle."

Waiting until I had lowered the sword Guillaume then began to explain everything he had placed on the table.

"This shield bears the emblems of the snake and of the dragon. It is not just for your protection Young Warrior, it is also for the protection of your sisters as you begin the process of changing them back."

"I don't understand, Guillaume, how is that?"

"You will understand should it be necessary, hopefully it will not."

Opsis had walked up and was standing just to my left, his hand resting on the table. "Your sisters, as you noticed on the field that day, are not in the best of terms. You may even need to protect them from each other until they are returned."

"This shield," Guillaume continued, "is made of the same steel as the sword. It is strong and will hold up well. You will see that the eyes of both dragon and snake are Grandite. Do not allow yourself to become careless and lose this, it is important."

I nodded my understanding as I reached across the table picking up the crimson cloak. "What is this for Guillaume? One can not hide wearing such a color, it would stand out in the worst of fogs and darkest of nights."

"That much is true." Guillaume said as he looked at the cloak. "As I said, your training has not been as it should, because of that exceptions must be made. Think carefully of your training, think of the times that you felt a presence, but yet could not see who was there. What do you remember about all of those events?"

I stood at the table thinking, trying to remember. It wasn't that long ago and yet so much had happened that it was just a ripple in..."Ah, always before anyone or anything that I felt but couldn't see appeared, there was a ripple in the air. Like the waves in the water, barely there but spreading outward, Unnoticeable to most, to others nothing more than the slightest of stirring in the dust."

"Correct, you remember well. We do not have the time for you to learn how to do that without aid. But you must be able to do that very thing if you are to succeed. This cloak is mine. I have not worn it since- for a very long while. On you it may be long, but that we can fix."

"And the boots, with the laces?" I asked as I slid them across the table toward Guillaume.

"They matched the cloak."

I heard Opsis make a sound as if he were choking but once more I chose to ignore it and watched Guillaume.

Guillaume said no more about the boots, instead he continued on about the cloak. I watched him, listening carefully as he talked.

"You need no magic words or spells for this. You do need to be able to focus fully and concentrate solely on where you need to be. This cloak does not make you invisible to others, this helps you to slip through a doorway from one place straight to another."

"I'm not sure I understand this." I thought maybe I did, but I had to be sure.

207

Opsis stepped forward to explain, "If you are standing here in this room and realize that you need to be in Guillaume's chamber, if you focus and concentrate hard enough, true enough, believe strongly enough, then the doorway will open. When you step inside this opening you have the choice of either stepping straight into Guillaume's chamber or waiting in the doorway for no more than half a day."

"If I stay too long?"

"You are lost there forever. Trapped between time and existence. Only a ripple in the air will ever give evidence that you pass by." Guillaume was serious. I wasn't sure I wanted this.

"The boots help you to step quickly and with sure foot. In them, your footsteps are silent. They will also give you sure grip should you be riding your caTragon, or the dragon."

"Riding the dragon? I think not." I had turned and looked at the halter, understanding that now.

"You don't have to, as it is, you are right. In her state it would not do her well. You will however need to get the harness on her. The Grandite in the harness will calm her to the point of near tameness so that she can be lead. It will also give her the strength she may need in her weakened state. The net, is for the snake. Her anger and hatred has kept her stronger. The net can be tossed from the ground or dropped from above, it does not matter how it is delivered. As it falls over the snake it will grow to the size it needs to be to hold her. There are stones of Grandite all along the outside edge of the net, I just worry about if there is enough, she is very strong."

I reached over and dragged the hammer across the table making a horrible noise as it scraped. "Is this in case the net isn't enough?" When Guillaume turned and looked at me oddly I grinned. He wasn't amused.

"No, that is for after you have your sisters under control. I will explain that, once we have you trained in how to use the cloak." Guillaume said as he held the crimson cloak out to me.

Watching Guillaume walk across toward the center of the room carrying that bright crimson cloak I kept thinking I had seen it before. There was just something so familiar about it. It didn't make sense for Guillaume to have a cloak that color, in all the time I had been here, but for that first day, he had only worn plain, normal colors, brown or white even black. Not this really bright red. Realizing Guillaume was waiting on me I followed him across the room. I was still staring at that cloak, trying to understand why I thought I should remember it. When Guillaume held it out toward me a design on the inside caught my attention. Taking hold of the edge of the garment I pulled it up to where I could see. Stitched into the fabric were the letters DD surrounded by a crooked and misshapen heart.

"My sisters gave this to you. I remember, it was some special day they heard about or made up. This was a gift to you from them. I remember you even wore this thing around them. You told me it would probably be too long for me, of course it will be, its too long for you. This thing drags the floor three feet behind you."

I could hear Opsis laughing while Guillaume just smiled. He looked at the heart for a moment before commenting. "I remember seeing them peeking around the corner watching me as I came down the corridor. Their giggling could be heard through the heavy door after they disappeared into their room. When I drew close the chamber maid opened the door smiling, she told me that 'the girls' had something for me. They would bring it to me in their study room. So I walked the couple of doors down and waited. It was funny watching them come in carrying this between them."

"You should have seen the look on his face when he realized what they were giving him." Opsis spoke up.

Guillaume sent him a look that would have melted steel, Opsis just smiled.

"They actually made this themselves," Guillaume continued. "so yes, even with it overly long, I wore it. They worked so hard on it and I didn't want to disappoint them."

"Those two would laugh, whisper and giggle for hours after they saw you in this." I remembered that much. I also remembered how disgusted I would get at their actions but that part I didn't share.

"So how can a cloak that my sisters made, have magic?"

"Anything that is done in love has magic. And it is the magic of that love, that is what is going to help get them back." Guillaume held the cloak out once again and this time I took it. As I draped it around my shoulders Guillaume looked to Opsis, "Go into my chamber, we will practice going there first." Opsis nodded and disappeared down the corridor.

I looked up from trying to figure out exactly how to wear something I wasn't accustomed to and that was so over sized. "We?"

"Yes, we. I can and will go with you the first several times just to make sure you understand and don't get trapped."

Guillaume stood behind me, waiting until I finished fighting with the cloak before he told me to clear my mind of everything but his chamber. That was the only thing I was to think about, Guillaume's chamber. When everything else was gone, visualize a door opening. As the door opened expect to see his chamber. As soon as I saw the door open to his chamber, he told me quietly, I was to take a step forward immediately. Try as I might, I could not fully clear my head. The image of my sister trapped in dragon form, fear of losing her when I was so close.

"You are going to have to focus, you can do this."Guillaume spoke to me calmly, "believe in yourself and the abilities you have. Put your fears aside, focus, concentrate. Let your eyes see what your heart does."

When Guillaume fell silent I nodded and tried again. Mentally I pictured myself taking my hands and shoving all thoughts aside. I pictured them all locked away for now. Concentrating to the point that was almost painful I suddenly saw the door. Focusing on the door before me I watched as it opened. The only words allowed in my head, "Guillaume's chamber" repeated over and over. As it opened I saw Guillaume's chamber before me. Taking a step I found myself actually stepping through the ripples I had seen before. Opsis was waiting and caught my arm as I staggered slightly, turning to drag the rest of the cloak through I saw the look of pride on Guillaume's face.

"Good for a first try. Now lets return to the Great Chamber." Guillaume had quickly returned to business.

"Did you not say something about being able to fix this?" I asked him holding up the extra lengths of the cloak. "I don't want to risk this thing getting hung on something I didn't see and being dragged back into somewhere I can't get out of."

Before Guillaume could do anything Opsis

211

walked over and showed me how to fold the top back to where I was fastening the middle around my neck as the top hung half way down my back. "You won't be the best dressed knight in the castle, but this will work." Nodding my thanks I stepped away from Opsis and waited for Guillaume. As soon as he moved back in place I began to concentrate on the Great Chamber. Doing the same as I had before and first mentally pushing everything aside I was able to clear my mind quicker. This time it was much easier and almost before I realized it we were back in the Great Chamber.

"This time, you will go alone. The important thing to remember, when you step forward, do not look anywhere but where you are going. Look through the doorway to where you plan to step into, no where and I mean, no where else." Guillaume said as he stepped back away from me.

Taking a deep breath I began.

If it were not for the fact that I was doing this for my sisters, I would have grown weary and frustrated with how long Guillaume's insisted that I practice stepping through the ripple of this that he called The Inbetween. There was also the matter of not wanting to make a mistake and get trapped somewhere that no one could find me. Hearing Guillaume tell me that each step is an individual's journey. No one could come along later and take the same journey as another, making it impossible to find someone who gets lost. Stepping through the ripple into the Great Chamber it felt as if my knees were about to give way. Sweat rolled down my face and back, I could feel my hair stuck to my cheek. The cloak felt as if it had grown heavier with each trip, now it was all I could do to bear the weight on my shoulders.

"That is enough for now," Guillaume said after seeing my exhaustion. "we will rest, and then we will do more. Come and help me carry these things. You need to grow accustomed to the feel and weight of them."

Slowly walking over, my feet sliding more than stepping I reached for the sword and shield. As soon as my hand closed around the hilt of the sword it began to glow. I looked up in time to see Guillaume nod. "It knows you."

The first thought that slipped into my mind was that it was a piece of metal, but I immediately corrected myself when I again took in its beauty and craftsmanship. I wasn't about to ask Guillaume how it could know me, not yet. Picking up a few other things I followed Guillaume down the corridor. My eyes grew heavy and my body craved sleep. Reaching Guillaume's chamber I stumbled my way over to my cot and fell across it. Forgetting the crimson cloak, forgetting the boots, forgetting everything as sleep took me immediately.

FOURTEEN

I could hear crying. I tried to look around, find where it was coming from, but all I saw was dark. There was a thick musty smell as if the air never moved where I was. I stood in what felt to be a small place, but in the absence of light I couldn't tell. I still heard the crying, loud, heartbreaking sobs. I tried to walk but my legs wouldn't move. I attempted to call out, but no sound would come. I was stuck, or trapped. Had I stepped into a ripple in my sleep? Who, or what, was crying. Why could I not see? Then I noticed before me as two eyes opened. They looked in my direction, but seemed to be looking past me. In those eyes was the sadness, tears of gigantic proportions slipped out and down. I sat up straight on the cot, I had been with my sister. She wasn't just angry, she was sad and hurting as well. "I'm coming." I whispered into the air, knowing they couldn't hear, but still hoping that some how, they would know.

"You have to tell him. He needs to know." Opsis was talking with Guillaume. They did not realize I was awake.

"I will tell him."

"When? When will you tell him?" Opsis all but demanded.

"I will tell him..."

"When the time is right?" I said speaking up so they would know I was listening. As I stood I saw Guillaume tense, and then his entire body seemed to droop in resignation.

"It is this, Young Warrior,"Guillaume began, " while we can not be sure of this, our best assumption is

214

that the Molditians know that the precious stones scattered about the dragon's lair and on the dragon's body are not all of them. There are many places around where the dragon lives that hold these precious stones. Places where you can't just walk in and pick them up. Some must be dug for in various manners, others are said to be in places protected."

"So?" I asked him, already fearing what was to come.

"The Molditians are a lazy bunch, they want, but they do not want to work for it."

"They want to enslave everyone in the castle to do the work for them." I finished for him.

"It is a regular practice of theirs, one they have done many times before. It does not matter to them who it is, what their station in life may be, how old or young they are. The only thing that matters is that as slaves you dig for the stones, and turn in every one you find. To do otherwise, would be a grave mistake." Opsis said, watching me.

"Have they appeared again?" I asked looking from one to the other.

"No, not yet. I do know that there are still many of them left, but they are hiding, and they are planning something. The warnings are on the winds. What or when, I do not know." Guillaume answered.

"Which means that we have to work quicker, as time may be shorter than we think." Crossing the room I sat down at the table across from Guillaume and remembering the sounds of my sister's crying, asked him, "What is my next lesson?"

Guillaume watched me closely for a few moments, "Are you sure you are rested?"

"I am rested." I said while waiting and watching

Guillaume as he decided whether or not I was rested enough.

"Then we will go further. Opsis, will you go to the pool and watch for him?"

"I will." was all he said just before he disappeared through the doorway.

Guillaume motioned for me to follow him as we moved to the center of the room. "The instructions are the same. Concentrate, focus, think only of where you want to be. Remember to look straight through the door and no where else."

"I will remember." I told him as I began to think of the pool.

Opsis greeted me as I stepped out through the ripple. "You are getting this down very well."

"I must, my sister's very lives are at stake here. There is also the fact that it may come in handy at other times."

Opsis stood looking at me for several long moments, when I looked at him quizzically he smiled. "You have come far in a short time. You should be proud of yourself."

"I will be proud of myself, when I have my sisters back."

Opsis nodded his understanding, "Guillaume will be wondering where you are."

It was my turn to smile as I turned away from Opsis and opened my mind once again. All through the day Guillaume had me going to various places in the forest. As many times as I stepped through the doorway of the Inbetween, only once did I make a misstep. On one of the many trips to the pool instead of stepping out onto the bank, I stepped out into the water. On my return when Guillaume looked at me questioningly I shrugged and told him I felt like a swim.

As the day grew late Guillaume was relentless in sending me through again and again. Then he decided to increase the risks. On one trip, unknown to me, he hung a glass globe on the cloak, as I stepped in, the globe dropped shattering. I held my concentration and looked straight ahead, stepping out into the Great Chamber with Guillaume right behind me.

"Just making sure." he said as he shrugged and turned away.

After that I never knew what little trick he set up to try and distract me as I entered the passage. Every time one of his attempts went off, he was always right there when we stepped out.

Finally he handed me the sword and shield. "You need to know the weight and feel of the weapons as you go through."

I looked up at him for just a moment as I settled the shield onto my hand. The sword felt almost as if it came to life in my grip as I slipped my fingers around it's hilt. It began gradually to glow and grow warm. It felt ready for battle. Turning away from Guillaume I again concentrated and stepped into the ripple of the Inbetween. I could feel the difference immediately. The weight of the weapons seemed to grow and even slow my step. Stepping out on the other side I looked at the weapons. They looked no different, but they felt different. "Strange"

"Magic and magic will at times rub against each other, almost as a competition for dominance. Weight that is added, fully or partially may cause an imbalance. There may be a drag or even a push just depending." Guillaume spoke from behind me.

Not surprised to know he was there I turned to

face him. "Magic is jealous?"

"It can be, yes."

I looked down at the sword in my hand as I shook my head. "Nothing surprises me any more around here."

"Don't say that, Young Warrior. One never knows what may be waiting just around the corner. You could also be inviting the ones living on the magic side to a challenge, and they, my young friend, can most assuredly surprise you. Come, let us go back, this is enough of this. There are other things you must learn, and time is short."

Stepping into Guillaume's chamber I realized just how tired I was. My body ached from all the walking I did. It felt as if my muscles were tied in various knots while my head hurt so badly it was difficult to see. I removed the cloak and carefully hung it on a peg out of the way. Just getting its weight off was a great relief. I looked over at the table and saw Guillaume and Opsis talking so I decided to remove the boots as well. Sitting on the edge of my cot I reached for the first of the laces.

"Do not remove those just yet." Guillaume said as he looked at me briefly. "You may not be finished traveling for the night."

"Is there a problem?" I asked as I stood and started to cross the room. "Are my sisters still well?"

"We're not sure," Guillaume answered honestly. "Opsis has seen pieces of something that has him concerned. The problems is that he has not seen enough to understand what is going on."

"I am not being allowed to see very much at all." Opsis explained. "Usually when I have a vision, I see it clearly. This is dark, foggy, making it impossible to see. It is more feeling than anything else. And the feeling is not good."

"We need to go to the Great Chamber and see if the crystals can enlighten us as to what is going on." Guillaume said as he rose from the table.

Together we all walked down the corridor to the Great Chamber. As soon as we entered the crystals began to glow. To me, they did not seem to glow as brightly as they ordinarily did. Crossing to the table we examined each different crystal.

"They look dim, almost dark." I spoke aloud, wondering if I were the only one that observed this.

"There is magic somewhere that is preventing them from working. The crystals try, but it is as if a cover or a blockade has been placed to prevent them from showing us what is going on." Guillaume answered my comment.

"Can you tell anything? Where it is or what it is causing this?" I asked as I tried in vain to see anything at all.

"Nothing, it is impossible to tell." Guillaume said still watching the crystals.

I looked at Opsis who had grown very still. "Opsis, are you well? Do you see something?"

"I am well, Young Warrior. No, I can not see anything. Yet there are strong feelings and they are growing. I feel hate, fear, anger. But I can not tell you from whom or why."

"Without knowing that..." I began

"There is nothing we can do."Guillaume finished. "You don't know where it is, so you have no idea where to

219

go. You don't know what it is, so you wouldn't know what to be ready to do. All we can do is wait. Hope for a lapse in the magic that will allow us to see what is being planned or that is actually about to take place. If it isn't already taking place as we speak."

"We will take turns at keeping watch here," Guillaume continued. "you two return to my chambers and get some rest. Decide among you who will be next, when it is your time you will come and relieve me. If it clears to where it can be seen, who ever is watching will alert the others quickly."

Nodding, Opsis and I turned to leave the Great Chamber, Guillaume had already turned back to the crystals and was watching them intently.

It was agreed that I would take the next watch. Stretched out on the cot I tried to sleep, my mind however would not slow down enough to allow it. Even though my body still ached, muscles trembling from the exhaustion, my mind was restless. My thoughts jumped about from what we had practiced all day to this new problem. What was going on that had Opsis so concerned and who was blocking the crystals and why. It was just too much to allow a mind to slow down I thought with a yawn.

I awoke with a start when I felt Opsis hand on my shoulder. Sitting up I struggled to come fully awake.

"It is time, you must go relieve Guillaume." Opsis said as I stood and stretched.

"I'm on my way." I turned and walked away. Traveling down the corridor I could see the Great Chamber was fully lit. The light from the torches bright enough to keep anyone awake. One day, I thought to myself, I am going to ask Guillaume how all of these torches can burn so brightly and not make the room unbearable. Entering I crossed to the table and stood beside Guillaume.

"Have you been able to see anything at all?" I asked him.

"No, nothing." Guillaume answered, "and that is very odd. I was trying to remember, but I do not recall any other time that the crystals have been blocked like this."

" I will take over now," I told Guillaume, "you go ahead and go back. If I see anything you will know."

The rest of the night passed slowly as I stood in front of the table carefully watching the crystals. They still glowed, but it was impossible to see what they were trying to show us. The monotony of the task made the time seem to pass even more slowly. Standing here in one place, doing the same thing began to get difficult. My legs still ached from the previous day. "I am young, I can do this without complaint," I spoke aloud as if to reaffirm to myself my strength "but a chair would sure be nice."

When I felt something against the back of my legs I jumped to the side, trying to turn and see what was there while not falling on my face. Confused I stood looking at a chair sitting where nothing had been before. Looking around the Great Chamber I confirmed that I was still alone. I knew I had not heard anyone come in, so where did this come from? Walking over carefully I placed my hand on the back of the chair. It was real and not a creation of my imagination. It was also a chair like those in the castle, not like the ones in Guillaume's chamber. Puzzled I sat down in the chair to watch the crystals and try to figure out just how the chair got here.

As the night progressed and the crystals still glowed darkly I began again to fight sleep. I was standing in front of the table attempting to watch something that I wasn't being allowed to see and growing more drowsy by the moment. "A cup of Guillaume's bitter brew would be good right about now." I said aloud, again talking to myself knowing there was no one here to hear me. When the mug suddenly appeared on the table, steam rising from it invitingly I simply stood and stared for several moments. Slowly reaching out I wrapped my hand around the mug. It was as real as the chair was, but the best thing was that the brew it contained was hot and welcomed.

"Such a strange thing." I said into the cup I held. "I mention a chair, and I get a chair. I mention this mug, and now here it is. How can this be?" I stood watching the crystals as I pondered on this strange turn of events. After a moment of thought I came upon the idea to give this new thing a test. Looking around the room my vision settled on one of the torches. "I would like for that torch to burn low." The fire in the torch dropped to a place where it was almost but not quite out. "I would like it to burn brightly again." The flame on the torch returned to its previous level. "Strange."

Looking at the crystals and seeing no change I tested to see if more would happen as I asked. Looking at the many torches around the chamber I said aloud, "It would be nice if the torches would in an alternating pattern lower their flame to almost out and then return to brightness while the torch beside it begins to burn low. It would be nice it this happened all the way around the chamber one after the other."

The first torch slowly burned down very low, and then began to flare up once again as the torch beside it began to burn low. This slowly made its way all around the chamber. I watched amazed as the torches continued to do this. Watching the torches I said,"It would be nice if the torches would speed up and slow down at different times," The torches immediately began to do just that. A quick look at the crystals showed no change but when I reached for the mug I found it empty. "More of Guillaume's brew would be good about now." I said as I watched the mug, immediately it was filled. Smiling now and enjoying this I thought for a moment. "It is growing cool in this room, a cloak would be good to have, along with just a little warmth from the torches." The room began to grow comfortable just as I felt the weight of a cloak settle about my shoulders. Looking down I saw it was Guillaume's crimson cloak. Shrugging I draped it better across my shoulders as I watched the torches.

"What are you doing?" Came Guillaume's voice rather loudly from the opening of the corridor.

I cringed inwardly and then turned to face Guillaume and Opsis standing just inside the Great Chamber staring at me. Opsis looking as if it were all he could do not to laugh.

I knew I was in so much trouble. How was I going to explain something that I didn't even understand? I watched as with a mere wave of his hand the torches grew still, burning as they should while everything else I had some how spoken into being disappeared.

"Have you even been watching the crystals?" Guillaume asked me as he walked toward the table.

"Yes, Guillaume, I have." I answered honestly. "I may have allowed momentary distractions, but most of the time I did watch the crystals."

"There has been no change in them?"

"No, there has been no change. They remain glowing, but darkened. As if someone has placed a coverlet over them."

Guillaume looked up from the crystals to me. His expression was of one lost in thought for a few moments.

"Go and rest for a while,"he instructed. "I will come and get you when it is time to learn more of what you will need to know."

I wanted to argue. I wanted to tell him that I wasn't tired. I wanted to remind him of how short time was. Yet I stood, fighting to hold my tongue not wanting to face the consequences of my rashness when I was already in trouble for what I had been doing.

"Would that we could wish the dark away. Instead of the things that were happening here tonight, to speak the words 'it would be good for the covering to be gone so that we may see what is hidden from us.' And it be so." I turned to leave the room when Guillaume spoke.

"Come, Young Warrior and look."

Turning back I looked from Guillaume to the crystals on the table. Glowing as they had been, only this time the darkness was gone. In its place were the clear images we had waited to see. As I looked I noted that each of the crystals were showing a different location. A couple showed two different locations on Fire Mountain, one held the image of a portion of the forest, in another was the dragon's lair, one was a view of the castle. In all of them there was no sign of life, nothing moved across the landscapes giving each image an almost eerie feeling.

"What ever was going on, has stopped for now." Guillaume said.

"Or it is known that they are no longer hidden." Opsis said.

While I listened to them discuss possibilities I watched the crystals. While I feared to hear confirmation of what I already knew I still had to ask.

"Those places on Fire Mountain look familiar. Like I should know them or of them. What is there?"

Guillaume did not take his eyes from the crystals as he answered. "Molditians."

Looking at the crystals again I searched carefully, there was still no sign of any life. It could not be right. "There is something wrong here." I spoke out loud as I still looked at the crystals.

"Why do you say that?" Opsis asked.

"There is no sign of life at all. No people around the castle, no birds, rabbit or even butterflies. There is no sign of any life around the dragon's lair or on the mountainside where the Molditians live. It is almost as if the dark was replaced by a picture of what we hoped to see."

"While still hiding what was really going on."Opsis finished for me. "We are no better off than we were when it was dark."

Except for the fact we realize this is not real, and not fooling us, while whoever is doing it thinks it does." Guillaume said with a thoughtful tone to his voice.

"Could someone be trying to make us believe that the Molditians are planning something?" Opsis asked.

"Or could they be planning something, and knowing we are watching be trying to throw us off trail by acting innocent?" I asked them.

"We could guess all day and still not know the answer. Even if we guessed it we wouldn't know. Opsis, if you will keep watch on the crystals, I will take our young warrior with the budding gift of magic and go over more of what he is going to need to know."

Opsis nodded and turned to the crystals as Guillaume and I made to leave. "Now, about what I saw when I came in this morning." Guillaume said as we walked down the corridor. "Do you want to explain that?"

"I would if I could Guillaume. All I know is last

night I was watching the crystals and happened to say something about how a chair would be nice. Suddenly I had a chair. Later I said something about a mug of your brew would be good and a filled mug appeared."

"And the torches?" Guillaume asked.

"I hoped you wouldn't bring that up. I guess I was seeing if it was really working because of things I said, or if you were providing them. So I said something that I knew that you would never do," at Guillaume's sideways look I added, "and I guess I was playing with it a bit as well."

Guillaume was silent for most of the walk down the corridor. Entering his chamber he looked at me as if debating about something. "Do you remember anything odd about your sisters?" he finally asked me.

I first thought what a strange question to ask of me. Then I remembered something. "There was the time with that tapestry they wanted me to help them get it down from the wall. I refused and left the room. I could hear them shouting that they wanted the tapestry down. That was the first time they called me Adwr. I wasn't gone long, I went back to tell them that if they were going to call me names I was going to forget they...." I stopped for a moment as that memory sank in, then as that wave of remorse passed I continued, "I was going to forget they were my sisters and not speak to them any more. When I went into the room the tapestry was down. They both had a funny almost confused expression on their face. I asked them how they got it down, when they looked at me and told me it came down by itself I thought they were telling me an untruth. I even told them that. The whole time they swore to me that it came down all by itself. After the things I saw last night, I believe I owe my sisters an apology."

Guillaume stood silent for a moment after I finished. "Your sisters learned early that they had the gift of magic. I was told to dissuade them from using it, which I did. I tried to get your father to understand that by denying the gift, by ignoring or refusing its existence he was inviting problems. I wanted to teach them how to use it in a safe manner, but your father would hear nothing of it. He came very close then to stopping me from being around any of you. He wanted to send me away from the castle. Thinking that by keeping me away, there would be no threat. That your sisters would lose interest. Instead of sending me away, he allowed me to stay as long as I promised to do all I could to turn them away from any interest in magic. Instead of causing them to lose interest it, in fact, it brought on just the opposite. They were attempting to understand something all on their own and with them not knowing what they were doing when they got my book or understanding how to do things properly, that was when the worst happened and the transformation was made. If only he had allowed me to teach them as I had wished, this may not have ever came about"

"They were a lot younger than me when this happened. Why am I just now showing signs of any gift?"

"You showed some signs of being able to do things even then. Small things that you probably did not even notice. I did not give you the caTragon. I did not yet know their temperament and wasn't about to allow you or your sisters around something that could be dangerous. You were determined to have one, and end up with one you did. I remembered having them in an enclosure, safely locked away. Suddenly here you come walking down the hall attempting to carry one and barely managing it, but carrying one in your arms none the less. You were smiling telling me thank you that you would take good care of him. I knew how you had obtained this caTragon for your own, but I said nothing. After the change, when I was sent away I had hoped that Opsis would be able to remain at the castle and keep an eye on you, but your father sent him away as well. He wanted nothing around that would remind you of what had happened. He did everything he could to insulate you from past pains."

"Then why did everyone continue to call me by that name?" I asked.

"That was all you would answer to. You refused anything else. It was the one thing you had left from them. Even if it were a curse of sorts, it was all you had."

"Is the magic still with them? Will we be able to use what ever they may still have to help them turn back to themselves?" I asked Guillaume holding my breath for the best answer.

"That, is what I am hoping for," Guillaume answered "and what we will find out soon enough."

Turning away he walked toward a table under his shelves of books. On that table were the rest of the things he had gathered before. "Come over here," he said, "we will discuss these things and how you will use them."

Walking over to the table I looked at the items, "Guillaume, why can we not just speak them back?"

"Magic is an odd thing. It is also an orderly thing. To bring about this, you must do this. To bring about that, you must do that. If you do this and wish to undo it, you cannot undo a this with a that."

I could see Guillaume watching me from the corner of his eye. I could have sworn he was laughing at me again. Not allowing myself to be drawn into what ever he was setting me up for I motioned at the halter, "Instruct me, oh great one."

228

FIFTEEN

Guillaume reached for the halter, lifting it from the table, "She will not like this, but one cannot reason with a dragon."

"I thought you said that the Grandite will calm her."

"It will"

"And we know that she is growing weaker."

"That is true."

Then it should not be as difficult to get this halter on her as it would if she were well."

"It may not be as difficult, but that will not change the fact that with a halter, she is being led like a trained pony. Her pride is at stake."

"While her pride may be important, her life is more so."

"You have grown wise Young Warrior, you are correct in what you are saying."

"So even if she does not like it, in the end, when she is again my sister, she will understand."

"One would hope that in the process of the change all things before or leading up to it will be forgotten."

"How does one forget being a dragon?"

"You have to first believe that she knows she is not really a dragon but a human transformed into one. You would have to think that she remembers the time before the change."

"But Guillaume, if she remembered that, then she would not have attacked the castle would she? What is going to happen when she returns and has to face the past?"

"One could not begin to guess or to understand her reasons if she did remember and still attack, as there could be many, or none. There are things that have happened during this time that we do not know, things that may never come to light. As I said, one would hope that she does not remember, or if she does, can come to terms with it in some way."

Standing silently looking at the halter I worried over what she would have to face, remember or not. Either way, it was not going to be easy on either one of them. "You are right, Guillaume. One would hope they do not remember."

Guillaume looked at me, "And if they do not, you would never speak of it?"

"And I will never speak of it."

Nodding Guillaume handed me the halter, "and if at any time they remember, we will handle it then, as we have handled your returning memories."

Taking the halter from him I watched as the Grandite began to glow softly. "How will I get this on her?" I looked from the halter to Guillaume.

"When the time is right, and everything is ready, you will need to step through the doorway from here to her. Timing is important as it will be much easier if we manage to do this while she sleeps. Once the halter first begins to slide over her head the Grandite will begin to work and you will be safe. The Grandite will calm her while the crystals will give you the ability to control her, get her to go where you need her to go. That way you can lead her from the back of your caTragon."

"And the one that is the snake? How will we catch her? She, I think will be the more difficult of the two."

"In this, I agree with you. Her inner strength has kept her physically stronger. It would be impossible to get a halter on her because of that strength. That is why I chose to create the net. As I told you, once you drop it on her, it will grow until it is large enough to hold her entire body." Reaching across the table Guillaume took hold of the net and handed it to me as well. "look here, there is a strong cord that runs through the length of the net. Once you have her in the net, pulling on this cord will draw it together, trapping her inside. The Grandite around the edges will calm her long enough to move her."

"And just where is it that I need to take them?" I asked Guillaume, thinking I knew what he was about to say.

"To the castle, to the room where the change happened. It is important that they be where the change took place. The door was opened there, it is only there that it can be closed."

I stood there, net in one hand, halter in the other contemplating what I was about to do. In some ways it should have felt the prefect revenge on their treatment of me so long ago. Instead, there was just a determination to do what ever I had to that would bring them back. I would ask forgiveness later if I must.

"Guillaume, once they are back to being human and not creatures, will they remember how to be human?" I asked, because I had to know.

"That is one of the many things that we will find out once we have them back." Taking the net from my hands he turned to walk away, "Follow me, you will need practice with this until you are comfortable in how it feels in your hands. You will only get one chance, you must not miss." Knowing he was right I followed him outside. Walking until we came to a clearing large enough for practice Guillaume handed the net back to me and moved to set up a target. As he finished and turned to walk back we heard the roar of the dragon overhead. Together we watched as it passed, then circled around coming back.

"This may not be good." Guillaume told me as we watched. Reaching over he pushed me back into the trees on her approach. As she circled the clearing she occasionally looked off in a direction that appeared odd and then back to the clearing. Finally she seemed to give up, turned and disappeared across the tops of the trees.

"I do not understand that," Guillaume said still looking toward the sky. "Over the course of time I have seen her do many things, never anything such as this. It was as if she were looking for us, but why?" He stood for several long moments contemplating what had just taken place. Looking around to me he motioned back toward the clearing. "Practice with the net on the target. I am going to the crystals."

I watched as he left, quickly disappearing into the trees. I thought it an odd thing about how he chose to use his magic only sparingly, only it seemed, in the instances where he had no choice. I wondered if it was due to what happened with my sisters, or if there were other reasons. Mentally shrugging off the questions I walked into the clearing and began to practice.

Throwing that net was more difficult than I had imagined. I had thought that I would be good enough I could just toss it over, it would settle on the target and I would be done. I thought that I was talented enough that I would immediately be able to do this without effort. Instead, I would throw the net, it would twist up and land short of the target. Or I could throw the net and watch it sail over the target into the trees just past it.

Once it fell onto the target but only partially, causing it to slide uselessly to the ground. Each time I would cross the clearing to where it had landed, collect it and move back to try again.

"There has to be a way to do this that I do not know." I spoke as I once again walked back from collecting the net.

"Practice makes perfect, prefect comes from practice." came the sing song words of a voice I remembered. "Practice, practice, shield yourself from ignorance. Shield yourself from inability. Practice perfection in practice." the words came from nowhere, and everywhere.

I stood turning circles in the clearing searching for the source. "Collectif, where are you?" The only response was laughter fading away into the distance.

Turning back to the task at hand I was mocking the words I had heard, "Shield yourself from ignorance, shield yourself, shield.." then I began to wonder. Picking up the net I thought of how I had been throwing it. I would simply just throw the thing. I didn't think of how it was bunched up or folded. Whether it was in a knot or flattened out. Turning the net in my hand, I examined it thoughtfully. I folded it in half and then half again. Throwing it across the clearing it sailed better but did not open as I needed it to. Going after it I again examined it as I walked back. I had forgotten about the lead line. Pulling it free from where it was entangled in the net I considered my choices. This time I folded it at an angle making sure the stones lay side by side with none overlapping. Picking it up, holding the line I looked to the target. Throwing it once again it was better, but not exactly correct. It still did not open as I hoped for. I also had lost grip on the line, watching as it slid from my hand. Once again I went for the net. Walking back I examined the net contemplating how to fold it. Instead of a fold, this time I held it so that as I gripped the center of the net the edges dropped together, the stones falling one beside the other. Looking at the line I slipped the loop over my left wrist and tightened it. I heard Collectif's words 'Shield yourself'. Memories of childhood games came to mind. Standing sideways to the target I picked up the net and held it at an angle. With a sideways throw I watched the net as it sailed across the distance to the target. It opened better but my aim was wrong and the net settled on the ground beside the target. Shaking my head I pulled the net back to me and picked it up for another try. As I gathered the net together I wondered about the size of it. Deciding to try something I held the center of the net in my hand, gathering half of the net I considered various ways of holding it to finally simply drape it across the hand holding the center of the net. Reaching down I caught hold of the edge of the net and again turned to one side. Turning and releasing the net in one smooth arch I watched as it sailed across the clearing to settle onto the target perfectly. Having finally figured out the method to do it, I now needed to prefect my abilities.

I lost all track of time as I stood in the clearing practicing over and over. By the time the sun was setting I was getting the net over the target perfectly every time. The satisfaction I felt was in the knowledge that this was going to help my sister. When I heard a noise it broke my concentration and I turned to see who or what was approaching. Guillaume walked out of the woods, the expression on his face impossible to read.

"I was watching, you have done well in learning this." he said when he stood beside me.

Nodding to acknowledge his comment I immediately asked "Guillaume, do you know why the dragon was here?"

"No, Opsis and I have done everything that we know to try and see what is going on. He still has the feeling of something about to happen, but it remains hidden. Even when I managed to get an image that was not covered I could not tell what would have caused her to act in such a manner."

"Guillaume," I began and then hesitated for a moment and then continued, "Collectif was here."

"Here? Are you sure?"

"Yes, I heard him clearly although I did not see him. He was here."

"I believe you." Guillaume said as he turned and looked into the trees. "Strange things are going on, unexplained things. I cannot help but believe we need to proceed with haste. Come, it has grown too dark to see and you have practiced enough for this day."

Entering Guillaume's chamber I crossed the room to place the net on the table. As soon as I released the net the glow from the Grandite faded. Turning away from the table I watched as Switch approached.

"Feeling better friend?" I asked as I rubbed my hand across his head. When I looked around I noticed that I was alone in the room. Turning I headed down the corridor to the Great Chamber. I could hear Guillaume and Opsis talking as I approached.

"Nothing, there is nothing here." Opsis said his voice filled with disgust. "I have tried everything I know. I can still see nothing myself, and I can get the crystals to show nothing."

Guillaume stood looking at the crystals. The glow proving they were trying to show something. The frozen images preventing that from happening. "There has to be a way to see. Something we have overlooked. Something not thought of, not tried."

"We have tried everything but going out there ourselves and look." Opsis said slamming his fist down hard on the table causing the crystals to rattle together. His frustration and anger overcoming his usual calm. "I know there is something going on. I know that some one is doing some thing that they do not wish us to know about. But what?"

Backing out of the room before I was noticed I made my way back up the corridor. I could try stepping through the ripple to look around, but not being sure where to go that was not an idea that would work. Switch and I could slip out, take a quick look around and come back and report anything we found. All I had to do was make sure Switch was up to it. Entering Guillaume's chamber I crossed the room to where Switch lay stretched out before the fire. As I was checking to see how well he was healing I heard someone enter behind me.

"Planning something?"

I turned to see Opsis watching me. Knowing that it is impossible to lie to a Cyclops I told him the truth. "I thought that since you and Guillaume could not get the crystals to show you anything, that if Switch were up to it he and I would take a quick look around to see if we could see anything."

"No." Guillaume said as he entered the room.

"Guillaume, we would only be gone a short while. I would be very careful and not take any chances."

"Going out there at all would be taking a chance.

236

If anything happens to you now your sisters are doomed."

"Guillaume, hear me out." I began

"Hear me,"Guillaume interrupted, "if you go out there, and you become injured, captured or worse killed, to where you are delayed or prevented in doing, what must be done, your sisters could and most likely will- die. You would have then fulfilled the vow you made before coming out here. Is that what you wish?"

"No, Guillaume, you know it is not."

"Then we will hear no more about you going out there."

"Yes, Guillaume." I turned away to see Opsis watching me. "I'm not going any where." I told him. I couldn't, Guillaume was right and I knew it. Sitting on the floor next to Switch I stared into the fire lost in thought. Collectif was out there somewhere. The Molditians were afraid of Collectif. If we could manage to talk with Collectif some how, get him to understand what was happening and that we needed to know what was going on. But I had no idea how to get in touch with a spirit, trapped, lost or just visiting. Then too there was that thing about me killing him. Because of that I wasn't sure he would want to do anything for me. Thinking that since it was magic that was preventing us from seeing anything, obviously there was someone with who ever or what ever was planning trouble that was strong. Preventing us from seeing was most likely not the only thing they were doing. If they -whoever they are-could be distracted then we could see. But how does one distract someone whose identity they do not know? Turning to where I could rest against Switch's back I still pondered the problems we were facing. I suddenly realized I wasn't seeing the top of Guillaume's chamber but a clear, starlit sky. I could feel the coolness of the wind blowing across my face, not just

my face, but also the dragon's face. The speed I or we
were moving causing the wind to roar in my ears,
blocking other sounds.. What was going on? I was still in
Guillaume's chamber, wasn't I? Was I actually riding this
dragon, my sister? Or was I just seeing what she was?
On we traveled through the night sky, the trees far below
seemed very small. Looking ahead I saw we were
approaching Fire Mountain. The dragon turned as if to
look and make sure I was watching. I must be there in
some form I thought, feeling as if I should laugh at myself,
until I saw what she had brought me out here for. The
entire side of Fire Mountain looked like an encampment
of some sort. Campfires burned everywhere. All manner
of shelters dotted the hillside. It looked like someone had
stirred an anthill setting them into action. Only this was
not ants, this was much more deadly.

Leaving the mountainside the dragon flew
onward. Crossing the lands I could see this was a vast
army that was forming. It was not just Molditians that
were here. I did not know some of these, others I
recognized from descriptions in the tales told around the
castle. The one thing I was sure of, there were thousands
of them spread out through the forest and they were
surrounding the castle. The castle that I had to get my
sisters back to.

"Are you going to sleep there?" Guillaume asked
pushing me with his foot. Turning slowly I looked at him,
blinking rapidly, feeling a little confused. "Well?"
Guillaume asked, "are you going to sleep there?"

Standing I looked from Guillaume to Opsis. "We
have a problem. I have been with my sister the dragon. "

"You have had a dream, you have been here ."
Guillaume said.

"I don't know how she managed it but I *was*

238

with her, somehow. She even looked back at me at one point."

Opsis sat at the table watching me for several moments. "Come and tell us what happened."

Crossing the room to the table I could see the doubt on each of their faces. If I had been in their place, I would probably doubt as well. However after what I had just witnessed, I had to get them to believe me. Taking my seat at the table I was grateful when Guillaume placed a mug of his bitter brew before me.

"Start at the beginning, and tell us everything, leave nothing out." Guillaume instructed as he too sat down.

"I was over by the fire trying to think of ways to find out what was going on. Its obvious that something is, otherwise the crystals would be working. I was even contemplating ways to contact Collectif, and see if he would help us. Even though I was the one that killed him or sent him to what ever level of death he is, I had hopes that he would help my sisters, or at least you Guillaume. I turned and was staring at the ceiling of your chamber when suddenly I was no longer looking at your chamber but the night sky. I remember seeing the stars and feeling the cool air. The wind passing my head deafened me as we were traveling so fast. She took me first to Fire Mountain. The entire hillside was covered with encampments. It isn't just the Molditians. Everywhere you look there are people and creatures, camps and campfires. Weapons are propped in stacks like they do the cornstalks in the fields. Strange beasts the likes I have never seen before wandered among them. At times fighting amongst themselves over a bite of food tossed their way or over some infraction by the offending beast. The fights, all seemed to be to the death, no matter what it was about. That was when she looked back to make sure I was seeing everything. I saw it, and all I could do was stare at what was before me. Thousands were on that mountainside." My hands had gone sweaty at that point and my mouth dry. Taking a swallow of the hot brew I collected my thoughts.

"What happened then? What did you do then?" Opsis asked, the calm in his voice an attempt to cover any apprehension.

"We left there and flew across the forest to the areas around the castle. All through the forest I could see campfires, all around these fires was this army of creatures. We reached the castle and they have it almost fully surrounded. They are not close yet, without magical intervention that will take several days travel on their part, what with everything they are traveling with. But that is where they are moving toward. It was as we made a large circle around the castle that I realized I was back here."

"Young Warrior..." Opsis began but was interrupted

"The boy speaks truth." Collectif's voice, but where was Collectif? I turned searching the room but he was not to be seen.

"The boy speaks truth. The enemy gathers and moves, moves and gathers. Time is short for all." Collectif, dead, alive or somewhere in between, still talked in that sing song voice.

"Collectif.." I began, I had to say I was sorry some how.

"Do not fret, Young Warrior, I was wrong." Collectif's voice seemed to come from everywhere and nowhere. Did I actually hear it? Or simply feel it inside? Collectif continued, "I allowed greed and hunger for things to cloud my mind, turn my thoughts and actions to where they need not have went. You did what you had to do to protect someone special, even though you did not know, nor did I did not know it at the time. If I had, I have the hope that I would have acted differently. As it is, I am here, in the only way I can be, to help. In the hopes of making amends in some manner."

I looked over to Guillaume and Opsis, from their expressions they had heard him as well.

"So, now what?" I asked them. "We have to catch and get my sisters in their snake and dragon forms to the castle. To the very room where they were first transformed, a room that has been repaired and sealed off. On top of that, the castle where we need go, is about to be besieged by an enormous army made of creatures I had thought merely created from the bottom of too many mugs of strong ale."

"You have made that mistake once before Young Warrior." Opsis said looking at me. Reminding me of when I said almost the exact same words to him, about him. I felt the betraying heat creep up my face as I turned away.

"It is obvious that if were merely an army of that size we were up against we would still have problems just with the numbers alone." Guillaume said, the look on his face showing him deep in thought. "Adding to it the fact that there is strong magic in this army only causes me more concern."

"The thing that I am concerned with is getting my sisters back. Then I will worry about this magic army." I said, showing my frustration at the possible interruption of what I knew I needed to do. "I have to save my sisters, otherwise, I don't know if the rest will even matter."

Guillaume sat staring at the table, lost in thought

241

for several moments. Looking to Opsis he seemed to make up his mind on something. "We can do both." he said with new determination.

Opsis watched him for only a moment before asking him, "Are you saying, what I think you are?"

Guillaume shrugged, "It will not be the first time I have ignored a royal command."

I looked from one to the other, "Guillaume, what are you saying?"

"When I was told to leave the castle, I was told to never return and to never use any of my magic any where around it."

Something in his tone and the look on Opsis' face caused me to ask, "And have you obeyed that command?"

Guillaume showed no guilt or remorse when he answered, "Mostly."

Thinking what ever he had done dealt with me I didn't want to know any more. I looked over to the table that held the tools of the change and asked them, "So what is it that we are going to do?"

Guillaume rose and walked over to the table. He picked up the halter and then turned back to me. "We will see if we can get the crystals to work enough to show us when the dragon, your sister, sleeps. When we know that she does, you will use the cloak and taking Sir Switch with you, step through the doorway to her lair. Once there, as quietly as possible you will slip the halter over her head, like so." He then began to show me how the buckles on the halter worked. Making certain that I knew

242

how to get the halter tight enough to hold but not so tight that it would cause injury.

"Are you sure that I still need to do this?" I asked Guillaume, "she did come and get me to show me the gathering army."

Guillaume looked over at me then turning to face me, crossed his arms over his chest. "Do you want to take the chance that she may not always be able to remember who you are? That it could only be a moment by moment memory?"

"I'll use the halter."

Nodding Guillaume reached for the net pulling it across the table. "Once you have the halter on the dragon you can look into any of the crystals on the halter to see if the snake is in her den or if she is outside. Once we know where she is we can then set out for her capture. You can ride Switch to where ever the snake is located, leading the dragon by the reins on the halter. She will follow, that I am sure of."

I watched Guillaume carefully as he spoke. In my heart I knew that I was only going to get one chance at this. If I wanted to bring my sisters back, I had to do this correctly from the beginning.

"When you find the snake it will depend on where she is on how you can use the net. You will have to use your judgment. If she is in an area that has brush or boulders, you may have to get her out into a clearing or attempt to drop the net from above. The lead rope that is on the net, when you throw the net at the snake, will lengthen on its own should you not be able to get close or should she try to escape."

"The net will go after her?" I asked more than a little confused.

"It can go so far, but only so far. If she gets past its

reach, we have lost."

Opsis walked over to stand at the end of the table. "You have to know this. You have to capture and return to the castle with both sisters. It will not work with only one of them, you have to bring them both."

"After I have caught them both and I am on my way to the castle, then what? The wall of the castle was repaired only a short while after the change."

Guillaume picked up the hammer from the table handing it to me. I was surprised at its light weight. I remembered it as being heavier on that first day.

"When you are just outside of the room where the change took place, strike the castle wall one time with the hammer. It will create an opening big enough for you, Switch, the dragon and snake. Once you pass through the opening swing the hammer again and it will close the wall, effectively confining everyone in the chamber."

"And you?" I asked Guillaume.

"Opsis and I will meet you in the chamber. I was told to never return or use my magic around the castle, but nothing was ever done to block me from there."

Taking a deep breath, I looked down at the items in my hands. "When do we begin?" I asked.

"We begin now." Guillaume said as he turned and walked down the corridor to attempt to get the crystals to work.

After Guillaume walked away Opsis and I gathered everything I would need. Packing it all carefully in a large bag we draped it across Switch's back. He did not look happy about it being there. Several times he reached around and tried to use his teeth to remove it from his back.

After moving the bag back in place for the fourth

time I was getting tired of the game. "Do that one more time Switch, and I'm putting a muzzle on you." I learned then that caTragons do not like threats. Reaching around as far as he could he grabbed the bag with his teeth and pulled it from his back, backing away from it he prepared to remind me of his fire breathing capabilities. Stepping between him and the bag I held my hand out. Speaking in as calming a voice as I was capable I talked to Switch. "You know this stuff is to help my sisters. I need it, and I need you to carry it for me, just for a little while. Once we get all of this changing them back stuff out of the way you'll not have to carry anyone or anything ever again if you don't want to."

"You're talking to a caTragon." Opsis said, watching me and fighting a smile.

I paid Opsis no mind as I watched Switch. He finally relented and moved forward for me to return the bag to his back. I could tell he was still uncomfortable about the bag being there yet he allowed it. I knew he was not going to be happy at all about the chain lead and collar I was going to have to place around his neck before we went into the ripple of the Inbetween. While we had practiced with it, and he allowed it, he did not like it. Once the bag was in place we moved down the corridor to find out if Guillaume was able to see anything with the crystals. I carried the sword and shield and kept an eye on Switch while Opsis carried the cloak and boots. As we walked I felt Switch fighting with the bag. He would stop and tug at it, he would even growl and snarl at it, but he didn't remove it again. Entering the Great Chamber we saw Guillaume standing at the table staring into one of the crystals. Moving up quietly we watched as he managed to get the crystal to work from strength of will alone. Sweat broke out on his face, his eyes narrowed with his mouth a thin straight line. His hands trembled as he fought to maintain concentration. For a brief few moments the crystal worked, showing us that the dragon was in her lair and from all appearances if not asleep she was so close to it she would be by the time I got there. Then the image was gone, the crystal was back to the way it had been for the past days. Guillaume closed his eyes and held onto the table while he sought a return of his strength. While we waited Opsis assisted me in getting the cloak on. With the cloak once again folded and tied in place I shifted and moved around trying to get accustomed to the extra weight. Turning I saw Opsis holding the collar for Switch out to me. Taking it from his hands I moved to fasten it around the caTragon's neck. He backed away from me snarling.

"Switch, "I said almost in a hiss myself, "I told you, this is to protect you and make sure we don't get separated in the Inbetween. Once we are out of it, this comes off." Switch still backed away from the collar, his eyes taking on a red cast, the smoke slipping more heavily from his nostrils. "If you do not do this for me and my sisters Switch, I will find myself a new caTragon friend." I turned away from him as if to go off in search of another caTragon. "Guillaume should have attached Grandite to this also." I muttered as I moved away.

Seeing my actions Switch moved to my side and leaned against me heavily. As he did I fastened the collar with the chain lead attached around his neck. Switch slowly shook his head a time or two and then was still.

Opening his eyes Guillaume looked to me, "Are you ready?"

"I am."

"Then lets begin. Focus on the dragon's lair. See it in your mind, hear the sounds of the dragon, smell the dragon, her sulfur and smoke. Concentrate. See the door, keep your eyes on the door, as it opens into the dragon's lair, step inside and get your sister. Go in grace Young Warrior, go in grace." Guillaume fell silent as I slipped into an almost suspended state as my mind focused on the dragon and the dragon only. I saw the ripple beginning to move, starting directly before me and then traveling outward. Inside the ripple was a door opening slowly. Once it was open far enough I saw the dragon's lair. Tightening my grip on Switch's lead I stepped into the ripple. As soon as I was inside the ripple I felt the weight change. Everything was heavier, it seemed as if I moved slower. I stared at the door before me. The words 'concentrate, focus' repeating over and over in my mind. Suddenly Switch stopped and jerked the lead from my grasp. I reached for it but it was gone. Turning I looked for Switch, he stood a few feet away fighting and pulling at the bag. Reaching out I grabbed him and turned back. The door was no longer there.

"No." Just a whisper, that was all I could manage. I stood rooted to the same spot where I originally stopped . The same place where Switch had pulled from me causing me to turn away from the door. Just for a moment, but that moment was all it had taken. My concentration had been broken, now the door was gone. Turning my head only, I looked to my left . For as far as I could see there was nothing but a misty gray color. It acted as a fog would, shifting and moving, almost dancing in some unseen wind to some unheard music. Turning I looked into the mist on my right, trying to see something. All I saw was the same as what was on the left. A never ending shade of gray, stretching out into forever. Looking down I watched as it swirled around my feet. Despair seeped into my soul, dragging at my spirit. I had failed. I was trapped here in this place, doomed forever to wander but get nowhere. Guillaume had warned me, repeatedly, not to look away.

"Now what Switch?" I asked the beast, "now what?" Switch stood silently by my side, seeming to know that something wasn't right. "I'm forgetting something. I've seen something, heard something I'm forgetting. What IS it? Something that if I could only remember..." I searched my memory, trying to recall the elusive knowledge that was teasing me. Taunting me just outside conscious thought.

Time moved slowly as I struggled. The gray mist growing thicker the longer I stood still. A cold feeling crept up my legs into my very being. Shivering I pulled the cloak around me tighter, this time thankful that my sisters didn't know anything about measurements and cutting to size. The cloak's extra weight helped to hold off the cold.

"How could I have been so stupid?" my anger at my own mistake grew. "It was a simple task, step into the ripple of the Inbetween and through the door on the other side. Watch the door, focus on the door. It was simple. How could I have messed it up so easily?" Switch shifted by my side, pushing against me as if trying to comfort me. I wanted none of it, shoving him away from me into the mist. When he stumbled and almost disappeared into the swirling mass I grabbed the chain and pulled him back to my side. The bag on his back had pulled slightly open, allowing me to see that the Grandite stones inside were all glowing. Looking down at the sword and shield the stones set in them also glowed. Lifting the sword up to where I could see the stone and crystals I watched as a ripple began in one crystal and moved, spreading outward. As I watched I remembered Guillaume's many tests and lessons. More than once he and Collectif moved about causing the ripple to flow. But how? As I stood staring at the stones they continued to glow brighter by the moment. The mists surrounding me took on a purple hue as it settled down around my feet. As the mist settled so did my emotions. Calmed of my anger, I realized that a feeling was there that was stronger than the anger. I tried to separate it from the confusion but could not. Despair threatened to drown me. Pulling the cloak tighter I thought of my sisters. "I tried, I tried," I whispered into the cloak. Suddenly, gently everywhere that the cloak touched I felt an energy, much like I had felt the time I had been close to a lightning strike. The hair on my arms and the back of my neck stood as a tingle ran through me. A roar filled my ears, while a much gentler sound filled my heart.

"Brother?" a whisper. Startled I did not respond. "Brother, can you hear me?"

"I can hear you." I whispered, barely able to breathe. Trembling at the sound and feelings.

"Brother, help me."

"I tried, but I am lost here."

"Brother, follow your heart."

"My heart breaks because I failed you."

"You have not failed, brother. Follow your heart."

"How? Do you know how to get out of here?"

"Follow your heart, Brother, follow your heart."

The feelings faded away slowly, lingering in my chest. "Follow my heart." I whispered. Clutching the cloak to my chest I didn't know whether to scream out my frustrations of give in to tears.

"You will fail if you do not stop this." I was talking aloud to myself again. Taking a deep breath I slowly exhaled. Holding the sword up again I looked into the crystals. The ripple was still there. Concentrating I slowly,

249

methodically cleared all thoughts out of my mind. Opening my mind's eye I looked around me. The mists had ceased to swirl, leaving me standing in an open area. Concentrating I waited, focused on the dragon.

"Brother."

Hearing the whisper I took one step forward. "You are my family, you are my heart," I whispered, "speak to me, help me get to you. Guillaume said you have magic, use it to help me if you can."

"You have the greatest magic about you, Brother. Follow your heart."

"What do you mean?" I asked, but was greeted by silence. I have the greatest magic? Somehow it seemed that all I had about me at the moment was questions and no answers.

Frustrated my sarcasm slipped free, "I just love th..." I closed my eyes and shook my head slowly from side to side. Love. Even Guillaume had said that love was the greatest magic. Wrapping the cloak tightly around me I concentrated. Focused on one thought only, my sister. In my mind I saw her, not as the dragon but as herself. She was smiling and motioning for me. Tightening my grip on Switch's lead I took a step forward, then another. Just to the right of where I was a door began to open, slowly. The crack around the opening growing with each step. I watched the door with my physical eyes, but with my mind's eye, I watched my sister. Stepping through the door I found myself in the dragon's lair. The dragon lay against a far wall of the lair sleeping. Wanting to stop and rest, wanting to get my emotions and muscles back under control I knew I did not have the time. I had to get the halter on the dragon. On the inside she was my sister, on the outside she was still a dragon. Reaching into the bag I slowly withdrew the halter.

Walking slowly and carefully across the lair I watched the dragon. Dragons are supposed to have very good hearing, I had to be silent in my approach. Holding the halter close to my chest, wrapped around my hand to keep it from making any noise, I moved forward. Step by agonizing step I approached. Fearing that at any moment I was going to make a noise to awaken her. Fearing that I may die in this attempt to save her. My palms were sweating and I fought the tremble that was beginning in my hands. How could someone that I remembered being so small, now be this big? I was within feet of the dragon when I stumbled over something on the floor of the lair. The halter in my hand slipped, tumbling untangled toward the floor. The noise was slight, but it was there. I looked up as the dragon raised her head and turned to look at me. Not taking any chances I lunged forward. Slipping the halter over the slightly sluggish dragon the Grandite glowed brightly as I tightened the first buckle. Even with the Grandite she struggled. Backing away from me she swung her head from side to side, trying to dislodge this unwanted thing I had placed on her. I had only gotten one buckle tightened, I held my breath and prayed it would hold as she attempted to remove it. I looked to see that Switch had moved away from the dragon and was watching its attempts for freedom closely. The close confines of the lair kept her from being able to stand or to spread her wings. Instead it was posturing and shaking, standing only as tall as the lair would allow as she tried any way possible to remove the offending object..

"I thought she was weak." I grumbled to myself as she continued to fight. When it appeared that this battle of wild beast against controlling halter was going to go on for a while I knew I had to try and end it. Hugging the sides of the lair I approached the struggling dragon. My recent misstep in the Inbetween left me leery of attempting to use that to get closer. Because of that I moved slowly along the wall, doing all I could to not draw the attention of the very angry dragon before me. A dragon so involved in her attempts to dislodge the thing on her head she did not see me until I was beside her. Moving swiftly away from the wall I reached for the flailing sections of halter. Slipping the end into the buckle I held tightly as she lifted me off the floor. I did not look to see how far up I was as I tightened the last buckle. Once it was done the last of the Grandite began to glow brighter. Letting go I dropped to the floor and backing away quickly watched my sister -the dragon- before me. Unable to roar thanks to the halter she shook her head a final time before turning to glare at me. Her great tale swinging around as if in a last movement of defiance.

"Forgive me, it is necessary" I told her as I reached for the reign attached to the halter. "We must now find Delwen, and time, grows short."

Holding tightly onto the reigns I stood watching the dragon, wondering if she would actually allow herself to be lead around. I looked as well as I could, to see if all of the Grandite stones were glowing. When I saw that they along with the crystals were glowing brightly I turned and started across the lair. The dragon followed as docile as a tame cat. I didn't rush it though and slowly lead the dragon over to where Switch stood waiting. The dragon and the caTragon watched each other warily for several long moments. While they stared at each other deciding whether or not they could trust each other and just who was in charge, I took advantage of the dragon's distraction and moved to where I could see the crystals embedded in the halter. Not a single crystal showed an image, they each glowed, but I could see nothing in them. I thought that maybe if we got outside of the lair the crystals would work. I hoped that they would. Moving again I lead dragon and caTragon outside.

As we stood in the entrance to the lair I again looked at the crystals. Each and every one glowed, but they were clear of image. I moved away from the dragon and stood looking out across the area before me. She could be anywhere and I had no idea how to find her. With the crystals blackened out as they were, it looked as if I were doomed to fail. Propping my foot up on a boulder I rested my arms on my leg. The hilt of the sword was pushing into my side in this position. When I tried to move it over it didn't help. Sliding it out of the sheath I gently placed the point of the sword on the ground and let it lean back against my knee. Resting my arms back on my knee I looked out across the area. As my gaze came across in front of me I noticed something different about the sword. The crystals encircling the Grandite stone glowed as did all the crystals, but their glow was not as bright. The Grandite itself was glowing, but the glow was fading. As I watched the Grandite's purple color cleared to where I could see into it as I could the crystals. The sword grew warm to the touch, as I held it I felt a vibration begin. It felt as if the sword was struggling to break free of my grasp. Curious I removed my foot from the boulder and lay the sword flat across the boulder's top. It lay still but for the vibration. Retrieving the sword I sat down on the stone and propped the sword in front of me. Leaning forward Guillaume's cloak fell across my shoulders and over my legs. Only my lower arms remained bare. Resting my head against the sword I exhaled deeply, frustrated yet again. I felt my head brush against the Grandite, while the sword was warm, the stone was cool to the touch. Closing my eyes my

253

body threatened to give in to the exhaustion it felt. As I let my thoughts drift, thinking of and rejecting possible solutions I felt the energy from the sword flowing into my arms. As the energy flowed upward I began to feel better, ready to try again and to keep trying. But how, what could I do now? As I sat there with my eyes closed all I saw in my mind was dark. It was restful, peaceful and quiet here. I thought I would rest here for just a moment. Suddenly out of the dark appeared a giant yellowish eye. In it was the expression of anger, a hatred so fierce and strong that I backed mentally away. Turning slowly the snake struck without warning. 'Show me where you are." I thought over and over, "show me where you are."

The snake moved through her tunnel, traveling away from me. As she slid through she picked up speed as if to try and leave me somewhere far behind her. "I'm trying to help you," I thought desperately. "Help me to help you. Show me where you are."

From the pitch solid black of the hole she burst forth out of the ground and moved across a field at an amazing speed. I stayed with her, angering her even more. As I followed her I searched desperately for a sign as to where she was. I looked every where and every way that I could for some sort of landmark to help me. Finally beginning to slow in my mind I hesitated, stayed back a short way, waiting to see what she would do. The snake turned to search for me. She knew I was close, she did not know how close and that bothered her. Looking for me she rose up and searched the field behind her. Standing half as high as the trees she was an intimidating figure. As she searched the area I slipped into her head and saw what she was seeing. I knew this place, and while it wasn't as close as I would have liked, it wasn't that far away either.

"Switch," I stood and called the caTragon over to me, "I know where she is, lets go." Climbing onto Switch's back I wrapped the lead for the dragon around my hand. As Switch left the ground, so did the dragon. Amazingly she didn't fight, she stayed right with us. What ever the reason, she followed so readily, I wasn't complaining.

"Switch, she is in the Field of the Golden Crystals. We need to hurry." Holding onto Switch's mane I leaned forward and watched the world pass as we made our way to her.

SIXTEEN

Fearing that she may have left the field in an attempt to hide I watched the ground below me for the snake that was my sister. At her great size it would be difficult for her to hide unless she went back underground. That was the last thing I wanted but for now all I could do was search, and pray she stayed above ground. Switch carried me the fastest route to the field, but it was still a long distance to travel, even by air.

At one point I felt more than heard Switch growling and snarling. Looking over in the direction he was watching I saw an encampment of the army advancing on the castle. Pulling my legs up tighter to my body I leaned down closer across Switch's back in the hopes that should anyone look up all that would see was a caTragon being chased by a dragon. From the position I was in I could see parts of the army as we passed. No one paid the passing creatures any attention. Letting out a breath I didn't realize I had been holding I sat up and looked behind us. There looked to be several hundred assorted creatures in this group.

"That's so strange," I told Switch, "I didn't think that all of these creatures could tolerate each other. I thought that several of those were sworn enemies. Yet, there they are together." Turning back to watch where we were going I resumed watching for the snake. The trees below passed by in a green spotted blur such was the speed of my caTragon. Suddenly the dragon pulled back on the lead nearly pulling me from Switch's back. Grabbing his mane and managing to get safely back in place I turned to look back. She was pulling backward, fighting the lead when before she had followed so well.

"Go back Switch."

Turning the caTragon went back. As we returned the dragon then began to lead us. Flying over a grouping of trees we crossed the river and then began flying up along the side of a mountain. Boulders and scrub brush passed so quickly it was near impossible to tell what they were. As we went over the top, spread out before us was a large, almost desert area. Slowing down as to be almost stopped she looked to me. I sat staring out across the ground before me. There had to be dozens of snakes, dozens of giant snakes slithering their way back and forth across the field. Each and every one of them looked exactly alike.

Looking out across the field of snakes I knew with everything I was, that only one of them was real. The problem, was deciding which one. "Guillaume said I'm only going to have one chance at this. She knows that and has decided to play this game. But why? Why delay changing back? I know she isn't happy this way. I simply do not understand." Switch's ears moved to the sound of my voice, but he too was watching the scene before us. As I watched the snakes I remembered my battle with the Molditians. When I had created the rain army Each one of the fighters in that army had looked like me, had my sister done something similar here? As I watched I saw that my thoughts of the snakes moving back and forth across the field were wrong. They all were moving in the same direction, they went to the left or right or even doubled back as one. There was just so many it looked as if they were moving independently. Shoving Guillaume's cloak back out of my way I reached into the bag for the net. I still did not know which was the right snake, but I wanted to be ready. When my hand grasped the net I tried to pull it from the bag but it wouldn't slide out. Pulling and tugging did no good, it would not move. Twisting to the side so I could grasp the bag to drag it around I noticed the dragon quietly fighting against the halter again. It was also acting so very strangely. Something just wasn't right. Using my knees I tried to maneuver Switch over closer to the dragon. The dragon kept backing away. Taking a tight hold on the lead I pulled hard, the dragon caught unaware was pulled very close to where I was. With the lead still wrapped around my hand and arm I reached for the halter to check the buckles. I needed to make sure they were tight. Just as I took hold of the halter the dragon opened her wings and with one motion pulled backward, pulling me off of Switch's back. Falling the length of the lead I was jerked to a stop when I reached the end. Hanging there in the sky I looked for the caTragon. He was nowhere to be seen. How far had the dragon managed to move with just that one motion of her great wings? When she started fighting the halter in earnest all I could do was hold on and pray she tired quickly- and that she didn't get the halter to come off.

I held on with everything that I had as the dragon fought with everything it had. I had come to the conclusion that her memory was there in an on again off again way. Just as Guillaume had suggested. At the moment, she was all dragon and she was determined to get free. The one thing I was glad of was that the way the halter fit she couldn't open her mouth far enough to use that fiery breath of hers. Her movements were at times jerky, making me dance and swing on the end of that chain lead. I could feel the metal digging into my skin but if I wanted to live, I just had to bear it the best I could, ignoring what pain I could. When the blood began to run down my arm from the cuts I began to wonder how much longer I could take this. With a twist and a jerk of her head I was sent sailing through the air again just to fall downward to the end of the chain. Over and over again she did this. Over and over she would fly straight to suddenly turn causing me to move erratically in the air. She started flying straight toward the mountain. As I swung at the end of the chain I could see the mountainside growing closer. I could also see the boulders and trees just waiting for me. As we approached in that wild erratic flight, in an act of desperation I moved the shield around before me in vain hopes of protection from the trees. I watched amazed as instead of crashing into and being pulled painfully through the branches the limbs actually slowed, then slid away beneath the shield. My relief was short lived. The pain I was feeling was fast becoming more than I could tolerate and I almost welcomed the thought of the boulders when she started to slow down in her flight. The farther she flew, the slower she flew until she finally, simply, stopped. With all of her strength gone she quietly folded her wings against her body and slowly dropped from the sky. I managed to crawl out from under her and away before she settled onto the ground. Laying flat on her belly with her head drooping she fought to drag in enough oxygen. I wasn't about to loosen the halter after what had just happened, but I decided to just wait it out until she was breathing normally again. While I waited I watched for Switch. I had hoped that he would have found us by now. The reasons he had not found us could be that we disappeared so quickly he didn't see the direction in which we went. It was possible that who ever was blocking the crystals could be somehow preventing him from sensing where we were. Or the one I didn't like was that something or someone was preventing him from coming. Standing I walked over to the dragon and again tried to use the crystals on the halter to find Switch. As before they glowed, but were clear of any sort of image.

I stood near the dragon looking around. Nothing here looked familiar at all. After all of that sky dancing I had completely lost sight of where we were. Looking to the sky I spoke in a barely audible voice, "Come on Switch, I need you to find me here."

Turning in slow circles I watched the sky while trying to come up with a plan. At the moment, all I had to work with was an exhausted dragon, a pouch full of Grandite pebbles, a borrowed crimson cloak and hope for a miracle. Change that, an over sized borrowed crimson cloak. Untying the laces on the cloak to loosen it somewhat I unfolded it to its full length and then tightened the laces back. Taking the extra fabric I stretched it across a nearby boulder. Looking back over my shoulder at the dragon she appeared to doze. Opening the pouch I poured the pebbles onto the cloak. One by one I lined them up in a pattern that formed a directional arrow. The arrow pointed toward the dragon and me. Sitting cross legged in front of the arrow I concentrated on Switch. Trying to find him with my mind's eye I scanned the countryside. The ache in my arm causing concentrating to be difficult but I finally began to focus away from the pain and onto the caTragon. If I could just see him, I knew I could get him to come to us.

Staring at the stones on Guillaume's cloak I was growing frustrated that nothing seemed to be working. Guillaume's words came back to me, "Some times, magic works against magic.." Maybe, that is the problem, I thought as I gathered up all of the pebbles and them pulled the cloak from the stone. Taking the pebbles and placing them one at a time back on the boulder I watched as they finally came to life. This time, following the leading of something from deep inside, carefully placing them side by side forming a large circle. Once the last stone was in place completing the circle the glow began to grow brighter, spreading inward until the entire inside of the circle glowed in that deep purple hue. Resting my hands on either side of the circle I began. Concentrating on Switch I watched as the colors swirled inside the circle. Starting out a deep, dark purple that with each swirling wave began to grow lighter. Once it reached the shade where there was barely any color at all I could then begin to see images. It was working, this was not blocked as the crystals were.

Excited I watched as what had once been a field full of snakes appeared. It was now empty, the only thing there were a few shrubs and a boulder or two. I watched as the image did not change. After several moments of nothing, out of a guessed desperation I moved my right hand, the image moved in that direction. Now that I knew what to do I set to work. I began searching where we were when the dragon attempted to escape and dragged me off of Switch's back in the process. After searching the field from every direction I began to search the surrounding area. There was no sign of the snake or of Switch. When the dragon made a noise I turned to look, as I did I moved both of my hands off of the stone. When I looked back I wasn't sure what I was seeing at first. After several moments of watching I realized I was looking at the sky. Leaving my hands away from the boulder I was still able to use them to maneuver the images in the circle. Moving slowly back in the direction of the field I thought I saw something in the distance. It was moving so swiftly, I feared with my inexperience in this that it was going to be difficult to catch the image clearly. Stilling my hands, I stopped the circle from moving and watched what approached my view. It was Switch and he was looking for me and the dragon. I sat watching Switch and wondered how I was going to let him know where we were. With him moving as he was, it was impossible to use the doorway of the ripple. Getting trapped once was more than I wanted to happen I wasn't trying again. Not this way anyway. As he passed the place where his image was the most clear I noticed that the bag was still secured to his back but the top was open from where I had tried to remove the net. This allowed me to see that the Grandite stones around the net were glowing brightly.

"I'm not sure if this will work or not, but it can't hurt to try." I said more to make myself feel better than anything else. Slowly and carefully so as not to damage the circle I placed my hands to where they touched as many as possible of the pebbles along the ring of Grandite. The moment I made contact the glow brightened growing darker. I could feel the energy from the stones in my hands and moving up my arms. The last image I was able to see was of Switch, he had stopped moving and appeared to be looking directly at me.

Leaving my hands where they were I stared at the circle. I could no longer see anything other than the swirling purple hues but I trusted it to bring Switch to where I waited. For what seemed like hours I remained where I was, even when the position I was in had my body aching. I longed to sit upright or even stand, but I ignored the feeling as best I could and waited. The energy feeling had reached my shoulders, still, my arms trembled from the strain of holding the uncomfortable position. My legs were beginning to feel numb as the circulation had ceased to flow. Just as it seemed I couldn't hold out any longer I heard a familiar roar. Looking up I watched as Switch made his way to where I knelt at a speed I didn't know he possessed. Standing I waited.

I watched him as he landed right in front of me. Pushing his massive head into my chest I grabbed his mane. "Oh yes, I'm glad to see you as well. Now that we have found each other, let us see if we can find one very large and ornery snake."

Moving back to the boulder I again sat in front of the circle. Carefully I again placed my hands in a way that my fingers barely touched the stones. The Grandite once again began to glow. I carefully searched the field working my way in the direction of Fire Mountain. There was a feeling drawing me in that direction, having learned to pay attention to those feelings I followed them now. When the image left the grass of the field moving onto the sandy, rock strewn landscape I saw it. "That trail can only have been made by one very large snake. As the Fate's would have it, we are looking for one very large snake. This one, is headed for Fire Mountain. After seeing the way you were flying Switch, I trust that you can get us there first."

Securing Guillaume's cloak once again I gathered up the Grandite pebbles and returned them to their pouch. Climbing carefully onto Switch's back I noticed something I had not noticed before. I was not wearing Guillaume's boots. In the haste to depart and begin the rescue of my sisters I had forgotten to change into them. Searching the bag I found them hidden under the net. Quickly I changed boots hoping that they would keep me safely and securely on Switch's back. Shoving my own boots into the bag under the net I signaled to Switch that I was ready. "Let's go Switch, we have a snake to catch."

As Switch made ready to take flight I wondered how the dragon was going to react to my tugging on the lead chain. Knowing I couldn't put it off and it was better to find out while on the ground I pulled steadily on the chain until I could see it moving against the dragon's neck. Carefully tugging on it enough to wake her I waited and watched warily. Opening her eyes she looked at me. In that one look I saw several different emotions. Fear and sadness yes, but for the briefest of moments, there was trust. "I'll get you back my sister," I told her, "I'll get you back." Turning back around I patted Switch on the neck, "let's go." Taking to the sky the dragon followed better than I thought she would. Together we headed for Fire Mountain and sister snake.

I had kept a fist size crystal out of the bag and held it carefully. Once we got close I planned on trying to use it to help find the snake. At this point I had no idea how hard she was going to try to hide from me. I could only hope that this crystal would not be frozen out here as they have been elsewhere. Switch was traveling swiftly across the sky, I was beginning to believe that we would actually get there first. As I held onto his mane I noticed the familiar glow in my hand and felt the crystal growing warm. Opening my fingers enough to see I watched surprised and over joyed as an image of the snake appeared. She was stopped, coiled up in the shade of a large grouping of trees. It was obvious though that she was not asleep as her head turned continuously, her tongue flickering in and out without stopping. As I watched the image moved, crossing the open area to the side of Fire Mountain. There, a few yards up from the base of the mountain was one of the snake's many hideaways. How was I going to keep her from getting back inside there, making it all but impossible to catch her? Leaning forward I rested on Switch's neck as we traveled, trying to think of a way to keep her out. "Or," I thought out loud, "we could allow her to enter her den thinking she had escaped us when in fact we have used her own little game against her. Hurry Switch, we really need to get there first, and without her seeing us."

At the touch of my hand Switch changed his direction and we moved in a wide arch around where the snake rested. The dragon was co-operating so well I had to keep looking to make certain she was still with me.

I watched as Fire Mountain rose up out of the flat lands around it. The sides of the mountain were harsh and hard. Covered in boulders, and not much else, you could see the air around the mountain shimmering in the heat. As Switch got closer to the snake's den I managed to pull the net from the bag while struggling with my wounded arm. Carefully I lowered the net to the point directly over the opening. Closing my eyes and concentrating hard I repeated my thoughts over and over, if I could somehow get the torches back in the Great Chamber to dance, surely I could do this. Mentally I watched as the air before me began to shimmer and ripple. Then several feet in front of the side of the mountain an image replicating the mountainside formed, effectively hiding us and the net. The net itself became shaped in the form of the snake's hole. All we needed to do, was wait.

As time passed my already tired and weakened

body was showing signs of exhaustion. I fought to hold onto the concentration needed to keep the image up. The heat from the mountain left me feeling even more drained with each passing moment. Just when I was about to succumb to the heat and exhaustion Switch moved jolting me back to reality. I watched as the snake made her way toward us. She was still cautious, watching in every direction. I waited, holding the lead line and my breath. As she approached she seemed to sense something was wrong. Stopping less than a foot from the image she looked at the hole in front of her. Forcing myself to concentrate on keeping the fake mountain image up and net looking like her hole, I watched her. After what felt like an eternity she began to slide through the image into what she thought was safety. As soon as most of her body was through I jerked hard on the lead rope closing the net around her.

I thought my battle with the dragon was hard. As long as any of the snake was outside the net she fought. Thrashing and twisting around inside the net she made it almost impossible to hold onto. The net held tightly to the snake not allowing any of her that was inside to slip free. All she could do in her attempts, was pull more of herself inside hoping to overcome the net and me. Instead, as the last of the snake slipped into the net the Grandite stones came together and began to work their magic in calming her down. Once the net was completely still and the snake calm, Switch moved down and grasped the net with his teeth. Watching him lift the net I could only think of how the powerful magic of love can give one great strength indeed. Turning he spread his wings out and with a single move rose into the sky.

"To the castle Switch," I said looking from snake to dragon back to caTragon, "let's go home."

266

SEVENTEEN

Switch wasted no time in turning toward the castle. While my sister the snake was at the moment somewhat calm, I worried that as large as she was the stones may not have the strength to last the entire way. My sister the dragon was also, for the moment docile, flying along almost at my side, allowing herself to be lead. It was going too easily. I kept telling myself we just needed to make it to the castle, that was the important thing. To get to the castle.

I fought to ignore the pain in my arm from the many cuts and bruises caused by my hanging from the chain, even as it grew in intensity as we traveled. I could feel the throbbing in my wrist, pulsating, pumping my blood out the many cuts. My hand was sticky from the amount lost. I wanted to unwrap the chain from around my arm and hand, to try and wrap a bandage of some sort around it in an attempt to stop the flow of blood. I did not as I could not take the chance that the dragon would see it as as opportunity for an escape attempt and try to take it. I forced myself to watch the landscape passing rather than see the damage done to my arm. It was bad enough I could feel the blood flowing out, I did not need to see how bad the damage actually was..

Looking over Switch's shoulder I looked down at the snake. Her eyes were almost fully closed, leaving only small slits open. This gave her an almost evil, plotting look. That worried me. I could see that the net was pulled tightly closed, the Grandite stones all coming together to form a seal over the opening. The glow from the stones was still strong and dark assuring they would hold, for now.

Allowing myself to lay forward I rested on the caTragon's strong neck. Weary to the bone I allowed my eyes to close as I pulled my arm in close to my chest. Tightening my grip on the chain causing pain to burn stronger keeping me from sleeping. I knew, I had to stay alert, even though I was so very tired. Below us the landscape passed quickly, changing moment to moment. Trees, fields and rivers blurred together, becoming a mass of greens and browns. My arm ached unbearably, growing heavier by the moment. I fought to stay awake and to keep my arm held up against my chest. Sleep threatened to take me as we traveled. I could feel a dampness against my chest, I knew that it had to be my own blood seeping through my clothing, I was losing so much, and yet, I could not stop. We were too close to being there. I would get my sisters to the castle and pray that Guillaume and Opsis was there. Pray that they could do something to change them back. Weakness was overtaking me as I tried to focus, tried to concentrate on getting to the castle. I could not get my mind to stay on one thought, it flipped as the pages in a book in the wind. Images passed through, memories of good times. Things I had forgotten for so long. Opsis teaching me manners, I was barely able to climb up to the table by myself, but he insisted I did it properly. "You are a prince, someday you will be king, you need to know how to act." Opsis preventing Guillaume from taking Switch away from me. "He will do well with this creature, leave him be with it. Look, watch them together, they are a kindred soul." I remembered asking Opsis later what kindred soul meant. He had told me that it meant we understood each other in a special way, that we had a connection with each other that was rare and one that should be allowed to grow, that some day, it could be important. I heard Guillaume's voice, "You are stronger than your weakness." I had fallen on the castle steps. The stones had scraped my knees and blood was flowing down my legs. "Think beyond the pain. Your strength lies in your will." Giggles, I was hearing the giggles that had haunted me for so long. "I win, you lose."We were playing a game, I don't remember what, it was among the many games they loved to beat me at. "Will you play again with us brother? Or will you and your dreams of knighthood give up?give up, give up?" "Where are you son?" my father called for me. I was hiding in the lowest room in the castle, as far away from everyone as I could get. It was right after the change. I was afraid, I was crying over what I had witnessed and I didn't want anyone to see. I felt then, I should have done something. I should have stayed, I should have grabbed the book, I should have ran faster. I watched as I slid back further into the darkness and hid from my own father.

"Where are you, son? I know you are here. Come out of the dark and face this. Together we will overcome what has happened." He called me something else, what was it? I heard, but couldn't understand. I refused to answer to that.

"My name, is Adwr." I remembered telling him that from the dark corner where I was crouched. "I am a coward. I did not try to stop them, instead I ran away."

"You ran for help, you did the right thing."

"My name, is Adwr."

"Come out of the darkness my son, we will fight this as a family."

I saw myself crawling out of the dark corner. I felt my father pull me close. There were tears in his eyes as well. We didn't fight though, we gave in to despair and the rooms were sealed away. Memories were just fleeting thoughts, and then they too disappeared. Only the heart remembered, longed for and never gave up on possibility. "You are stronger than your weakness."Guillaume's voice. But the darkness was pulling me, sleep was dragging me under.

"What are you doing? Young Warrior? Do you hear me? Warrior! Hear me. I am asking of you just what it is that you are doing."

"Go away Collectif, I need to rest."

"This rest you do not need. Open your eyes Warrior, or you will open them no more."

"I'm tired Collectif, I'm tired and I wish to rest."

"What of your sisters?"

"I will take care of them once I've rested."

"You can rest later."

"Collectif, I thought you were dead, how are you here? Why are you not acting dead?"

"How does one act dead Warrior?"

"Collectif, GO AWAY"

"No, not going. Your sisters need you, Guillaume needs you, family need you..I'm not going. Not going away, not acting dead..Open your eyes Warrior."

"Collectif, I'm sorry."

"Be sorry later, be alive now. Open your eyes Warrior or you will force me to act. I will. I will act and you will open your eyes. I do not wish to, but I will."

"Collectif, just go away. Act later after I have rested."

"As you wish Young Warrior, as you wish."

Silence, a peaceful, quiet silence. I felt as if I were floating along, drifting to somewhere. There was no pain, there was no sound. Just the feeling of floating. The darkness was a soft bluish gray, not black like I would have thought. I felt as I had that night so long ago, floating on a raft on the lake near the castle. It wasn't moving anywhere, just floating. That was how I felt now, just floating in this soft darkness, going nowhere. It was a subtle change at first, like a small bump in the road. An action easy to ignore. Then there was another, instead of floating I was now rocking. I did not open my eyes, I allowed the rocking to carry me, moving with it. There was a peace here that I had not felt in a long while. It called to me, tempting me to simply let go. I felt myself giving in to the release of self as I knew it.

Then without warning the darkness was shattered by brilliant flashes of light brought on by the unbearable pain in my arm. Sucking in air fighting the urge to scream in the agony I opened my eyes to see the dragon fighting the halter, jerking hard on the chain, still wrapped around my arm. She appeared to be trying to back away from something unseen by me. She fought frantically, bucking and kicking against the halter and what ever was there frightening her.

"Collectif!" I shouted weakly into the air. "You win! My eyes are opened. I am awake! Leave the dragon alone, please I beg you stop this!"

After a few moments of searching the air around her the dragon calmed. She stopped fighting, desperately trying to get away from what ever was in the air frightening her. Once again she allowed herself to be lead, moving closer to me and the caTragon. I looked down at the snake, she was moving, but slowly. The stones were still glowing, but not as darkly. We were running out of time. I searched the landscape around me, trying to place where we were. Crossing over the top of

yet another hill, lands I recognized spread out before me.
I could see it in the distance, my heart jumped in its
excitement. It was growing late in the day, the sun on the
edge of setting below the horizon. Its last fire red rays
caught the moat and sent reflected light all along the
walls of the castle.   We were almost home. So intent was
I on watching the castle I missed what I should have
seen. I watched the castle growing ever larger as we
approached. The sun slipped silently below the horizon
and the last of its rays faded. I watched for the first lights
to show inside the castle but there were none. What I did
see were campfires flaring to greater life all around the
castle. Hundreds upon hundreds of campfires burned
openly. The castle was fully encircled by the enemy army.

"The castle is under siege Switch. It looks as if they
are trying to starve them out." I watched the ground
below me carefully, hoping and praying we weren't seen
as we flew past.   "Be silent Switch, be silent." I
mumbled, my fear of being seen growing. Looking down
at the net Switch carried I saw that the Grandite stones
were slowly growing dim. The difficulty in containing and
quieting the giant snake using up their magic swiftly. The
snake was beginning to move about more. Not now, I
thought, not now.

Using my free arm and knees I managed to get
Switch to understand where I wanted him to go. Silently
as possible we moved around to the far side of the castle.
After all of this time I could still see where the wall had
been repaired. The location appearing as a scar from a
wound would on a body. Nudging Switch with my knees I
reached into the bag and pulled out the hammer
Guillaume had provided just for this. The caTragon
moved up as close to the wall as possible and still allow
me room to swing. My sister the snake began to move

272

and struggle even more inside the net. When I looked I saw that the Grandite stones were barely glowing now. I had to hurry. Holding onto the hammer as tightly as my weakened state allowed I drew back my good arm making ready. In a wide arch I brought it back around swiftly, striking the wall a solid blow.

In a silent yet brilliant explosion of light a large section of the wall vanished leaving a hole large enough for all of us to get through. Grateful that in the silence there was nothing to alert those around the castle of our presence. No stones fell into the moat below, nothing crashed into or from the castle, with one blow, there was simply a hole created for us to enter. Switch slipped easily through this hole and after placing the net holding the snake on the floor landed silently beside it. Slipping from his back I pulled the lead steadily. Staggering somewhat from loss of blood my determination was back. The dragon would come all the way up to the hole in the wall but refuse to enter. Fighting hard she was dragging me toward the hole in an attempt to pull me from the room and escape back across the forest. Just as my feet touched the outside wall another pair of hands grabbed the lead and began to help me pull.

"Its about time you arrived." I told Guillaume as we managed to pull the dragon up close to the wall.

Once the dragon was close enough Guillaume reached out and grabbed hold of the halter. Once his hands closed around the halter, his fingers brushing against the dragon's head she calmed instantly.

"Yes, there you are." Guillaume spoke soothingly to the dragon. "I've been waiting for you here." Quietly he continued to speak to her as he gently pulled her toward the opening. After much coaxing and gentle words she passed through the opening that was barely large enough for her. I had succeeded in what I had set out to do, they were both back in the room where it all began.

With a simple wave of his hand, Guillaume signaled for me to again swing the hammer and close the hole in the wall , sealing us all inside the room.

While Guillaume calmed the dragon Opsis moved to my side. He carefully unwrapped the chain from my arm as I simply stood watching. When the chain was completely unwrapped Opsis lead me over to a basin of water and carefully rinsed the blood from my arm. I watched feeling almost detached from the scene. The only thoughts going through my mind at the moment was that I had made it. I had brought them back as Guillaume instructed. Turning away from Opsis ministering to my wounds I watched as the snake began to twist and turn in the net causing a small opening to appear as the last of the Grandite stones went cold. Shoving her head through the opening the net fell away and she rose up, her head reaching almost to the ceiling of the room. Angrily she looked down at us, coiling up as if to strike. As she drew back Guillaume moved around the dragon to look at the snake's head so high above us.

"You can cease your theatrics now, you are here. Once you are changed back, then you can deal with what comes. This is not going to change that." I watched surprised as the snake also calmed at Guillaume's voice and words. Dropping down to the floor she lay waiting and watching.

"You suffered some nasty wounds Young Warrior, but you will be well." Opsis said to me as he rubbed a salve of some sort over my wounds. I watched, waiting for the pain to begin but there was none. Once he had all of the wounds covered he carefully wrapped my arm with a bandage.

"From the looks of you, one would think you had been in a great battle." Guillaume said as he crossed the room. I turned from observing Opsis's ministrations and faced Guillaume. I watched as he took in my blood splattered appearance.

"In many ways, I was." I answered.

When Guillaume reached where Opsis and I stood he placed his hands on my shoulders. Looking directly into my eyes he nodded and smiled, "Well done Young Warrior, well done."

"Thank you Guillaume," I said then turned to look across the room, "now that they are here, how are you going to change them back?"

"I'm not," Guillaume answered me, "you are."

"I AM??" I nearly shouted as I turned back quickly to stare wide eyed and open mouthed at Guillaume. "How??"

"Do not looks so surprised Young Warrior," Guillaume said. "you can do this, just as you have accomplished everything else that has been needed of you."

"I am glad that you have confidence in my abilities.. especially those that I do not know of." I was still staring at Guillaume, waiting on an explanation.

"You are aware of your abilities, just unsure of what to think of them." Guillaume motioned at Opsis as he spoke to me, "we have watched your struggles and your victories. You are strong and wise in more ways than you realize."

"Accepting that as truth," I said as I turned to look at my sisters, the dragon and snake waiting, "I still do not understand how I can bring about the change back."

275

Guillaume stood near the doorway out of the chamber. Holding his book close to his chest he watched me carefully before asking the question. "What is the last thing you remember hearing your sister shout as you left the room?"

"That my name was Adwr and would always be Adwr." I answered without hesitation.

"And is it?"

"It is what I have long answered to, but it is not my name."

"Do you, Young Warrior, remember your name?"

"How is that important now Guillaume?"

"It is important, do you remember?"

"No." I admitted. "I remember everything else it seems, but that."

"You must remember." Guillaume said in a matter of fact tone.

"It is lost to me." I answered. I hung my head as I turned away from him, not wanting to see the condemnation and disappointment in his eyes at my failure.

"It is no more lost than all of your other memories that have returned to you."

"Then why can I not remember it as well?" I asked him, honestly wanting to know.

"Because you still blame yourself. You still feel as if there was something you could have done. Even as you now know differently."

"How, Guillaume, do I not blame myself? I ran from the room leaving them. I allowed them to do the thing that has them in this state." I said, still not looking at him while motioning toward the dragon and snake watching us.

"It was not your fault this happened."

276

Guillaume insisted.

      Not wishing to argue any longer I began to pace the room. Ignoring them all as they watched me. As I walked, I would stop at various places in the room, examining items along the way, picking some of them up from where they rested, heavily coated in dust. I carefully brushed the dust away allowing memories to return. I remembered being in this room so long ago. The games that were played. Listening to Guillaume's stories. Watching the people passing in the halls, they would always smile and speak or wave in passing. The knights that would stop and allow me to see their swords and shields. Opsis, always trying to teach me manners and respect. Calling me away from the knights so they could go about their duties. Memories flooded my mind, but not the memory of my name. It yet alluded me. Slowly circling the room I made to pass by my sisters, still trapped in their changed state.

      "Brother..our brother." the voices spoke in unison. I stopped to look at them both, waiting.

      "I am sorry brother. Forgive me, forgive us. It was childish jealousies and anger that caused us to call you by that name."

      "I do forgive you." I said, starting to turn away, to move past them.

      "Brother, remember please. This was never your fault. You are not to blame. We need you. If you forgive us, remember."

      I could see the fear in their eyes. I was desperate to remember now. Standing before them I held out my hands toward them, "If you know, then tell me."

      "You must remember...you must remember." the voices grew quiet, yet they still watched me.

      Scrubbing my eyes with the heel of my hands

277

I turned away. Continuing around the room I reached the exact place where the change had happened. I felt a cold like I had never known before. Backing away the cold followed me, circling, enclosing me in a time frozen in this room. I was running from the room, yelling something, I was yelling for Guillaume to come help. I could hear my young voice echoing off the walls. The panic I felt was heard in the sound. My bare feet slapped against the cool stone floor, the walls passing in a blur of color. I burst through the doorway shouting for Guillaume to come, to hurry..I watched as Guillaume turned abruptly from his work, looking confused and concerned at my entrance. I heard his voice as he spoke to me. "What is it Young Warrior?" Guillaume asked, " What is wrong, Ewan?" The images in my mind faded back to where they had been. I was again standing in the room where everyone waited on a memory.

"Ewan, my name is Ewan." My voice sounding more assured even to my own ears.

"It is indeed Ewan..now we can proceed with what must be done." Guillaume smiled, his ever present, calm reserve and lack of emotions were gone. I could see the relief dancing in his eyes and shining in his every action.

"Come over here to me," Guillaume instructed. "and take my book."

EIGHTEEN

Walking across the room to Guillaume it seemed strange. I had answered to Adwr for so long I didn't know how I would remember to answer to anything else. Stopping before Guillaume I waited.

Guillaume had watched me cross the room, now that I stood before him he seemed to be deep in thought. Clearing his throat he began to explain what we had to do. "You had to remember everything, for this to work. From before the change, when the change happened and after. No memory, no knowledge could be skipped or left out. That is why you had to remember your name."

I did not speak, merely nodded my understanding.

"As before, with this you will only have one chance. If you make a mistake, if you so much as say one word wrong, they will forever be this way. Until death grants them mercy." Guillaume said, still watching me. "What you are going to do, is give them the ability to speak. You will have to keep repeating the words in a conversational level until both can and do speak clearly. Do not stop once they begin, you will step back out of the way, but you will continue to say the words I give you quietly, just above the sound of a whisper. Do you understand this Ewan?"

"I do." I answered with the only possible response. My whole being was trembling, but I had to do this. I could do this. I would do this, I would have my sisters back. Hearing a noise I turned to see Opsis moving something across the room. As he turned it I saw that it was the large mirror that my sisters had loved covered by Guillaume's crimson cloak. He moved it carefully across the room to stand it in front of the dragon and the snake. Both I saw, were watching him closely.

"Guillaume, " I said as I turned back, "why do they need to speak? What is going to happen?"

"Once you have said what I am going to give you and they begin to speak, they will repeat the words that they said so long ago, only in reverse."

"They have been changed a long time Guillaume, will they remember the words?"

"They will see the book." Guillaume answered.

"But how will they be able to read backward Guillaume?"

"With a few words of my own Young Warrior."

At my confused look he added, "With a few words spoken by me, they will see the words in the book, but for them they will appear in reverse."

I stood looking at Guillaume, considering what he had said. I had to ask, "How will they know they are saying the words correctly?"

Guillaume looked at me for a moment, understanding that I was asking out of concern and not to be an annoyance,he answered, "I can read the words with them the first time and only the first time. After that they must say them without me. As they repeat the words the change will begin. They must keep repeating the words until the change is complete. There must be nothing left of the creature that they were before they stop chanting. That is the reason for the mirror, so if need be they can see, and they will know when they are fully changed back. It is important that you keep repeating the words you are given so that they will be able to speak until it is completed. If you stop and they lose the ability at any time, they will be forever frozen at that point of change. Your sisters will be part human, part creature. That will be a much worse state than they are in now as wholly snake or dragon."

I looked over my shoulder at the dragon and snake waiting, watching. "One would think they would be able to feel the difference."

Guillaume chose to ignore that comment. Opening his book he then asked me, "Are you ready?"

"I do have one more question,"

Guillaume closed the book and looked up waiting, his expression one of tolerant patience.

"You said once that my sister said something wrong, that was the reason that she is a snake not a dragon,"

"Yes, that is true." Guillaume answered.

"Then how can she be changed back, if you do not know what she said?"

'I know what she said Young Warrior, I can not use the crystals to see much of the present or any of the future, but I was able to go back to the day of the change. I do know where the mistake was made."

"How can you correct this? How can she be changed back?"

"They will have to do this one at a time. I will work with the dragon first, once her change is complete I will help your sister the snake. Hers will be a little more difficult, but not impossible." Guillaume watched me, waiting for a few moments to see if I had any more questions. When I said no more he asked, "Are you ready?"

Taking a deep breath I straightened to my full height. Releasing the breath I turned to face Guillaume face to face. "I am"

"Then let us begin." Opening his book he
turned to the page he sought. "Remember," Guillaume
told me, "No matter what happens, keep repeating the
words, do not stop for any reason." When I again nodded,
he began. I listened carefully to the words that Guillaume
read. Making sure that I heard each word and syllable. I
carefully remembered where his voice changed and
where he spoke with emphasis. When I was sure that I
knew what I was to say and how, I nodded. Guillaume
stepped aside and I began.

At the sound of the first words both the dragon
and snake turned to me. Watching me closely as I
repeated again and again the phrases Guillaume had
instructed me to say. When the snake drew back away
from me, its eyes closing into mere slits I closed my own.
Thinking that if I didn't see anything, I would be less
inclined to stop talking. That changed when I heard what
sounded like a cry of pain come from the dragon.
Opening my eyes I watched as she too drew her head
back, shaking it from side to side as if in pain. Great tears
fell from the dragon's eyes as the snake twisted and
turned appearing to wrap itself into a strange knot against
a far wall. A gray smoke lifted from the floor, raising
upward to cover them both. Quietly at first I began to
hear their voices. They were hesitant at first, as if afraid.
Their voices scratchy and rough from being long unused.
Over and over I repeated the words Guillaume had given
me, listening to the voices of my sisters grow stronger.
Once their voices were clear, I backed away watching
Guillaume as he stepped forward. I heard him saying
something but I couldn't make out what he was saying as
I repeated the phrase again and again, concentrating
only on those words and saying them correctly. Opsis

stood beside the mirror, waiting for the right moment to remove the cloak.

I watched, hearing the voice of my sister as she read from the book. Repeating carefully, word for word what Guillaume was saying. The gray mist grew thicker, darker. It swirled about the room, slowly at first, then began to move quicker. I watched as the Grandite stones on the net and halter again began to glow. Their purple hue adding a strange light to the mist. The crystals on the halter came to life, glowing brightly while growing so warm that I could feel the heat from where I stood. As I watched the halter fell away from the dragon. She was then able to speak even more clearly. Streaks of light like the lightning bolts from the sky streaked and danced about the room. I heard the cries and the moans coming from the mists that kept growing dark, even as I heard the words being said. I stood where I was, fighting the desire to rush in and help, reciting the words as I had been instructed. The dragon suddenly appeared, her eyes wide and frightened as the voice of my sister spoke the words. The dragon's wings outstretched reaching from one wall to the other across the room. The dragon's tail thrashing about, knocking furniture across the room and items off the shelves. Swallowing I kept talking, carefully watching what was taking place before me. In the midst of the mist I saw the snake, twisting around and around, as if impatient, and yet at the same time afraid. Then I saw the light, a soft golden glow like that of a candle beginning. It started at the dragon and grew outward. As it spread, it grew brighter until it was the point that I was blinded and could see no more. I brought my hand up shading my eyes from the brilliance while I still carefully recited the words. It was then I heard Opsis move the mirror. I could hear the cloak sliding across the metal covering. In the room was the smell of sulfur and smoke, but something else. Something gentle. The room went from a comfortable feeling to extremely hot, a red glow like that of a fire appeared then changed to blue and the room became unbearably cold. I shivered in the cold but I kept repeating the words just as I had been told, fighting any desire to stutter. The room returned gradually to a comfortable temperature. Through the thickness of the midst I could see movement. As the midst began to settle and the brilliant glow began to fade away, I watched as the dragon began to shrink away before my eyes. Smaller and smaller, changing from dragon ever so slowly into human form. I listened as I heard the words still being repeated until the midst was gone. Then crumpling to the floor my sister fell.

Still speaking I started to move forward only to see Guillaume's hand come up stopping me. Staying where I was I kept speaking. I watched my sister the snake as she writhed on the floor, knowing it was her turn. Guillaume called to her, first she drew back away from him, her head turning from side to side as if seeking a way out. Guillaume spoke to her soothingly, calming her as he called her again to him. This time slowly she moved forward. Before she got close, she turned and looked to me. Her voice so long unused still a song to my ears. This is what my dreams had been telling me I was missing. My sisters, my family, and I had almost killed them at one point, now I almost had them back. He held the book again in a position where she could read the words. She listened, repeating word for word, sound for sound what Guillaume said. Her eyes only left the book once to look again at me. Then she turned and concentrated fully on reading.

The mist returned, growing, swirling, darkening as I watched. Again the temperature in the room changed from comfortable to a feeling so hot as to have me tugging at my tunic. Before the red glow of the heat could subside the cold came. Again I fought the desire to shiver and stutter my words and my teeth wishing to chatter together. I watched amazed as the flashes of light came from the center of the mist streaking outward only to disappear into the air. I heard the moans and cries as she still managed to struggle through repeating the words of the book. The Grandite stones slowly began to dim, taking the slight purple hue with them. The mist began to lower to the floor finally disappearing altogether. Looking about the room I watched the snake become still, it too began to grow smaller, changing slowly, incredibly slowly to human form. Finally before me, laying still on the floor was my other sister. They were returned to human form, but were they alive? Had the return done them harm?

I stood where I was afraid to move. I did not want to know that after all of what we had been through that the worst had happened. I watched, not realizing I was holding my breath until my chest felt as if it would burst. As time passed and still they did not move I began to tremble, fear growing in my heart. I looked from my sisters to Guillaume and Opsis who also had not moved. Guillaume saw my movement and turned slightly toward me. He made a slight motion with his hand for me to stay where I was. He must have known how badly I wanted to rush to them. I wanted to pick them up from the floor and talk to them, ask them of they were well. Switch moved up beside me. I had forgotten all about the caTragon. Not taking my eyes from my sisters I lay my hand on the caTragon's head. His presence was a small comfort, but it wasn't what I wanted right at that moment.

As we stood waiting a large explosion of sound rocked the castle. The structure shook and trembled at the blow. The caTragon beside me snarled and growled but did not move. 'Not now, please not now,' I thought desperately. I looked to Guillaume and Opsis, the look on each face told me what I feared. The castle was under attack.

Again the castle shook and trembled under a massive blow of some sort. Dust rained down on us from above. I heard the crash of something falling out in the castle somewhere. Where were the knights? Where was anyone? I remembered when we approached the castle that it had been darkened with no sign of life anywhere, other than the enemy surrounding it. Another explosion, not as loud, coming from a different side of the castle. The structure still shook and trembled at the blow.

I looked to Guillaume, "Why," I asked him in a low voice. "Why are they attacking the castle?"

Guillaume briefly glanced from my unmoving sisters to me. "They seek among other things; ruler ship of the lands, and slaves to mine the precious stones on and around Fire Mountain and the many dragon's lairs in the land."

This is what you spoke of that time before?" I asked him.

"It is, but your sisters,"he said quietly, motioning toward them, "needed your full attention first."

The next hit on the castle caught me unprepared and I was knocked off my feet, causing me to slide across the floor right into the folds of the discarded net. Picking up one of the crystals I looked, trying to see if it would work. If it would show me what was being used against us. As the attack was under way and secrecy no longer important the crystals worked quickly. A bright glow brought out the image of the grounds around the castle. As far back as the crystal allowed I saw a massive army. Creatures from all the land surrounded us, evil filled their eyes. I watched as they loaded an enormous catapult and prepared it for firing. All around the castle the enemy gathered, moving in slowly and carefully. Pushing before them several of these large catapults. It looked that there were no less than two on each side.

I looked up at Guillaume, "Catapults."

He nodded, it was as he had thought. "Fire?" he asked.

"No, not yet."

"Give them time, if no one appears, they will use fire to burn us out."

"Can you do anything?" I asked him. I could not hide the hope in my voice.

"Not alone." he answered. "there are too many of them, and too many with magic enough to combat mine."

As the castle shook once again I looked back to my sisters. They had yet to move from where they lay. The only thing I knew was that they were breathing.

"Why have they not moved Guillaume?" I asked, my voice still low but worried.

"To have changed once, was difficult enough on them. They changed emotionally and mentally as well as physically. Yet, the change did not take from them the full memory of having been human. It was that memory that was haunting them, and slowly killing them. For they knew that they had trapped themselves and could not escape the nightmare of their existence alone."

Guillaume stopped and tried to hold his balance as the

castle was struck again, shaking and trembling under the blow. "They needed help, they needed you. They did not know that over time you had made yourself forget what happened because you blamed yourself. As time passed they grew weaker. They knew each other, but could not tolerate each other. I can not help but believe, that they each blamed the other. They have fought often, and with each battle lost strength, both physical and emotional. They were swiftly losing the desire and will to continue."

The next blow struck the wall just outside of the room where we were. The castle shook as if moved and broken free from the cornerstone around which it had been built. What had not already been knocked from tables fell as everything slid and rolled, scattering across the floor. The mirror fell over with a crash as debris rained from the ceiling. And still, Guillaume stood watching.

Standing, and untangling myself from the net I looked to Guillaume and Opsis. Neither moved, neither took their eyes from my sisters. Even though they did not say the words, it was obvious from their expressions they thought my sisters should have awakened by now.

From outside the castle came the battle cries of the surrounding army. They were yelling as loud as they could possibly yell. All the while they struck any and every object they could that would make a noise, the louder the better. When a boulder from the catapults would strike the castle the noise came even greater.

"The walls of this castle are thick," I said aloud, "but even they can only withstand so much." Not able to stand it any longer I crossed the room, circling wide from where my sisters lay, unmoving but for their breathing. Guillaume watched me for a moment but said nothing and returned to watching for any signs of movement from Delwen and Delyth.

There was no open window in the outside wall since it had sealed along with the hole when I swung the hammer after we entered. I leaned my head against the wall, with my hands flat on the surface on either side. The cool temperature of the wall cooled the heat of my face brought on by the frustration of waiting. I was so tired, the exhaustion threatened, but I knew I could not rest yet. There was too much at stake here. There was too much yet to do. Opening my eyes I removed the crystal from my pouch and watched the enemy just outside. The darkness of the night did not stop them, they seemed to prefer and even thrive in it. They were all a nasty bunch in appearances and in actions. Moving about, laughing, drinking what ever ale or brew they preferred. In their drunken state they were more dangerous as they now felt no fear, if they had felt any before. Many were eating, something. Their manners were non-existent. They carried around large legs of beast, some that had been cooked over the campfires while others just consumed it raw, blood running down their chins. The skins and rags they wore were dirty and torn. Many were stained with what could have only been the blood of their enemies. I watched, picking out the various creatures that lurked in the darkness, attacking my home.

The Molditians, vile creatures that I wished now more than ever I or Guillaume had defeated. I felt that this group were the ones most responsible for the attack.

Algans, they preferred to be around the water. What has brought them here? Their thick skin, scaly and tough has a tendency to dry out easily becoming very uncomfortable if not painful. To look at them one would believe them related to a dragon. They had the long face, but could not breathe fire nor fly. Their bare feet and hands were webbed, giving them amazing swimming abilities. They did not have a tail as a dragon does and they walked up right as a man. With eyes a strange yellow -green color I did not wish to look into. A vicious bunch that would just as soon tear an enemy apart as not.

Rantganees, every time I had ever seen or heard of this group I thought of a rodent. While they walked upright on two legs their arms were short ending in hands that were small with long slender fingers. Having a flat face yet long nose with protruding whiskers on either side. They also had a mouth full of razor sharp teeth that could tear a man apart quickly. Covered in hair that looked like a long coat of fur. This protected them from their enemy making them hard to injure and almost impossible to kill. They did have a long thin tail that they had been known to use like a whip, causing serious injury to their victims.

Garrmensh? If these were who or what, they looked to be, they were a long way from home. A fish like race they could breathe in or out of water thanks to having both lungs and gills. Walking upright like a man, the bright colored cloak they wore covered the fin that ran down the center of their back. Like the Algans their fingers were webbed. Their feet were without toes, wide and webbed as a duck's feet. This was a group that preferred to be near the sea, thriving on the abundance of the salt they crave. They had no need for precious stones or slaves from inland. Tales that I had heard whispered told of how they would find ways to wreck passing ships. Either by tricking them close to shore and onto rocks or creating giant whirlpools in the sea sinking the ships quickly. The crews on board were doomed, some becoming slaves, others meals. What ever the cargo on board becoming treasures to the Garrmensh to use or to trade.

As the crystal moved from camp to camp I grew more ill. How were we going to fight, and defeat such an army?

Grantiants lurked just beyond the campfires. Giants, the smallest among them stood no less than twelve feet tall. Their arms alone were the size of the trunk of a tree. With three eyes they missed nothing. The fingers on their hands were long enough to close around a gathering of knights and crush them easily. They stank of death and decay. Grantiants were known to have magical powers. It was no doubt they were the ones that had prevented us from using the crystals for so long.

Glowing from the limbs of the trees I could see the eyes of the Baltrist. This was most likely the smallest of the races so far. With tiny eyes and near nonexistent ears they were the only race here I had seen so far that could fly. A bat like creature and nearly fully blind they had an instinctual way of knowing where they were at any given time. I wondered if there were any other race here, hiding or just not seen that could also fly.. An adult Baltrist barely reached three feet tall, yet they had leathery wings that would stretch out six feet on either side. On these wings were claws that could and would do great injury to a victim be they man or animal.

Having seen more than I wished to I returned the crystal to my pouch just as I heard the first soft mumble come from one of my sisters. Turning swiftly away from the wall I watched as she lifted her hand to her eyes.

NINETEEN

I started to rush forward only to see Guillaume raise his hand to stop me. I glared angrily at him but obeyed. As much as I wanted to help my sisters, I did not want to risk causing any harm now.

Drawing her legs up, she turned and pushed herself up into a sitting position. Leaving one hand resting on the floor beside her, helping her keep her balance, she raised the other trembling hand to push her hair from her face. Raising her head she looked from one expectant face to the other. We stood waiting, prepared to rush forward at any hint of distress. Finally she took a deep breath, then looking at me smiled. "Brother."

"Yes Delyth?"

"You did it Ewan. You did it." Delyth's voice soft and barely audible. Her actions showing she was yet weak.

I had not asked Guillaume, but I had wondered about how old my sisters would be when they were changed back. I did not know whether they would be the children they were when they first changed, or if they would have aged. Before me now I could see that they had aged physically as time passed. Only time would tell how they had matured emotionally. I still wondered, but had not asked again, how much they would remember of their past. I knew that I would not ask now either.

I looked to Guillaume who simply nodded. Walking forward I knelt down on my knees before my sister. Reaching out I pushed her hair back, then ignoring Guillaume and Opsis pulled my sister close for an embrace. The feelings of relief that it was finally done threatened to overwhelm me.

"Ewan?"

Pulling free from Delyth I turned and looked across the room to Delwen.

"Ewan I am sorry. You are no coward." Delwen was standing unsteadily, her hand against the wall in an attempt to remain upright. She was watching me, the expression in her eyes one of pleading and regret.

Smiling I stood and helped Delyth to her feet. Walking slowly beside her, making sure she kept her balance we approached Delwen. Reaching where she stood waiting, I held out my hand to her. When she took my hand I pulled her and Delyth slowly into an embrace. I only hoped that both were too weak to notice my own trembling, or the tears that rolled silently down my cheeks. We were only allowed a few brief moments before I heard Guillaume call my name.

"Ewan..."

Before he could say more there was the sound of a boulder striking the castle. The structure shuddered and shook around us. Dust and debris fell again from the ceiling. The caTragon looked to the outside wall. He was listening to something but I could not tell what.

"Ewan, what is happening?" Delyth asked.

When another boulder struck, causing the castle to shake, I knew I couldn't lie. "The castle," I hesitated, "Dragon's Doom, we, are under attack." If I had expected fear from my sisters, I expected wrongly. Instead of becoming afraid, they became angry.

"Who is attacking us?" Delwen asked, looking toward the same wall as the caTragon. The expression on her face one that would have caused trained knights to back down and tremble.

"From what I saw through the crystal

everyone that the Molditians could talk into fighting. Most of them bloodthirsty warmongers anyway."

"Where are the knights?" Delwen asked.

"The castle was dark when we got here. I do not know where anyone is. Or if anyone is even still here." I answered her honestly.

Delyth had been standing listening, then appearing to have come to a decision asked me. "What are our plans to stop them, Ewan?"

"Our plans?" I turned to her. "What do you mean, our plans?"

"Just tell us what we can do to help." Delwen said.

Watching them I was surprised to see how quickly they were regaining their strength. If I had not witnessed the change only a few moments before and seen for myself their weakness I would have never believed them ever weak in any way. I looked to Guillaume and Opsis for assistance. Standing side by side on the far side of the room they only smiled.

"We can not allow this attack to continue without fighting back." Delwen was pacing back and forth across the room. Her bare feet made no sound on the stone floor as she walked. Every word she said emphasized with movements of her hands. "We need a plan."

"Their army is so vast, I don't see how the five of us alone can defeat them. Delyth said. She was standing in the center of the room watching Delwen pace. In her hands she held my crystal, the images within it of the attacking army clear.

"But they do not know it is just the five of us." I said as I stepped forward. "Truth is," I added, "we do not know it is just the five of us. The others are possibly hidden somewhere in the castle. The knights working to protect the innocent until they can find the best way to fight back. We do not have time to go search for them, but it is possible that once we begin fighting back, they may come out from where they are hiding and assist us."

Crossing the room I set a table back upright and poured the pebbles in my pouch out onto its surface. The Grandite began to glow softly as I lined them up once again in a circle. When the purple hue filled the center of the circle an image began to form. Delwen and Delyth moved closer and watched the image grow clear. The army outside had grown since I had last looked. They had been joined by other races. The most surprising being the Trook. This group is normally solitary having nothing to do with others. Their size and large colorful wings along with the ability to fly giving them an arrogant air. Their hands and feet both held deadly talons. They were a brutal enemy to go into battle against as they had no morals or compassion. They would attack any one or anything and once they caught their target, what they did was gruesome to say the least. Even with their arrival this army did not seem to be in any hurry. They milled about laughing and drinking. Some were from the looks of it asleep or passed out, while others were occupying their time by playing strange games. It was obvious that more than one was drunk in what ever ale they were consuming. As we watched they fought amongst themselves. Words would become shouts that would move on to blows. Those watching would encourage the fight which most times did not end well at least for one. Several of the combatants died at the hands of their allies, the bodies left were they had fallen. It was only occasionally that they would place a boulder in the catapult and send it into the castle walls.

295

"They are trying to intimidate us into giving up, either by starvation or fear, because they know we are far out numbered." Delyth spoke as she watched.

"Are we?" I asked them.

"Ewan? What are you thinking?" Delyth asked with a suspicious yet curious, almost anticipatory, tone to her voice.

I smiled and turned to face Guillaume and Opsis, "I have an idea."

TWENTY

"I have an idea," I said again looking up to Guillaume, "But it will take all of us together using our various talents in order for it to work and for us to defeat this enemy."

"Let us hear this plan of yours Ewan." Guillaume said as he and Opsis moved across the room to the table. Guillaume picked up the crystal and watched the images while I retrieved my bag from against the wall.

"The Molditians have persuaded every race of beings they possibly can into helping them with this war. I think some how that there is more here than just wanting slaves and becoming ruler of the land. That Opsis is where you come in. Your gift of extra sight will show you more than the crystals or the Grandite are able to show us."

"I can walk among them and they will never know it." Opsis said as he alternated between watching the images and watching me. The smile playing across his lips giving way his pride in what he was watching unfold before him.

"Guillaume, I can not help but believe that there was more to your battle with the Molditians than you have shared with us. I will not ask you now what you have kept silent about, but I may soon. As it is, they know of your ability to create armies out of weather. But, in our favor, is that they should not know that you, or in truth, any of us are here. What I need to know is this, can you create armies that work independently of you or I?"

Guillaume stood silent, his expression one of serious consideration. "That would be difficult, Young

Warrior as they need someone to follow." Guillaume answered.

"Then can you create an army, out of their sight?"

"The leader would still need to be with them at their creation. Otherwise they would not know where to come to."

"Then I can cross over the forest on the caTragon, create this army and return to fight."

"You must remember, if you are injured, if you die, the army is gone." Guillaume spoke, reminding me.

"Yes, I remember, but I discovered something about this sword and shield." I told him as I picked them up from the table. Taking hold of the shield's grip I held it before me. The sword held tightly in my other hand. Concentrating I focused my thoughts on the shield for a few moments, then turned to Guillaume. "Strike me."

Without hesitation Guillaume picked up a piece of broken furniture and swung in my direction. Before the piece of wood reached the shield it's momentum was quickly slowed, stopping in midair. When Guillaume tried to draw his weapon back, it would not move. He tried to make it go further forward, it would not move. When he released it, the wood fell harmlessly to the floor. Watching the shield Guillaume reached out his hand, just before he reached the place the wood stopped he felt a change in the air around the shield. Smiling he looked to me," That will help keep you safe I am sure. How did you discover this?"

"Let's just say I was hanging around and happened to discover it by accident. The only problem with it is that I must be prepared, so as to prepare the shield as I did just now. In battle I will be."

"How do you plan on getting out and away from

here without being seen?" Delwen asked.

"I will use the doorway of the Inbetween. Switch and I will step across to the other side of the forest. Once we step out of the ripple we will return here in the normal fashion. Just before we come into the enemy's sight I will, with Guillaume's help, create my own vast army."

Delwen looked momentarily confused at the mention of the InBetween, but instead of asking about it, asked instead, "And us?What of Delyth and I?"

"Delyth can you speak to them in their mind? Have them thinking they are hearing spirits or possibly that they are going mad? Even if they simply believe that the person next to them is playing strange mind games and have them fighting each other would help."

"I can do that easily." Delyth said.

"Delwen, can you cause them to see things that aren't there?" I asked hoping her answer was the one I wanted.

"I can." she said and smiled. Then asked, "what would you like them to see?"

"First answer this. Can you cause each group to see the thing that they fear most...all at the same time?"

"That is more difficult, but with Delyth's and Guillaume's help I can do that, yes."

"Can you have them believing that I and my army are those things?"

"I can do that," Delwen answered thoughtfully, "but I am not sure how long I can hold it. If I lose concentration or grow weary, it may fail."

"So we will waste no time." I said as I motioned for Switch. "Opsis, watch for my return. As soon as you see me appear leading the army here, tell Delwen and Delyth so that they may begin." I watched Opsis nod thoughtfully and then I turned to Guillaume.

"Is it possible to create an army, out of more than one type storm at the same time?"

Guillaume caught my idea immediately and smiled. "Yes, Young Warrior, it is possible and it is a good idea."

"Can you do it from a distance? Or will I need to learn more words to create them myself?"

"I can do it from here. I will watch for you and Switch to step out of the Inbetween. As soon as I see you safe, I will begin. You will go ahead and start on your journey back this way. Before you are half way across the forest, you will have your army. Do you by any chance remember the words that I once instructed you to forget?"

Smiling slightly I ducked my head in a pretend attempt to hide my grin, "I remember the words."

With a nod of acknowledgment Guillaume told me,"When you reach the designated area, begin to recite the words. I will begin here at the same time. Together, we will create an army capable of anything and everything needed to defeat this enemy around us."

Slipping the lead around the caTragon's neck I made ready to go. I looked up from Switch to see Guillaume and Opsis solemnly watching me. I returned that look for just a moment before I turned and picked up the sword and shield. Looking quickly around the room one last time I took a deep breath and sliding the sword into its sheath at my waist I said solemnly, "Now, it begins." Hearing Guillaume's nearly inaudible, 'go in grace', I turned away. Closing my conscious thought to what was going on around me I mentally saw where I needed to be. Within the space of a heartbeat, I was leading Switch out of the Inbetween on the far side of the forest.   I took several steps away from the doorway still leading Switch when he suddenly stopped.

His unexpected move nearly pulling me off of my feet. Turning to see what was wrong I saw one angry caTragon. His dragon's head had smoke streaming from his nostrils, while flame was beginning to spark from his mouth, his lips drawn back in a fierce snarl showing row upon row of razor sharp teeth. The claws on his feet extended and ready for use, his tail slowly swung back and forth. Seeing him crouching low as if preparing to pounce, I knew he was sensing something that I couldn't see. Just as I made ready to turn back around I felt the movement in the air behind me. Twisting in a half circle I raised my shield as I ducked low to the ground. I felt the blow on the shield and saw the sparks that came from metal hitting metal. I was being attacked, but by who, or what? Regaining my feet I searched the air around me for any sign of movement. I could feel them now. I knew they were here, but where? The feeling wasn't overwhelmingly strong so I guessed there to be only one. I only had to find them.

Moving back to stand beside the caTragon I used his great sense of awareness to help me find my attacker. Where Switch looked I looked. I could feel them moving about. It was strange, one would have thought they would be still so as not to give themselves away. Yet this one moved around constantly, possibly trying to confuse me or throw me off my guard. Or- the thought came to me, they may think that they are here to get rid of a boy. An easy target that would be of so little trouble that they could play for a while first.

I began to look confused, turning in needless circles. I looked behind trees, up toward the sky. I even dared to use the point of my sword to move aside the greenery of a bush. I could feel their presence, they were close by.

301

Shrugging my shoulders I turned to the caTragon, "Who ever was here is gone now Switch, lets go." I allowed my sword to lower slightly. Then from the corner of my eye, I saw the ripple in the air. I kept my face turned toward the caTragon but I could see the ripple growing. I was also beginning to smell the dank, putrid, odor of death and decay. Grantiant, I was going to have to fight a Grantiant. I could only hope this one was not the usual fifteen feet high. Halfheartedly tugging at the lead still around Switch's neck I watched the ripple from the corner of my eye, waiting for it to begin opening.

The moment the Grantiant began to step out I swung. Screaming like a madman I swung the sword. Blocked by the Grantiant's shield he then grabbed for me. Ducking away from his hands I swung the sword again, this time striking the outstretched hand. The sword sliced into the Grantiant's hand inflicting serious damage. Blood poured as the giant looked at his hand and then to me. Rage filled his eyes, his mouth drawn tight in a thin line, his eyes no more than slits in his face. I could see his jaw working as he ground his teeth together. Not waiting I swung again, blocked by his shield he pulled his own sword out from behind him.

It was sword against sword, metal against metal as we fought. Sparks flew from the swords each time they made contact. The noise of the battle ringing through the forest, echoing off the mountainside. Sweat ran down my face and down my back. My tunic under the chain mail clung to my skin. I could feel the sweat drop from my hair onto my face and into my eyes. The salty taste as it ran into my mouth an annoyance but not a distraction. The burn in my eyes making it difficult to see, so when need be I fought by sense of smell. The raw stench of the Grantiant making him easy to follow whether my eyes were open or closed. My arms ached from the fierce blows as sword repeatedly struck sword. Each time I could feel my arm shake all the way up to my shoulder. My legs hurt from the stance needed to maintain my balance and still fight as I wanted. I was at the disadvantage, fighting against his great height. Vital organs were safely out of my reach as he held my attacks at bay. I refused to allow the thought to enter that he was only playing with me, that at any time he could end this. I had to win, there was no other option. Too much and too many depended on me for me to lose now. If I could only get close enough, I could strike him in a manner that would disable him enough to allow me time and opportunity to attack and win. Time and again he held me back. The length of his sword alone making getting close impossible. The ability he had in using it made it even more so.

 I saw him as he drew his sword back, he was going to swing straight down. I had intentionally been swinging low and close. I hoped to give the illusion that my abilities were limited and I could only fight with in a certain range. All while trying to remain alive. Wondering if it had actually worked I watched as the Grantiant drew back.

 "Today, you die." was all he said as he made ready to swing.

 I waited until his arms were drawn fully back, holding his sword in a manner meant to do massive damage to the target. I knew I would only have one chance, if I missed, I was dead. As soon as he was fully vulnerable I drew back my own sword and sank it deep into his belly. As the sword sank into the Grantiant all the way to the hilt I heard his scream of pain and of anger. Quickly pulling my sword free I backed away, waiting to

303

see what he would do.

Placing his good hand over the wound he watched himself bleed. He looked from his wound to me. Disbelief filled his eyes.

"Not possible," he said as he shook his head, "Not possible to be killed by a boy." Falling to his knees he hesitated and then pitched forward onto his face.

I waited several long moments, listening and watching for any sign that the Grantiant was not dead. After a reasonable amount of time had passed I carefully moved forward, holding my sword at the ready. As soon as I was close enough I pushed at the body with my booted foot. When he did not move I was sure he was dead, but I could take no chances. Slowly I pushed my sword into his back and all the way through his chest, right where his heart would be.

Pulling my sword free I looked to the caTragon, "Thanks Switch, that was good knowing this guy was here. You saved us." Backing away I cleaned his blood from my sword as I thought out loud. "How did he know we were going to be here? Or was it just coincidence? Could he have just been passing by on his way to the battle and happened upon us? No, I do not think so. I think they have a suspicion that some one is up to something. But how- how did they know I would be here exactly? And what else do they know?"

I moved over to where Switch stood waiting. I removed the lead and prepared to climb onto his back when I heard a noise. " Now what??" I said in a tone that gave my exhaustion and frustration away.

Out from among the trees came an army of caTragons. They were all shapes and sizes, mixed in whether they bore the head of lions or dragons. Snarling and growling, giving way with a roar that shook the ground around us they came. The odors that were specific to this creature, permeated the area. The smell of smoke and sulfur, along with the scent of singed fur and something that was akin to death drifted in the air around them. By the dozens they came into the clearing around us. The largest that I saw was the size of a dragon. Bearing his lion's head proudly his dragon's body stretched out to be fifty feet in length at the least. His footsteps thundering through the wood as trees were pushed from the way of his massive body. His lion's underbelly just clearing the ground, yet anything that he happened to cross went unnoticed. The branches of the trees scraped harmlessly against his dragon's scales along his sides. Even though using the lion's head he maintained the ability of breathing fire. Flames cleared the grounds before him, leaving a scorched and smoldering earth in his wake. On his back, was an old friend.

"Collectif!" I shouted out. Watching as he dismounted and moved to stand before me, brushing away the soot and ashes that comes from riding a creature that breathes fire. Taking one of those deep sweeping bows I had so hated he smiled. "You, look quite well for someone who is supposed to be dead." I said.

"As you can see now, I am much alive, alive and not dead..no not dead." Collectif responded with a smile.

"How is it, when I stood and watched you die, when your blood dripped from my sword as your eyes grew dim, that you are in fact not dead?"

Laughing joyfully Collectif walked forward and placed his hand on my shoulder. "Think Young Warrior, what is one of the first things that Guillaume taught you?"

Shaking my head slightly I looked at Collectif, "That things may not be as they seem."

305

Collectif smiled and nodded.

"So why was I left to believe you were dead? And how is it, that you are not?"

"You fought an image created by Guillaume. I was there, so that it would do as it should, but it was not me you fought. No, not me but me. When the wound was inflicted, you saw what you expected to see." Collectif hesitated to take a breath and watch to see I was paying attention. "You had to know how it felt to kill. You had to understand what it was to see death up close. It had to be real. It had to be a death that would effect you or there would be nothing learned."

"And it had to be someone that I knew? Was that also to make it more real? Something that would affect all of the emotions that go with death?"

"You are an intelligent one Young Warrior. You have grown much, much you have grown in this journey that you have traveled."

Nodding to acknowledge the compliment I turned to the army he had brought with him. "I see you have lost your fear of caTragons. Where did you find so many of these great beasts?"

"They are not hard to find, when you search with belief. It is almost as if they wish to be found and to be put to use in ways of good." Collectif answered as he looked over the still growing numbers.

"How did you get them to follow you here?"

"That was simple. I told them Guillaume was in need."Collectif looked back at me and taking another of those bows, with a wicked look in his eyes that told me he knew it annoyed me, asked,"Shall we go to battle?"

This time it was my turn, bowing not nearly as gracefully as Collectif I answered, "We shall go to battle."

TWENTY-ONE

As I mounted Switch I watched as the giant caTragon lowered its massive body to allow Collectif to return to his place on its back. Almost as one, each beast spread its wings and took flight. I lead the way with Collectif at my side. I did not look to him, I knew he was there. His presence was a reassuring and calming one.

As we approached the designated area of the forest I could feel a change in the winds and the surrounding temperature. It had swiftly gone from comfortable to cold. The sun had disappeared and dark thick clouds formed above and around us, almost as if they had been waiting for our arrival. The sound of thunder joined the occasional roar of a caTragon. I could feel the vibration of the sound deep within my skin. The winds grew stronger, blowing my hair back behind me, often whipping it around to slap at my face. The feeling like being stung by thousands of bees. Instead of being painful, it was exhilarating in the anticipation of what was to come. My clothing tugged and pulled in the winds, showing its strength and speed. I could smell the rain in the air around me. It mixed with the sulfur smells, cleansing them and making them stronger.

At the exact point agreed upon I began to recite the words that I knew Guillaume was also speaking at that moment. The winds around me no longer blew straight back. They circled and swirled growing stronger by the moment. They changed as they swirled going from cold to hot from wet with liquids to dry as the dust of the earth below us. The clouds around us growing thicker, darker. Great flashes of lightning streaked outward as the thunder rumbled, growing in intensity along with the winds and rains. I could see an army forming in the clouds, marching with us, following us as we went. Their armor was the ice of the cold, their weapons were captured bolts of lightning. Their faces were formed in the clouds, dark and ominous with empty eyes that knew nothing but to fight. The closer we got to the castle, the greater this army grew. Among them began to form the image of me riding upon a caTragon, sword at the ready. The expression they wore one of determination, one of deliberation. There was no sign of fear among any that I saw, only the desire to fight, and to win. I turned my attention back to the sky before me. In the distance I could see the horizon, before that, was the castle. Looking below me I could see the outer edges of the enemy surrounding the castle. Their numbers had grown to enormous proportions. This group did not look as determined as those closer to the castle. They lay about their fires, by all appearances lost in their drunken slumbers, not even looking up at the army passing above them.

At the sounds of panicked screams I looked back toward the ground I had passed. There moving slowly and steadily was an army of which I had been unaware. Flowing rather than walking they slipped up on the enemy and overwhelmed them. Going from mobile creation, to the water they were formed from, drowning the unwary only to return to the form created for battle once the screams were silenced. In their wake lay many bodies as they marched forward as an incoming tide of death and destruction.

When I looked back to the army around me I saw that in the clouds were many in the form of Collectif. At my expression he smiled and shouted to me, "Remember, they think me dead. Many of those below fear the spirits of the dead. This too shall be at our advantage."

Nodding in understanding I watched the castle growing larger. As we approached yet another boulder fired from the catapult struck the castle, this one creating a hole in the wall that was within reach of the enemy's ladders. As they ran to get ladders in place, preparing to enter the castle, with the shouts of battle, we attacked from the sky.

We first thought we had managed to take them by surprise but quickly found that not to be true. Catapults that had been concealed were uncovered and revealed to be facing our advance. Loaded and ready they were fired and quickly reset for reloading. Hidden in the lower hallows of the fields archers stood and unleashed a barrage of arrows into the sky. The first streaked past us, one deflected by my own shield. As the archers prepared to fire the next volley of arrows a wind of horrific force began to blow. The army that had been created in the clouds advanced downward toward the ground. The winds they carried stirring up the dust of the ground creating a storm that blinded those in its midst. From the inside of this came the first sounds of battle as army met army. I could hear sword striking sword, while I could see nothing past the sands swirling below me. How I wished for some sign that all was still well with those inside the castle. That they all had been able to do what was needed of them.

Motioning with my upraised sword we made to move closer. I watched as the catapults were fired again, sending huge boulders across the sky toward us. The army of caTragons parted allowing the boulders to pass harmlessly. From the edges of the battle in the dust storm below us another line of archers fired on us. This time striking one of the caTragons. Bellowing in pain the creature began to fall. Several caTragons near it moved to its rescue, catching it upon their backs they turned to carry the wounded beast to safety.

Collectif saw the expression on my face and yelled across the distance between us, "It is a minor wound, one the caTragon can heal on its own. Concentrate on what surrounds us."

Returning my attention to the battle I signaled for Switch to fly in low. Followed by the army behind me we moved into the thick of the battle. Holding the shield before me I raised my sword. For the first time I noticed the Grandite stone in the hilt glowing brightly. Before my eyes the entire sword began to take on the bright glow, growing warm and vibrating in my hand. I felt the power and strength flowing from it to me. Just above the heads of our enemies we passed. Shouting loudly I saw the created army attack. Moving into the thick of battle swinging swords made of lighting they dealt many a death's blow. As the army from the sky continued to march toward the ground those watching the approach became less sure of themselves. This army from the sky did not die. Strike them as they might, the soldiers would part, then collect together again to fight once more.

Fire from the caTragons burned the fields, consuming the enemies supplies and for those unable or unwilling to run, the enemy themselves. I saw the moment the Molditians noticed Collectif and his many replicas. Apprehension replaced some of the iron determination that had been there moments earlier. When his images on their caTragons touched down on the ground attacking, the Molditians moved back, but did not flee.

Sensing something amiss I looked to the side to see Trooks appear from out of a ripple in the air. The caTragons closest had felt their approach before me and were prepared. As each Trook stepped forth they were attacked before they realized what was happening. Caught in the jaws of a caTragon all they could do manage was one final sound of death before they were no more. When each was done away with the caTragon would release them allowing them to fall unceremoniously to the ground below.

Feeling the familiar movement near me I turned in time to raise my shield as a Trook stepped ready for battle from the ripple. Striking at my shield its blow was slowed as the shield worked its magic. Turning I struck with my sword and watched the Trook fall.

"Keep alert!" Collectif shouted.

"I am!"

"Be more alert!" he shouted as he moved away.

"Be more alert," I mimicked, "I liked you better as a fool" I said as I shifted my weight on the caTragon to hold my balance better. Searching the ground I watched the battle raging below me. With each side determined no one was giving ground. Even as bodies of the enemy grew numerous on the ground those still standing fought on. A barrage of arrows flew past my position close enough I could feel the movement in the air as they passed. I looked to see Collectif watching me angrily. "I know I know, be more alert." I said just under my breath, yet knowing that he understood what I was saying.

"Brother! Hold your sword skyward." Delyth's voice sounded not in my ears, but inside my head. Doing as she instructed I held the sword aloft. A more brilliant glow grew from what that had already been there. Brighter and brighter the light became. From that light streaks of lightning flashed outward. Thunder rumbled angrily in the dark clouds still filling the sky around me. The lightning took on human shape as it reached the ground. Humming with an electric charge they advance on the enemy on the ground. The heat they produced singed the ground, everything they touched burst into flame. Be it plant, structure or any living thing. Following the lightning came great stones of ice. Pounding the ground and all that were unfortunate enough to be caught in the open. All that were struck had great gaping wounds opened. As soon as the ice touched the ground they too took on human shape, attacking the enemy around them.

"Ewan," Delyth called to me, "do not fear what you are about to see. Know it as illusion."

Seeing Collectif in the distance I made to cross to where he was. As I moved forward the ground below me came to life, rising up and then dropping back as the waves in the sea. Great creatures dropped from the sky, falling to the heaving earth below. Finally getting close enough to be heard I shouted to Collectif who look more than a little unnerved. " It is the work of Guillaume and my sisters." Relief flooded his features as we watched the ground rise again.

CaTragons swooped down attacking those battling the real and the unreal. The sounds of death filled the air around us. And yet still, the enemy battled on, refusing to give way.

Switch suddenly began to climb higher into the sky away from the battle. When I looked I saw why, Grantiants were moving close. Stumbling only marginally as the ground beneath them heaved. Reaching into the air around them, capturing caTragons with their bare hands they attempted to slam them to the ground only to see them disappear from their grasp. Frustrated they ripped trees out by the roots and grabbed boulders up from the ground. Drawing back they sent them skyward toward us. Moving back farther out of range we watched the rampage below us.

"We're getting nowhere this way!" I shouted to Collectif.

"We are going to need try something else if we are to defeat this army." Collectif agreed. As Switch shifted and turned in the air I saw something in the distance that gave me an idea.

"Collectif, leave your caTragon and come with me." I shouted as I held out my hand to him. Taking my hand I took us through the Inbetween into the room in the castle where the others waited.

"Collectif, it is good to see you old friend." Guillaume greeted him as we stepped from the caTragon.

"Like you didn't know." I said in an amicable manner.

"Why have you come here Ewan and not out there in the battle?" Delwen asked.

"We are not getting anywhere close to ending this in the manner we are going." I answered her. "I have an idea that I needed to ask Guillaume about."

"What is your idea Ewan?" Guillaume asked.

"Fire Mountain, would it be possible to bring it to an eruption? Would it be possible to flood the area with the lava that flows, and yet protect the castle?"

"Better yet I have an idea." Delwen spoke up. "What if instead of creating an actual eruption of the mountain, we cause them to all believe it is happening? Delyth can plant the thought in their minds that it is real, they will then experience what they expect to when faced with such an occurrence."

"In other words,"Delyth continued, "if they see the lava moving toward them, catching up to where they are no matter how they run then it will. If they believe they are being burned alive by the molten lava, doomed a horrible and painful yet mercifully quick death, then they will indeed die. Even though it is not real."

Opsis had walked away from the table where he had been standing and joined the conversation. "In that manner, the army would be defeated and the castle in the way of no harm and needing no protection."

"It can be done."Guillaume said, his tone thoughtful. "We will need to go up to one of the turrets where we are free of any and all obstructions. We can gather just outside the doorway where we will not be seen from below. Come let us go before your army begins to falter from your absence."

As we made to leave the room I grabbed the hammer Guillaume had given me to use to get into the castle along with several crystals. Leaving the room we made our way down the corridor. At the end of it our way was blocked by the stones used years earlier to seal off the corridor after the change. Moving ahead of everyone I drew back the hammer. With a single blow the wall gave way, crumbling before us. Passing through the opening we hurried down the corridor until we reached the stairway up to the turrets. Climbing the stairs we could hear the sounds of battle through the small openings in the thick walls. Not bothering to look out we hurried upward along the narrow way. Reaching the doorway I stopped and looked back to make sure everyone was together. Easing my way to the edge of the doorway I looked outside. No one was on the turret, looking upward all I saw were the caTragons swooping in on the army below. Peering around the outside of the doorway I saw that there was no one that could see us as we stepped outside. Motioning for everyone I left the stairway and stepped out.

When we all were outside we formed a circle with each of us facing outward. I gave each person a crystal. These should we chose, could be used to see what our enemy below was seeing. Delyth closed her eyes and began to repeatedly chant under her breath. Holding our arms outstretched, palms upward we concentrated on what we had planned.

The crystal in my hand came to life, glowing softly. Still concentrating on the image of Fire Mountain erupting I looked to the crystal. The image showed the army below hesitating, looking away briefly but repeatedly from those they were fighting toward the mountain. The ground beneath their feet began to tremble and shake violently, causing many of them to lose their balance. Falling to the ground they would try and return to their feet only to fall again as the trembling grew worse. Catapults overturned, stones that had been piled high tumbled to the ground scattering, crushing those caught in their path. The mountainside rumbled and shook, roaring to life with an explosion of magnificent proportions. Rocks and trees rained down upon them as smoke and ash filled the sky. The day quickly grew dark and all sunlight disappeared. Ash began to rain down as a choking snow. The ground was covered within the matter of a few moments, yet it kept falling growing ever deeper. The confusion and fear this brought on causing many to stop fighting, standing completely still as they stared at the mountain that was living up to its name.

Many began to gasp and choke on the ash filled air, unable to breathe they turned to flee. They did not get far as the lava began to flow. Instead of a slow, creeping movement it flowed swiftly, covering and incinerating everything in its path. The hiss and pop of things burning sang from the crystal. I could even smell the sulfur and gases coming from the lava as it moved closer. The heat could be felt long before the lava arrived. Plants and trees wilted and died from it. Animal and human alike searched for water but the water had turned to steam disappearing quickly into the air. As the created lava reached the army screams of agony were heard only to be cut off abruptly.

When all was silent Delyth stopped her chanting and we looked from one to the other. After several moments of silence I moved to the edge of the turret and looked to the ground far below. As far as the eye could see were bodies of what had been our enemy. Now nothing more than carrion for the buzzards already circling. When the others joined me to look over the edge the feeling of relief and accomplishment was shared.

"I do believe Young Warrior, that you have done it. You have stood strong and as strong have defeated those that wish to defeat you." Collectif said as he looked outward.

"I do believe, friend Collectif, that we all did it." I answered him.

TWENTY-TWO

"Well done indeed." came a new voice from the doorway.

Turning quickly at the familiar sound I could not help but smile. "Father!"

We all watched as he left the doorway and approached Delwen and Delyth. "Welcome back to us my daughters. You have been sorely missed." Reaching out he pulled both of them into his embrace. It was impossible to miss the tears that fell from his eyes. Trembling now he held them back at arms length. Looking from one to the other he could only smile as he drew them back into his embrace. After long moments he looked up to Guillaume. "Thank you, for bringing my daughters back to me."

Guillaume shook his head, "It was not I, but Ewan that has brought them back to you."

"Ewan, not Adwr?" he asked as he watched me.

"No Father, not Adwr any longer."I said. Shrugging slightly and with a ghost of a smile.

Stepping away from my sisters he walked across to where I stood. Reaching out he clasped my shoulder as he spoke "You have grown much since you left. I can see it in your eyes, how your wisdom has grown. You left us a child, and have returned a man."

"I have learned much since I have been away."

He nodded thoughtfully in agreement and then turned to face Guillaume. Looking across the length of the turret he hesitated. Then as if making a decision he walked across to stand directly before Guillaume. Standing silently for a few moments he then reached out his hand to Guillaume, "Brother, it is good to see you

317

again. I know that it has been you that has kept all of my family safe through this, for that, I thank you. And I know, that even though you argue the point, you have done much, to bring them back to us." When Guillaume started to speak he was stopped by an upraised hand. "For the way that we treated you all those years ago, I offer you my most humble and sincere apology. We should have listened to you then. Perhaps if we had, this would have been resolved long ago. If I had listened, possibly, this would have never happened to begin with. I have hope that you will return to us here, where you are most welcome."

I watched as Guillaume stood looking at his brother, his countenance much more relaxed than I had seen in recent days. It reminded me of a time, long ago sitting in a room, listening to stories of dragons.

"I do not know," he said, "that I can return here to live as I have grown accustomed to my simple and quiet home in the mountain. I do know that I would be most happy to visit on a regular basis."

As my father motioned for my sisters and me, I watched as his smile grew even more broad than before. "Then come and join us in the celebration of this victory in battle and even more importantly of my families safe return."

"That I will gladly do," Guillaume said, "but first, Ewan and I have some business back at my home. If you will allow us we will leave and return quickly."

Granting his permission with a simple, "go in grace," my father turned away, leading Delwen and Delyth back toward the doorway to the stairs. When I looked back to Guillaume he simply motioned for me to come close. As soon as I did I found we were standing back in the Great Chamber, just outside the door to the hidden room. The doorway was open and a light shone from within.

"The last time you were in here, what did you see?" Guillaume asked me.

Thinking back, trying to decide what he thought important for me to remember it came to me. "There was a tapestry hanging on the wall, but it was empty of design."

Guillaume nodded and then motioned for me to enter. Stepping inside I looked to the wall where the tapestry hung. Instead of the blank tapestry that had been there, it was now brilliant in color and design. The image was of me, standing in the center, the great sword held in my hands before me, my sisters beside me, the caTragon at my feet. In the background was the castle bathed in a golden glow. All around us were the bodies of the enemy we had defeated. The purplish hue of the Grandite swirled around our feet.

Guillaume stepped up behind me, "Some people have a destiny and for what ever reason, never see it accomplished. Others take up the challenge and see it to the end."

Standing in front of the tapestry I turned to look at Guillaume, "My sisters have called me a hero. I do not feel to be a hero, why would they call me that? I only did what I knew to be necessary."

"A hero, is one who will willingly go into what ever stands before them, no matter the danger, in fact, ignoring the danger to self, in the desire to do what ever is needed to protect those in need of it. They will fight until they can fight no more. They will fight, until the last of their blood spills to the ground, if that is what is needed to succeed in what they face. A hero is one who does, what they know to be necessary without thought to self.

319

That is what you are to your sisters." Reaching out
Guillaume took hold of my arm, pushing the sleeve of my
tunic up showing the wounds there. "You went into a
situation knowing the possibility of your death was great.
Yet you went, and you did what had to be done. Then
together you went up against impossible odds and won.
Inside that castle are people who will also look to you as
your sisters do. Remember this though Young Warrior, do
not allow the admiration and comments, the appreciation
of the people to turn your head. Do not allow it to change
you to where you are nothing more than a wasteful wind."

I had turned back to look at the tapestry when I
heard Guillaume's comment. "Guillaume, I know that
between you, Opsis and my sisters, there is no threat of
my possibly becoming anything resembling a 'wasteful
wind'.

Guillaume smiled and continued, "When you
remembered your name, did you also remember what it
means?"

Looking at Guillaume curious as to his asking, "No,
Guillaume, that I have not considered."

"It means, Young Warrior."

Laughing now I turned to look directly at Guillaume,
"So you and Opsis have been calling me by a form of my
name all along."

Smiling, Guillaume placed his hand on my shoulder
much as my father had done earlier, "This Ewan, is not
the end, as there is much more of your destiny yet to be
fulfilled. Understand that this, is just the beginning. Look
at the tapestry."

Turning I looked again to the tapestry. It had once
again changed. The Grandite purple swirled upward, its
various shades filling the entire surface of the tapestry. I
could actually see the movement of the colors as they

danced inside the fibers, much as the colors had in Guillaume's robes on that first meeting long ago. Taking a step backward I turned and followed Guillaume from the room. As the door closed behind us I saw the crystals on the table softly flickering. Walking over to the table with Guillaume we looked at the crystals, they too merely showed the purple of the Grandite.

"Something is approaching. Whether it is danger, an upheaval of what we have known or whether it is just a time of happiness; that we will have to wait to see. For now, come, let us return to Dragon's Doom, your family and a celebration await us."

R. S. Revels

www.ingramcontent.com/pod-product-compliance
Lightning Source LLC
Chambersburg PA
CBHW031158020726
47499CB00002B/407